Kate watched the unnatural colour in his face settle to its usual pallor.

'I don't need to say this to you, but there is *nothing* between Mrs Bliss and me. All I wanted to do was to please you.'

'I feel ashamed that you feel the need to reassure me. Of course I know there isn't, it never crossed my mind. But I'm grateful that you are attending to her house. It will make such a difference and I love you for it.'

'I didn't mean you to know until it was finished. You see, when I went to the house and saw ... Anyway, that's for another time. If there's something you'd rather be doing, I'll sit here a while longer.'

'If it's all right, I'll stay with you.'

There was nothing more to say on the matter without repeating herself so she sat silently, thinking. That he'd done as she asked amused her. Secretly repairing the house wihtout telling her was, in its own way, an acknowledgement that he had heeded her good sense and her compassion. But there was something more behind it, a further reason to do with his past perhaps, the past he didn't feel able to tell her about.

Educated at a co-educational Quaker boarding school, Rebecca Shaw went on to qualify as a teacher of deaf children. After her marriage, she spent the ensuing years enjoying bringing up her family. The departure of the last of her four children to university has given her the time and opportunity to write. The latest novel in the highly popular Tales from Turnham Malpas series is *Whispers in the Village*. Her latest hardback novel, *A Village Feud*, is also available from Orion. Visit her website at www.rebeccashaw.com.

By Rebecca Shaw

Intrigue in the Village

Rebecca Shaw

An Orion paperback

First published in Great Britain in 2003
by Orion
This paperback edition published in 2004
by Orion Books Ltd,
Orion House, 5 Upper St Martin's Lane,
London WC2H 9EA

Reissued 2005

A CIP catalogue record for this book is available
from the British Library.

Typeset by Deltatype Ltd, Birkenhead, Wirral
Printed and bound in Great Britain by
Clays Ltd, St Ives plc

The Orion Publishing Group's policy is to use papers that
are natural, renewable and recyclable products and
made from wood grown in sustainable forests. The logging
and manufacturing processes are expected to conform to
the environmental regulations of the country of origin.

www.orionbooks.co.uk

INHABITANTS OF TURNHAM MALPAS

Maggie Dobbs	School caretaker
Willie Biggs	Verger at St Thomas à Becket
Sylvia Biggs	His wife and housekeeper at the Rectory
Sir Ronald Bissett	Retired Trade Union leader
Lady Sheila Bissett	His wife
James (Jimbo) Charter-Plackett	Owner of the Village Store
Harriet Charter-Plackett	His wife
Fergus, Finlay, Flick and Fran	Their children
Katherine Charter-Plackett	Jimbo's mother
Alan Crimble	Barman at the Royal Oak
Linda Crimble	Runs the Post Office at the Village Store
H. Craddock Fitch	Owner of Turnham House
Jimmy Glover	Taxi driver
Mrs Jones	A village gossip
Vince Jones	Her husband
Barry Jones	Her son and estate carpenter
Pat Jones	Barry's wife
Dean and Michelle	Barry and Pat's children
Revd Peter Harris MA (Oxon)	Rector of the parish
Dr Caroline Harris	His wife
Alex and Beth	Their children
Jeremy Mayer	Manager at Turnham House

Venetia Mayer	His wife
Neville Neal	Accountant and church treasurer
Liz Neal	His wife
Guy and Hugh	Their children
Tom Nicholls	Retired businessman
Evie Nicholls	His wife
Anne Parkin	Retired secretary
Kate Pascoe	Village school headteacher
Sir Ralph Templeton	Retired from the diplomatic service
Lady Muriel Templeton	His wife
Dicky and Georgie Tutt	Licensees at the Royal Oak
Bel Tutt	Assistant in the Village Store
Don Wright	Maintenance engineer (now retired)
Vera Wright	Cleaner at the nursing home in Penny Fawcett
Rhett Wright	Their grandson

Intrigue in the Village

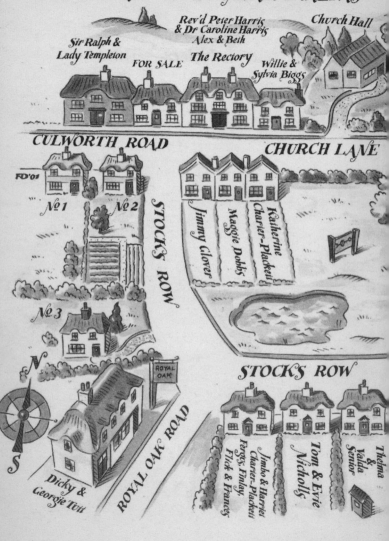

St Thomas à Becket

Bel Tott

Anne Parkin

Liz & Neville Neal Guy & Hugh

GLEBE COTTAGES

GLEBE HOUSE

CHURCH LANE

Village Store

STOCKS ROW

JACKS LANE

Swimming Pool

School House Kate Pascoe

Turnham Malpas School

SHEPHERDS HILL

Sir Ronald & Lady Bissett pond

Footpath

Alan & Linda Crimble

HIPKIN GARDENS

BECK

TURNHAM footbridge

Prologue

The bridegroom walked undetected down Church Lane, cursing the gaggle of geese engaged in their early-morning circling of the Green in the hope of being fed. He tried to squeeze past them but they hissed, stretched out their necks, spread their wings, and took rapid, threatening steps towards him. Softly he cried, 'Shoo! Shoo!' but they ignored him and continued their lordly procession. He never had and never would have this animal thing. He reached the lychgate, silently undid the catch and turned in. Should he wait here or go up to the church porch? He snapped back his impeccable white cuff and looked at his watch. Only fifteen minutes to go. Where was she? Where the devil were Peter and Mrs Peel? Surely they should be here by now. The bridegroom checked to make sure no one had seen him, then walked softly up the path to the church door and tried the heavy iron handle. It was open! He went inside, still unseen, except by the geese and they wouldn't tell.

The front pew was where bridegrooms sat awaiting their brides. She'd taken some persuading, and even now he wasn't sure he should have persisted in proposing. But she was just what he needed; whether he was just what she needed was another matter, but he had to have his own way, that was how he was made. She'd be dressed in a light grey suit, she'd said, no hat, hats weren't her thing, matching shoes and a small spray of flowers made by the florist in Culworth. He wished, briefly, that she'd be wearing a real wedding dress, romantic you know. He adjusted the rose in his buttonhole and checked his pocket for the wedding ring. Quiet, she'd said. No best man. No bridesmaids. What do either of us want with all that carry on? The fewer people who knew the better.

He'd been too long without a partner. Ghastly word that. Been too long without a *wife*. He daren't count how long, because it reminded him that he was much older than her. He certainly didn't behave like an older man, and she claimed she never noticed his age. There'd been a twinkle in her eye when she'd said that and it had boosted his ego, not that it needed boosting, that had never been a problem with him. He checked his watch again. A chill ran down his spine. Where were they? And more so, where was *she*?

The bride was sitting on the dressing-table stool in her bedroom, putting on her cream satin shoes. Had she got the right shade? She held the shoes, one in each hand, against the skirt of her wedding dress. Yes, she had. Exactly right. She put them on, stood up and went to the long mirror to examine herself now she was fully dressed. From head to toe she looked the perfect bride; hair held in place by a kind of fledgling tiara, classic high-necked, long-sleeved dress, with heavily beaded bodice, the glass beads catching the light each time she breathed. The skirt was slender with short slits each side at the hem so she was able to walk freely. Her bouquet! She picked it up from the bed and assessed the finished article. Yes! She'd got it right. Perfect! He'd love her in this. Grey suit indeed! For such an intelligent man he was easily fooled. So . . . within the hour she'd be married. It still wasn't too late to say no. Did she want to? No to all that money? No to limitless foreign travel? No to no expense spared? No to having anything she wanted? Worse still, could she say no to love? He loved her far more than she loved him. Was she being fair marrying him knowing that? She'd told him time and again and he'd listened, but he hadn't heard. There was the sound of a car engine. She walked sedately down the stairs and out of the door, put her house key under the flowerpot and graciously stepped into the car. The chauffeur held her flowers while she settled herself, returned them to her and they drove the few yards to the church at a stately speed.

When he opened the door for her to get out, the bride shook her head. 'Give me a minute.'

Was she doing the right thing? Should she? She gave a thought to pulling the petals from a rose in her bouquet – 'Love him, love him not' – as a test. Just a test. Marriage was a big step. He'd gone on and on proposing until, in the end, she'd had no resistance left. Why shouldn't she? He was lonely and so was she come to that. At forty-one, decisions needed to be taken. But as she'd said, no children and she wasn't giving up her work. Absolutely not. He knew that. She opened the car door to say, 'Drive me back home. It's off,' and instead heard herself saying, 'Hold my flowers, please, while I get out.'

In a dream, she stood in the church doorway, saw Willie Biggs give the nod to Mrs Peel at the organ to play 'Here comes the Bride'. The organ flared into sound, the majestic chords booming into the rafters. There ahead of her was Peter in his white marriage cassock and, turning to get a first look at his bride, was her groom resplendent in morning coat. Morning coat! He never said he'd wear one! His light blue eyes were bright with his pleasure at the sight of her. She walked steadily down the aisle, trying hard not to break into a run, placed her cold, trembling hand in his warm grasp, smiled at him and then looked up at Peter.

'Welcome to you both. God bless you.'

Chapter 1

Beside the tinned soup shelves in the Village Store, Greta Jones and Lady Templeton were discussing that evening's celebrations. 'Well, Lady Templeton, he's never invited *all* of us before, has he? I mean, just the nobs, begging your pardon, usually, but this time it's everyone. Even the Senior sisters. Everyone is going. I can't understand it.'

'I've no doubt Mr Fitch must have his reasons. I expect he wants us all to share his pleasure in his achievements. He has got something to celebrate, hasn't he? A major, international civil engineering company in twenty-five years and it all started, he says, with a couple of men, two shovels and a wheelbarrow. What a triumph.'

'I expect so, and he has mellowed lately, hasn't he? He gave all those computers to the school — state-of-the-art say those who know what they're talking about — and he saved us from having traffic lights and what not, year before last. That was a master stroke.'

'Absolutely.' Lady Templeton began to study the tinned soups.

'Is Sir Ralph going?'

'Of course he's going. It would be churlish to refuse.'

'But they don't see eye to eye, do they?' A gentle, questioning glance from Lady Templeton made Greta

Jones change her tone. 'Well, they do these days, see eye to eye, I mean, now he's mellowed.'

'He is a changed man, Greta. Those frosty blue eyes of his are not nearly so chilling as they were.' She smiled, took down two tins of vichyssoise from the top shelf and continued with her shopping. She wouldn't have said so for the world but Greta Jones was quite right; it *was* surprising. But she was looking forward to it, and had already got out the dress and jacket she'd bought for a visit to Japan and never found a use for since. It was a gracious cornflower blue, which Ralph said brought out the colour of her eyes perfectly. Dear Ralph.

Jimbo was at the till and as he began adding up her purchases, she said, 'You'll have a busy day today preparing the buffet.'

'I should say. Thank goodness for staff who know what they're doing. Where I'd be without Pat Jones, I do not know.'

'Don't forget your good training has helped.'

'No. Believe me, if the talent isn't there, no amount of training will do the trick. I've got Sir Ralph's cigars in, the ones he ordered. Will you take them?'

'How lovely. Yes, of course. They say just about the whole world will be there tonight.'

'And then some. Not seen anything like it.' Jimbo gave Lady Templeton her change and winked at her. 'Bye-bye, Muriel. See you tonight.'

'Indeed. Good morning, Greta.'

Greta Jones, who was now standing behind her waiting to pay, nodded and smiled, then put her wire basket on the counter, determined to get to the hub of the matter.

'Seeing as you're doing the catering, you'll be the man to ask. What is this do all about? I saw you wink at Muriel.'

'Just a friendly wink. That's all.'

'You know something, don't you? Out with it.'

Jimbo spread his hands and shrugged. 'I have no more idea than anyone else. It's to celebrate his company's twenty-fifth anniversary and he wants to give everyone a good time. No expense spared. More than that I do not know. Honest. Cross my heart.'

'You're a slyboots, Jimbo, and not half.'

'Eight pounds, thirty-five, please.'

As Greta Jones sorted out the money for him she said, 'I reckon there's a conspiracy going on. There, eight pounds, thirty-five exactly. Well, I expect we'll all find out tonight.'

'Best bib and tucker.'

'What else? See yer tonight.'

'Definitely.'

They'd opened up the field nearest the Big House for cars and ten minutes before the start of the festivities it was difficult to find a parking spot. But no one cared; they were there to enjoy themselves and eat as much as they could. Everyone always took advantage of anything Craddock Fitch had to offer, then laughed at him behind his back. He'd never been liked. Too high-handed, efficient and lacking in understanding of a countryman's life, that was his trouble. He thought money could buy everything, but it would never buy their respect. Even so, there were gasps of delight when they saw the fairy lights, which covered the front of the house, hanging like vast curtains over the walls and windows, and draped over

7

every tree of any size. A long table, illuminated by dozens of candles and bearing an array of drinks, stood on the gravel outside the front door and it felt smart to stand there admiring the lights, looking across Home Park to the floodlit trees, holding a drink in one's hand, snatching a few nibbles and seeing what everyone else was wearing. Some of the men like Jimbo, Neville and Sir Ralph, for instance, were in dinner suits, which added an extra effervescence to the gathering.

Eventually, people began drifting inside to make room for late-comers and they found the inside of the house was even more amazing. The hall was bedecked with flowers, or maybe, some thought, smothered would be a better choice of word. Swags of them were strung around the walls, columns of them stood beside every door, and the vast fireplace was filled with a magnificent display, backlit and utterly breathtaking.

Ralph Templeton said to Muriel, 'There's more than a twenty-fifth anniversary going on here tonight, isn't there?'

Muriel whispered, 'I'm sure of it.'

'He's in danger of over-stepping the mark, I think. Vulgar ostentation springs to mind.'

Shocked, Muriel whispered, 'Ralph! Really!' She smiled. 'He just tries too hard, desperate to do the right thing.'

'He wouldn't know the right thing if he met it in the street.'

'Ralph! Please. I thought you'd put all that behind you.'

'I have, until he reminds me. Where is he, by the way? Not like him to miss the fun.'

Peter and Caroline came up to them, drinks in hand.

'Good evening, Caroline, my dear.' Ralph greeted her with a kiss on both cheeks. 'Good evening, Peter. Now you might be the very man to tell us exactly what all this,' Ralph swept a disdainful hand around the hall, 'is about.'

Peter smiled and nodded towards the staircase. 'I think you might be finding out right now.'

Coming down the imposing Tudor staircase was Craddock Fitch, wearing quite the smartest suit and the sharpest tie they'd ever seen him in, but what was more impressive was his smile, which stretched almost from ear to ear and made him look ten or even twenty years younger. The polite hubbub ended as they all had their attention drawn to him and a round of subdued applause rippled through the hall, begun by Muriel and picked up by everyone else. This started a rush inside from the guests still enjoying their drinks on the terrace.

Mr Fitch arrived in the hall and turned to look up the staircase. 'Is he expecting someone else then?' asked Ralph, one of the last to join in the applause.

Muriel gasped, 'Oh look!' The gasp, like the applause, went round the hall and the people, crowded in the doorway, strained to catch a glimpse. Unbelievably, it was Kate Pascoe from the school, in a *wedding dress*. A wedding dress? *Kate Pascoe?* Was this a joke? Kate walked carefully down the stairs, looking for all the world like a princess, the glass beads on her bodice and her tiara catching the light from the myriads of tall candles, her face radiant, eyes only for Craddock Fitch.

As she reached him, he took her hand and kissed it in the manner of a courtier of old, turned to the astounded guests and said, 'May I have the pleasure of introducing my wife to you. This is Mrs Katherine Marguerita Fitch.

I hope you will be as thrilled and delighted as I am today. I'm a very lucky man.' He spoke from the heart, a shock in itself.

No one moved: they were too stunned.

A strained silence fell, which no one dared break.

Then Muriel, entirely due to her kind heart, squeezed through the guests in front of her, took the bride's hand, kissed her on both cheeks and said for all to hear, 'My dear, how absolutely wonderful. You look . . . perfectly gorgeous. Yes, indeed. A princess to behold. And you, Craddock, much love. You're right, you are a very lucky man.' Muriel kissed him on both cheeks too and took hold of his free hand and shook it. 'Congratulations, from all of us.'

Mercifully, Muriel's actions broke the spell. There was a rush of those nearest to the bridal couple to shake hands and offer their best wishes and congratulations. But they were scandalized. Old Fitch, with the emphasis on the *old*, marrying a slip of a girl like Kate Pascoe? She was still a newcomer to the village, but it felt as if they'd known her for years. Fancy her marrying that frozen old toad! She'd done it for the money. Oh yes. There couldn't be any other reasonable interpretation put on this wild venture. He must be mad. To say nothing of *her* mental state. She'd gone completely crackers. That brush with death and black magic years ago had finally done for her.

'Wouldn't mind getting *my* hands on his money though,' said Greta Jones, out of the corner of her mouth, to Grandmama Charter-Plackett.

Grandmama was having great difficulty restraining herself from protesting out loud at this utter folly. Grimly, she forced out the words she would later come to regret. 'I give them three months.'

'Well, fair's fair, I'll give them six months. But I must say she makes a beautiful bride. Very beautiful.' Greta continued to watch people wishing the bridal couple well, thinking Kate might as well make the best of it while she could. But the alimony . . . my God, she was no fool. Greta, who'd struggled all her married life with the family finances never stretching as far as needed, envied Kate with heart and soul.

Grandmama Charter-Plackett felt disgust. What was that ridiculous man doing marrying a mere girl? Kate was old enough to make up her own mind, she supposed, but really . . . If ever there was a recipe for disaster, this was it. She'd always known Craddock Fitch hadn't come out of the top drawer, much as he might like to think he did. He didn't quite carry it off. There were a few little cracks in his attitude that spoke volumes, and this was one; quite a big crack, actually. Still, *she* wouldn't want him, certainly not, and *he* definitely wouldn't want her. She smiled ruefully and said to Greta, 'Well, we may as well get what we can while the glow lasts.'

Greta nudged her and laughed. 'You're right there.' They helped themselves to a glass of champagne each as a waiter in tails and bow tie passed between them.

Then Jimbo stood on a chair and proposed the toast to the happy couple.

Greta's mouth dropped open. So, he *did* know all about it. Damn him! The secretive sod. She'd give him a piece of her mind when she went to work on Monday.

Everyone raised their glasses to the happy couple. Muriel toasted them with tears of happiness in her eyes.

11

She looked at Ralph and said, 'Oh, Ralph, isn't it lovely? I'm so pleased for them both. They make a shining couple, don't they? I've never seen her looking so charming, in fact beautiful. It must be love.'

Ralph downed his champagne and took a second one from a passing tray. 'Exactly.'

But there was something in his tone that alerted Muriel. 'Ralph?'

'She's married him for his money, my dear, make no mistake about that.'

'Shush! Ralph!'

'Believe me. No woman would want him for himself. It's the millions she's after.'

Muriel opened her bag to search for her handkerchief. 'Ralph! I've forgotten my . . . where is it?'

'Here you are.' Ralph gave her the handkerchief from his jacket pocket. 'Don't upset yourself. They've made their own bed and so far as I am concerned, they can lie in it.' He picked up a third glass from a passing waiter and sipped it with relish.

'Ralph! I'm ashamed of you. How very ungenerous. It's not like you at all.' She wiped her eyes, but before she'd managed to regain control, she saw to her horror that Mr Fitch and Kate were making their way between the guests, speaking to people right and left, and heading apparently straight for her and Ralph. Oh no! She so hoped there wasn't going to be a scene. Someone turned and knocked her glass with their elbow. Champagne ran down Muriel's bare wrist and up her sleeve. She dabbed at herself, desperate not to be looking a fool when the bride and groom reached them. The glass was almost empty. Ralph took it from her and picked up a second glass for her from

12

yet another silver tray making its way round. Well, he'd say this for him, he was more than generous. Ah! Here they come. He'd better not gloat, hadn't old Fitch. He, Ralph, had better take the initiative.

'Good evening, Fitch. Good evening, Kate. What a wonderful surprise! Such a very well-kept secret. I do hope, very sincerely, that you'll both be very happy indeed.'

Mr Fitch looked eyeball to eyeball at Ralph and they squared up to each other like boxers measuring one another's strength and intentions. Ralph kissed Kate on both cheeks and whispered, 'You look wonderful, truly wonderful.'

'Isn't she a treasure, Ralph? I'm a very lucky man.'

'Indeed you are.'

Mr Fitch put an arm around Kate's waist. 'She took some persuading, but I got her in the end. Didn't I, darling?'

Kate smiled.

Ralph continued with his self-imposed politeness. 'However did you manage to keep it such a secret? We all think nothing goes on in this village that we don't know about and here you are, inviting us to celebrate twenty-five years of commercial success when all the time it's a wedding party. Splendid!'

Muriel beamed her pleasure that there hadn't been a scene and decided Ralph really was a gentleman after all. Then she realized what the marriage would mean to the village. 'You'll be stopping teaching then, Kate, now you're married? The school will miss you. We'll have to start getting used to someone else. Oh dear!'

'I shall still teach, Muriel. Can't live without my children.'

'But won't you perhaps be having . . .' Muriel lolled her head teasingly to the side and smiled.

Kate answered as gently as she could, not wishing to upset Muriel who in her book was far too sweet to rebuff. 'No. We shan't.'

'Oh! I see. I hoped perhaps for Craddock's sake . . . and yours, of course, that you might . . .'

Ralph saw Muriel was getting herself in deep water. 'My dear, I'm sure it's perfectly possible to be married without children coming along. Lots of couples make that choice nowadays.'

'Well, you did, didn't you, Ralph?' Mr Fitch took a grip on Kate's elbow and moved her on. A fleeting look of, well, it could only be called hate, directed solely at Ralph, crossed Mr Fitch's face as he moved away.

Muriel took a moment to absorb the insult. When she did she paled and dared not look at Ralph for fear of what she'd read in his face. How could the man be so cruel on his wedding day? He knew she and Ralph hadn't married until the time to have children was long past. Ralph had endeavoured to be so thoughtful and it hurt her to the core. She felt like crying but didn't; she wouldn't give Mr Fitch the satisfaction nor Ralph the embarrassment. Her backbone of steel was brought into action and she stood, stonily listening to the orchestra, which had struck up, and wishing she could escape. Then she saw Kate and Mr Fitch head towards the dining-room door, and the guests begin to file through to the buffet, shaking hands with the bride and groom before they went in. Horror of horrors! Ralph and she would have to shake hands or it would be

14

round in a trice how rude they'd been and everyone would wonder why.

Muriel glanced at Ralph and saw he was white at the gills, straining to control his anger. She placed a timid, consoling hand in his and drew his arm through hers.

'We'll brave it out, the two of us together. We must or they'll all be talking. I don't think he realized what he'd said, you know.'

'He knew all right. Come, let's be the best of guests and smile. At least we can eat his food and drink his champagne without a qualm. The bad manners are all on his part. Come, my dear, forward!'

The buffet table looked so wonderful it seemed almost unreal. To say no expense had been spared was an understatement. It was dazzlingly colourful and so beautifully arranged it felt like a crime to disturb the design. Salivary glands were working overtime, however, and once the bride and groom had helped themselves, they all tucked in. The Misses Senior, having brought plastic bags hidden in their cavernous handbags, almost rubbed their hands with glee. They'd be able to steal enough food to last them a week and no one would be the wiser. There were four places where guests could pick up their plates and napkins and begin to load their plates, and it was surprising how quickly everyone had chosen their food and had wandered away to find space to eat.

Peter sought out Jimbo to compliment him. Jimbo was eating from a well-stacked plate but at the same time his eyes were constantly surveying the room, keeping a check on everything. 'Jimbo! Congratulations feels inadequate, but what else can one say? The buffet table is unbelievable.

15

What a triumph! We managed to keep the secret, didn't we? I don't know how. I didn't even tell Caroline.'

'Well, Harriet had to know, obviously, because there was the wedding cake to make. Wait till you see it. Fitch left the design to Harriet and she's as nervous as hell in case he doesn't like it. They'll be wheeling it in soon. I say, look at Ralph, over there by the fireplace. He looks livid and so does Muriel. I wonder what's happened?'

'No idea, I'm afraid. Best not ask.'

'Got to go,' Jimbo said suddenly. 'Harriet's signalling that the cake's about to be brought in.'

It was the most stupendous wedding cake that had ever been seen in Turnham Malpas or any of the surrounding villages come to that. Four tiers placed on a vast silver stand were smothered in peach and cream icing sugar flowers, and real matching flowers stood in small, trumpet-shaped silver vases atop each tier. It was truly magnificent. If it had been the wedding of a duke and duchess it couldn't have been more triumphant.

It was only when they were all invited outside to see the fireworks that everyone realized the perfectly wonderful evening of food, wine, dancing and jollity was about to end.

Fountains and rockets were spectacular and at the end, the intertwining of K and C in brilliant, multi-coloured Catherine wheels finished the evening in great style.

Filled to the brim with food, drink and bonhomie, the guests wended their way home on foot or by car, leaving Kate and Mr Fitch to make their own way up to his flat.

Kate sank into an armchair, drained of energy, while

16

Craddock went to the drinks table to make them both a nightcap.

'What a day, Craddock. What a day.'

He turned from the drinks table to look at her. 'But wonderful?'

She smiled. 'Of course. I'm glad the service was private and just for us. It felt so special. I was right, wasn't I?'

'Yes, you were. Here's your drink, just how you like it.' He slumped down into the other armchair, toasted his wife, then drank the whisky straight off. 'It's going to be different having someone to talk to in the evenings. That will give me such pleasure.'

Kate smiled again. Looking down at her glass, she swirled it about for a moment by the stem and then said, 'I wish you hadn't said that to Ralph.'

'Now, Kate, I say what I think fit.'

'It wasn't fit and you didn't think. It was insulting. You knew full well he has never had children and that Muriel and he married when it was far too late.'

'Well, the sod was inferring I needed an excuse not to have children, meaning I was far too old to father a child. Which I'm not.'

'He meant nothing of the kind. He was trying to get Muriel out of the big hole she was digging for herself and well you know it.'

Craddock made a dismissive gesture and tried to change the subject. 'I've been thinking—'

'I won't have it, for your own sake as much as mine. No wonder they don't like you if you come out with remarks like that.'

'Don't like me? *Me?*'

Kate nodded.

17

'But they've all enjoyed themselves tonight, loved it in fact. Thanked me for it. How can they not like me?'

'They have no respect and certainly no love for you, Craddock, and you're going to have to earn Brownie points with them somehow. They take all you give, then they go home and laugh at your extravagance.'

Craddock was stunned. 'How do you know this?'

'Because I take the trouble to listen to them and watch. I'm not a teacher for nothing. I can attend to the child I'm speaking to and still know exactly what's going on in the rest of the class, and it's the same with grown-ups. I see them talking out of the corner of their mouths about you. To your face they say what they know you want to hear.'

'That's a bit of a broadside for my wedding night. It was a splendid wedding party, went off without a hitch. How can you say they didn't enjoy themselves? I thought they did.'

'Oh, they did! Very much. And, yes, the party *was* splendid and the cake a dream. But they will take all you can give and still not respect you for it.'

'You've never said this before.'

'I've never been your wife before.'

'True. But you are now.' He stared into the distance, turning his whisky glass round and round in his hands. Kate stood up. Craddock looked up at her, overcome again at how beautiful she was in her spectacular dress. 'You looked so exquisite this morning. Your dress was a wonderful surprise. Grey suit, my eye.' He paused for a moment, then added humbly, 'Will you help me?'

'To stand up? Of course.' She crossed the hearthrug and stretched out her hand, a wicked grin on her face. 'Up you come.'

'I don't need pulling up! Heaven's above, I'm not in my dotage! I meant to get the village to like me, if not love me. Will you help?' He looked so downcast standing there, genuinely pleading.

She took his hand in hers and kissed it, squeezing it tightly. 'Of course I will. We've both been around a bit, seen the world, but today, for me, is like coming home into a safe harbour. We're going to have such fun. You and me together. Each doing our own thing out in the hurly-burly, well, you more than me, but married and happy. So happy.' Kate leaned towards him and kissed him gently on the lips. 'I nearly got the chauffeur to take me back home this morning, thought I couldn't go through with it, but I'm very glad I did.'

As they trailed upstairs, arms around each other's waists, Craddock Fitch decided his new wife was full of surprises. Life was certainly going to be lively married to Mrs Kate Fitch.

Chapter 2

There was a knot of people waiting outside the Village Store for the Saturday morning bus into Culworth. It was pouring down so they were huddled under umbrellas, comparing notes about the party.

Someone from Hipkin Gardens rolled her eyes and said, 'It was the desserts I liked. That meringue thingy with the nuts was superb.'

'And the chocolate sauce they poured over that wicked ice cream was out of this world.'

'Thank God it wasn't raining like this last night else we'd have been soaked watching that firework display. They're never the same in rain, are they?'

A neighbour nudged Greta Jones and winked. 'I slept like a log last night I was that tired. Bet I know two people who didn't.'

Rather primly for her Greta answered, 'Well, of course, I know nothing about that. I'm just surprised they managed to keep it so secret. No one I spoke to last night had the slightest idea something was going on.'

'Same here. Not an inkling. They say . . .'

Their heads grew closer. 'Yes? Go on.'

'They say she's not having any children. Put her foot down apparently.'

'No!'

'She needn't bother putting her foot down. It's not likely with him being so . . . *old*.' A burst of laughter emerged from under the umbrellas. 'There must be twenty, twenty-five years between them.'

'There is a limit, isn't there? Honestly! I don't know what she can be thinking of.'

'Maybe it's love.'

There was a chorus of disbelief.

'They also say,' someone shut their umbrella so they could draw closer, 'she's carrying on teaching.'

'No!'

'With all that money! Who the blazes would want to *work* with money like his on tap?'

'Once she gets a taste for sunning herself in the Seychelles she'll perhaps change her mind. I know I would. I hope Vera Wright's on the bus. She won't half have a surprise when we tell her.'

'You wouldn't catch me . . . here's the bus. Oh, look! Vera's on it. Come on! Mind my eye with that umbrella of yours. Wait till we tell her; she'll have a surprise and not half.'

Muriel saw the bus go by as she brought in the milk. She smiled to herself when she thought about how much tittle-tattle there'd be on the bus this morning and guessed it wouldn't be about shopping. Muriel almost wished she were on the bus like she used to be on Saturdays. There was a lot to be said for having a car, but somehow this morning she felt she was missing out.

Ralph had just come downstairs. They might have had a very late night last night but, my word, he looked handsome today. She went up to him and gave him a kiss.

21

'Good morning, my dear.'

'Good morning, Ralph. You're looking so handsome today.'

'Thank you. It's not how I feel. I think it was the champagne we had while watching the fireworks that finally did it for me.'

'It was a lovely wedding party. A tweeny-weeny bit over the top, but lovely.'

'Teeny-weeny bit? A lot I would have said. He has no idea, has he?' Ralph pulled out his chair and sat down.

'Never mind. The Senior sisters will have a beanfeast for the rest of the week.'

'A beanfeast?'

'I saw them popping food into plastic bags. They really are a disgrace.'

Ralph raised his eyebrows. 'Do they always do that?'

'Always. I used to see them doing it when I lived here as a girl. One Bonfire Night party, when your father used to have a big bonfire in Home Park, they actually had a shopping basket with them. They're quite unashamed about it.'

'I'd no idea. Tea?'

Muriel smiled and nodded. 'Yes, please.' Gazing out of the window, she said, 'I thought the wedding cake was so beautiful. I hate those dreadful bride and bridegroom figures. This one was so original and in such good taste.'

'You sound wistful, my dear.'

'Not really. But it was beautiful. Harriet is very clever.' Muriel sipped her tea. 'Do you really think Kate has married him for his money?'

'In a strange way, there's more to it than that, I think. Though I can't see it working for long.'

'That's what Grandmama Charter-Plackett said. She's given it three months.'

Ralph grinned. 'More toast?'

Muriel took a slice, examined it and decided they'd have to get a new toaster. 'No honeymoon and back teaching on Monday. It's not very romantic, is it?'

At eight-thirty precisely on the Monday morning, Kate's little car whizzed into the school playground. It was always there, parked by the schoolhouse, so when the children came to school that morning, things looked no different at all. It was quite disappointing. But all of them knew about the wedding and many arrived with small presents and flowers for her.

And there she was, as usual, standing on the doorstep of the main entrance ringing the original school bell, in use since the school opened 150 years ago, at ten minutes to nine as if nothing of importance had happened during half-term.

'Good morning, everyone!' she said and, as usual, they replied, 'Good morning Miss Pas . . .' Then they stopped and there was a jumble of 'Mrs Fitch' and 'Miss Pascoe', followed by an embarrassed silence.

'My mum says she hopes you'll be happy,' shouted Karen, the biggest and boldest of Year Seven.

'My mum says she can't believe it,' said a small innocent in Year One.

'Neither can mine.'

'Well, there's one thing for certain, I'm still your headteacher and the same person I was the last time you saw me. Nothing's changed really. So which class shall I choose to go in first? Mrs Hardaker's, I think. Quietly.

23

Next?' She surveyed the rows of children all hoping to be chosen. Lovely, bright, shining morning faces except for the Binns children. They looked ghastly. 'Miss Booth's class, please. Gently now, gently. We're going into school, not a football match.'

'Wish we were, Miss Pascoe.'

'Now the big ones, my class.'

'I've brought you a present, look.'

'Why, how thoughtful of you. Take it in for me and I'll open it straight after prayers.'

'Mine says, "Mr and Mrs Fitch". Look.'

'It does. In your handwriting too!'

'I've brought a card. I wrote it myself.'

'That's very kind of you. Thank you very much. Go inside out of the cold and we'll have a look after prayers.'

Kate watched her class go in, her mind elsewhere. *Was* she the same person? No, not really, there was something in her that had changed, but she couldn't identify what it was. She knew she felt warmer inside, in the very core of her, cosier, and at peace. Was that getting married or because she'd married Craddock? He'd gone up to London this morning full of energy, revitalized he said, loving marriage and reluctant to go, but business called. It always would. But even so, she knew she occupied a very, very special place in his heart. At last, during the year they'd been seeing each other, he'd found his heart. She was relieved he wasn't possessive and jealous, which wouldn't do for her. She couldn't bear those kind of chains. Love given freely, on the other hand, was wonderful.

'Miss Pascoe!' Karen from Year Seven interrupted her thoughts.

'Yes, Karen?'

'There's a lady called Mrs Bliss and she wants a word. They don't look our sort at all.'

'Karen! Where is she?'

'In the coat room and her kids are kicking the wellies about.'

'Go into the hall and ask Mrs Hardaker to settle everyone down. I'll be there in a minute.'

Karen was proved right. There were four children of varying ages, badly clothed and fed by the looks of them, doing just as Karen had reported.

'Children! Come here to me.' She waited in silence, fixing them with a determined eye, until one by one they had done as she asked. 'Good morning, Mrs Bliss. I'm Kate Pas . . . Fitch, the headteacher. You want to see me?' The hand Kate shook was lifeless, bony and chilled.

'Come to register them. All four. This is Philip and he's Paul, they're twins and they're ten. The two girls are Una and Della. Una's five and Della's seven. Is there space for them?'

'Only just. We're very full at the moment. Where do you live?'

'Little Derehams. That old cottage, the one that hasn't been occupied for years.'

'Have you walked here?'

Mrs Bliss nodded.

'There's a school bus at eight twenty-five every morning from the crossroads in the centre of Little Derehams. They've a right to catch it. They'll be home on it by four-ish each day. Will you write down their details for me; dates of birth, which schools they've attended and such? Can't stop, I've prayers to take. They'll need school dinner, we all have a hot meal every day, so we'll feed them today and then you can send the money tomorrow for the week. I'll give them a note. Say goodbye to your mother and come with me to prayers.'

The parting of mother and children was casual to say the least. They drifted away from her without the smallest demonstration of emotion on either part. She gave a slight movement of her hand, which almost said, 'Get off, and good riddance.'

Kate showed the children where to hang the thin, worn-out coats they wore and, taking the two smaller ones by the hand, she led them into the hall. 'Sit anywhere you like. We'll sort out classes later.' The boys squatted on the floor right at the back; the two little girls stood shyly, hand in hand, fingers in mouths, just looking. They each had enormous brown eyes set in deep sockets, and their cheeks were hollowed and their jaw bones well defined. Hungry, that's what, thought Kate. Downright hungry. Their fine brown hair, wispy and unevenly cut, had a distinctly unkempt look. She went to stand in front of the children and waited until Mrs Hardaker had finished playing her quietening-down music.

'Good morning, children.'

When she left the school, Mrs Bliss went into the Village Store. She crept in, feeling intimidated, having expected some half-hearted run-down village shop; finding it well set-up and packed from floor to ceiling with goodies too inviting for words, threw her. She picked up a basket and began wandering around the aisles, tempted beyond imagination to shoplift. Then the girl behind the Post

Office counter said something to a customer about getting a coffee to keep out the cold.

Mrs Bliss peered round the tall freezer, which was full of homemade ready meals, and saw the coffee machine. Her insides craved the heat of a hot drink and sugar too. That would help. Bravely, driven by necessity, she poured herself a coffee, stirred three lumps of sugar into it and two little pots of cream and went to stand by the side window to drink it. She sipped the scorching drink and thought of other coffees she'd drunk when the world was the right way up . . .

A man, surprisingly wearing a boater and striped apron, took her elbow and gently turned her round so she was sitting on a chair. 'Thought you were going to faint. Sit there for a minute. You're new here?' He stood, smiling down at her, waiting for her reply.

She took another sip of her heart-warming coffee before she answered. 'Yes. We've come to live in Little Derchams. Brought the children to school, their first morning. Thank you for this.' She wished he'd move away and let her enjoy the drink. 'Seems a nice school.'

'It is. My daughter Fran is in her last year there. She's been very happy. The other three did very well there too. How many children have you?'

'Four. Two boys, two girls.'

'Same here. Handful, aren't they?'

Mrs Bliss nodded. Thankfully, the man wandered away, but she noticed he kept glancing at her. Did he suspect what she was about to do? Someone called from the rear of the shop and he disappeared. Right! In a moment she had a large pack of mince from the deep freeze in her bag. She did buy some milk and a packet of biscuits, then made

27

to leave, walking as slowly as she dared. The jingling of the shop bell startled her as she opened the door, but no one came after her. She'd made it. Thank God. So now she'd finally reached the bottom, stealing to feed her family. But the bus fares to Culworth yesterday had cost far more than she'd hoped, and then the taxi, but they'd all been so exhausted . . .

Jimbo, who was seated with Harriet in the kitchen, said, 'She's going to steal.'

'Well, go and stop her.'

'Can't.'

'Why not? You know how furious it makes you. Go on.'

'No, Harriet. Not this time.'

'Why not? Who is it?'

'I don't know, but I do know she has four children to feed and she's desperate. She had one of our coffees and it looked to me as though it was the first hot food she'd had in days. She'd have eaten the cup if she could have.'

'You sentimental old thing you. And there was I thinking you were a commercial animal through and through.'

'Hmm. What are you doing, might I ask?'

'I promised Kate I would cut this tier of her cake into pieces so she could give the children a taste of her wedding cake. I'll take it across in a minute. She wants it ready for when they have their break.'

'By the way, old Fitch was delighted with the cake, my darling. So was Kate.' Jimbo watched Harriet counting the slices. 'Funny couple. Still, it might work out OK.

Though the odds do seem stacked against them, don't you think?'

'Definitely. But stranger marriages have worked out and maybe this one will too. I hope so for both their sakes.'

'So do I. When you go across to the school ask Kate about this woman.'

Harriet, having arranged the pieces of cake on a huge silver serving dish and covered it with foil, took off her statutory apron and head covering, put on her coat and set off for the school with a big smile on her face. She loved popping in to the school to see everybody. It was such a happy place to be and Harriet was almost disappointed that when Fran left there'd be no excuse for coming in.

She'd arrived just in time. The children were sitting at their tables while the milk monitors were handing out the milk.

'Wow! Just made it!' Kate said. 'Thanks for this, Harriet, I'd never have got the pieces all the same size, and then there'd have been terrible trouble. Napkins too! Lovely.'

They had a delightful ten minutes handing round the cake and giving the children a wedding napkin to catch the crumbs. After they'd all gone out to play, Kate took Harriet into her tiny office.

'We had someone in the Store this morning who'd come straight from bringing her children to school for the first time,' said Harriet.

'That would be Mrs Bliss.'

'Jimbo was of the opinion that she was intending stealing, and he left her to get on with it. Said she looked ghastly and he thought she was going to faint.'

'The children look hungry too. She seemed absolutely

29

lifeless. I can't quite put my finger on it; unaccustomed to poverty, I guess.'

'Jimbo is very hot on stealing in the Store. He won't even dignify it by calling it shoplifting. But this morning he allowed it to happen. Perhaps a bit of investigation wouldn't go amiss. Free dinners or something?'

Kate nodded. 'You've taken the words out of my mouth.' She stood up when she heard the bell for the end of play. 'Thanks again. Don't forget your serving dish. There's still a few pieces left, so take them with you. Craddock and I have plenty.'

Harriet had to ask. 'Happy?'

'Very. Very happy. Truly.'

'I'm glad. You're just what he needs. It's been a huge surprise.'

'Thanks for keeping it secret.'

'Believe me, it was the village's best kept secret ever. Everyone was stunned.'

'That was part of the fun. Must go. Thanks!'

Harriet went to collect her dish only to find that there were no pieces left for her to take home. She hoped it was the Bliss children who'd done the dirty on her.

When it came to dinnertime, the children ate in family groups with their teacher or a dinner lady at the head of the table. Kate insisted the children had school dinners and baulked at any attempt to introduce packed lunches. Some parents had argued with her about it, claiming their children were difficult eaters and they'd never eat a thing if presented with a cooked meal of meat and three veg. Her answer had been that they would be surprised how quickly the children grew to like school dinners when they saw how everyone else got on with theirs and enjoyed them.

She made sure the Bliss twins were seated at her table and noticed how rapidly they emptied their plates. It was jam rolypoly for pudding and their eyes grew large as their dishes were passed down to them.

'There's more custard if anyone . . .' She held up the jug and the first hands up were Philip and Paul Bliss's. They gobbled up their extra custard as though the whole jug would not have been enough. Kate made a note to see their mother about free school meals for the four of them.

After school, and before the minibus left, the Bliss twins came into the Store. Tom Nicholls was in charge for the afternoon and took their money for the five bars of chocolate they'd chosen, unaware that they were in truth penniless. He rather liked their good manners and the way they spoke so nicely.

After they'd gone, Linda said to Tom from behind her Post Office grille, 'Nice kids, aren't they? New, I think.'

'Could do with some new clothes. Kate won't take kindly to them dressed like that.'

Linda said, 'I know she won't. She insists on the full uniform right from their first day. It'll cost a bomb to kit out our Lewis, but I know he'll look lovely, even if the sleeves on 'is blazer will be too long. I can't be buying blazers any too often, not with our mortgage. He's reading already. Can't think where he gets it from. Alan was a dunce at school.'

Tom laughed. 'Weren't we all?'

'Enjoying working for his nibs, are you?'

'Grateful, let's put it that way. I couldn't bear having to move Evie, she's so happy here. Jimbo saved my bacon giving me this job, believe me. I like the days driving round collecting the homegrown vegetables and such from the farms. He's given so many people a livelihood, has Jimbo. Farmers' wives making cakes, meals for the freezer, jam for the mail order, pickles, you name it. Cooking hams for the deli. There's no end to it.'

'To say nothing of all the people he employs for events. The wedding was a smashing do, wasn't it? That cake! I'd have given my right arm for it at our wedding. And the food! Jimbo kept that quiet, didn't he? Eh!'

'All part of being a businessman, Linda.'

Tom continued serving people, slicing ham, giving change, keeping an eye open for any misbehaviour, and he'd just helped someone to load up their car when his arch enemy appeared from the mail order room to get her shopping before leaving for home. For some reason he didn't get on with Greta Jones, and he didn't know why.

Mrs Jones slapped down eight packages on the counter. 'Here we are, Linda, the last of today's parcels. What a day I've had.' She absent-mindedly stroked one of the beautifully wrapped mail order packages as though reluctant to let it go. 'I've packaged everything from lemon cheese to pickled onions.'

'Get on, you know you like it.'

Mrs Jones had to admit she did. 'Satisfying. I even enjoy admiring the red-checked covers on the jars. They never fail to make me smile! We've got a new line starting – bottled peaches. We're buying them from the greenhouses at the Big House and bottling them ready for the Christmas trade. Wonderful gold labels they're going to have, but it's still Harriet's Country Cousin brand name. Bottled in brandy so God knows how much they'll cost to buy. Jimbo's struck a good bargain with old Fitch though.'

32

'He'll have more on his mind than peaches at the moment,' Linda commented. She and Mrs Jones giggled. Their tittle-tattle, which amounted to nothing in the end, annoyed Tom.

'Maybe he was feeling magnanimite at the time, as he was courting!' Mrs Jones bent double with laughter but caught Linda's warning glance just in time. Linda's counter faced the outside door and she'd spotted Kate coming in. Mrs Jones straightened up, gave Linda the money for the stamps on her packages and waited for her receipt. It seemed ridiculous, this business of paying to post the mail order packages, robbing Peter to pay Paul as you might say, but Jimbo insisted on it to keep the accounts straight, he said, and to make sure the mail order was paying for itself. Mrs Jones shrugged. If that was how he wanted it, that was how he got it. 'Why, good afternoon, Kate. Married life suiting you?'

Kate, who was now standing behind her waiting her turn, said, 'Yes, thank you, Mrs Jones.'

'I was sorry none of your relatives were there on Friday.'

'They disapproved.'

'Ah! That's understandable.'

Kate looked askance and didn't reply. She had a pile of small boxes of wedding cake to post.

'Oh! They're going all over the world! How wonderful.' Linda enjoyed herself weighing them all and working out the value of stamps needed for each one. 'Three to Africa! Of course, that's where you worked before you came here. They'll be surprised.'

Rather tartly Kate replied, 'I haven't put our ages on the cake, Linda.'

33

'Oh! I didn't mean that. I meant surprised at you getting married. You know with you being . . . a bit older than usual. They'll be pleased though, I expect.'

'I hope so. I'd like a receipt, please.'

'Of course. A receipt. Got to watch the housekeeping, eh? Don't expect old Fitch lets anything slip through; mustard on accounts, I understand. Must have had to be, the way his business has taken off. Look after the pennies and the pounds look after themselves, eh?' Linda printed out the receipt for her and pushed it under the grille.

Kate felt as though she'd been beaten with a meat tenderizer. It really was abominable the way this woman gossiped. She wondered why Jimbo kept her on. She caught Tom's eye watching them and saw he too was annoyed.

As Linda dropped Kate's boxes into the postbag she said, 'We've had some lovely children in from the school. They must be new. No uniform, I noticed. Very well spoken.'

'That'll be the Bliss children. Yes, they are new, started today. Thank you, Linda.'

'Someone said there were new people in Simone Paradise's old house so it must be them. I saw them getting on the Little Derehams minibus when they left here. Bet it's in a mess. There's been no one in there since she . . . got burnt up, and it wasn't up to much even then.'

'Time you learnt to curb your tongue, Linda.'

Linda puffed up like a disgruntled turkey cock. 'I'm not a kid in your school.'

'Pity. I'd soon have you knocked into shape.'

'Well! Really!'

Kate slammed out of the Store, furious with herself for

having allowed Linda to anger her, but it was a shock learning that the Blisses were living in Simone's old house. In her heart, she had grieved for Simone for a long time. But her death had brought to an end an episode in her life of which she was not proud. Black magic! She must have been a complete idiot. She drove up to the Big House, hoping Craddock would be home early and she could heal herself by telling him all about her day.

The same thing happened each day that week. Immediately after school finished, the Bliss twins came into the Store, made a rapid choice of five bars of chocolate and then ran hell for leather to catch the minibus.

But the following week they didn't come in. Both Tom and Jimbo noticed them dithering by the school wall, as though making up their minds whether or not to come in the Store, but instead reluctantly climbing on to the bus with their sisters.

They'd told their mother that Mrs Fitch was giving everyone a bar of chocolate each day to celebrate her wedding. Mrs Bliss knew that wasn't true, but who was she to chastise them for stealing, when she'd done the very same thing each day to put food on the table? In any case, they were so transparently honest it hadn't occurred to them that five bars gave their game away. Mrs Bliss knew they'd either shoplifted the chocolate or stolen the money for it. Bless their dear hearts, thinking of her. How bad had things got that she was blessing them for stealing, when all their lives, honesty had been their watchword.

But on the Friday, the bell jingled and all four of them came in to the Store. Una and Della wandered off on their own, while Philip and Paul kept Jimbo in conversation.

The two little girls then headed for the outside door and the two boys abruptly ended their conversation and dived out after them. They rushed on to the bus and were gone.

'Mr Charter-Plackett! I think those girls have—'

'Thank you, Linda, I guessed.'

'But don't you want to—'

'I said thank you.' Jimbo's dismissive tone smarted. Honestly, thought Linda, for years he's been glad for me to tell him if I suspected shoplifting.

'I was only doing my duty as you see it.'

'I know.'

'But, you've always said—'

'Linda!' Jimbo thundered. 'Thank you.'

'That's an example to set our Lewis. I'll let him come and watch how to do it. He likes chocolate.'

Jimbo marched over, removed his boater and pressed his face to the grille. In a stage whisper he said, 'Will you leave it to me? I saw what happened, I have got eyes, and I shall deal with it. Right?'

There was something about the authoritative manner in which he clapped his boater back on that angered Linda. How was she to know? More loudly than necessary she said sarcastically, 'You'd better give me a list of who can and who can't shoplift, then I shan't make any more mistakes.'

Jimbo, already going back to the till, paused, recollected he'd decided not to sack Linda again because of the humble pie he'd have to eat to get her back, then continued on his way, fuming. For two pins he'd stop the Post Office; it was more of a service than a moneyspinner after all. But then he remembered it drew shoppers in, and that otherwise the superstore on the by-pass would get

36

their trade. No, he'd keep the Post Office, but pray he'd come across someone with Linda's skills. If he did then, bang! Out she'd go. He found it incredible that pathetic, gossipy Linda was indispensable to him. Still, her intimate knowledge of the goings-on in the village was a valuable asset. The customers all loved her for it, unless the gossip was about themselves. But he'd have a word with Kate on Sunday. Something had to be done about the Blisses. He couldn't afford to have both mother and children stealing, much as they might need it. Jimbo was convinced they were grindingly poor and, in addition, unaccustomed to it.

Chapter 3

Maggie Dobbs threw her shopping bag on to the floor and swore, roundly and loudly, as her cleaning shoes and apron fell out of it. There was no one to hear so it didn't matter. Her outdoor shoes she shoved off her feet and let them drop on to the tiles along with her coat and scarf. She'd have to give up this school job. It was more than a Christian soul should have to tolerate.

It was a wet day and the kids would kick off their wellingtons but not before they'd plastered her nice clean floor with muddy footprints. Anyone would think they'd done a day's work on a building site before they arrived at school. Thick mud here there and everywhere. So what does her nibs Kate Pascoe or rather Fitch, decide? 'Mrs Dobbs,' she'd said. 'This floor will have to be cleaned before you go or it will be all over the school.' She'd added please but only as an afterthought. Maggie hated wet days, because if the floor needed cleaning, which it always did, it meant moving all the boots and some of the children didn't have them named so how the heck was she supposed to know whose boots went under which peg? She wasn't a mind reader.

Maggie heaved herself up and went to switch on the kettle. Entering her kitchen always gave her heart a lift. It was so spanking smart and up to date it was unbelievable she was renting a cottage at least four hundred years old. Don Wright – and . . . Vera was it? – who'd rented it to her had done a great job of modernizing the place. The bathroom was to die for, you felt cleaner just walking into it. White from floor to ceiling, wall to wall. Wonderful! Such a pity that her Dave had died two weeks before they'd been due to move in. He'd have loved it here, after that ghastly flat they'd rented for fifteen years.

Maggie sat back with a cup of scalding hot tea and allowed herself to think for a moment. Feet propped on the coffee table, she ruminated on her job. It was very trying. Every morning by eight o'clock she was at the school sorting out the day for them all. Back at eleven-thirty to take delivery of the hot school dinners from the caterer's van, put out the tables, and keep a watchful eye on the ladies who served the dinners to the children, to make sure they cleaned up their own mess of spilt food before they went. She conducted a vicious war with them day in, day out.

Home again and then back at three, to begin cleaning ready for the next day. Then, lo and behold, there were sometimes evening classes. Like that embroidery group that rented a classroom once a week in term-time. She'd warned them about leaving needles around . . . There came a knock at the door.

She opened her front door to find a woman standing there. She pretended not to recognize her. She wore thick mascara and her hair was blacker than the night. She was slim too, like Maggie would never be in a month of Sundays.

'Yes?'

'Maggie Dobbs?'

'I live here, yes.'

'Can I come in?' The woman looked almost furtively around as though making sure she hadn't been seen knocking on Maggie Dobbs's door.

Maggie opened the door wider and let her in. A strong waft of a cloying oriental perfume hit her nostrils. She'd have to open a window when this woman left.

'I'm Venetia from the Big House.'

Unimpressed, Maggie nodded.

'I run the leisure centre for the staff training college there.'

'Yes, I know.'

'Oh! Right. I wondered if I'd be welcome . . . you know.' Venetia winked knowingly. 'I'd be very discreet.'

Why couldn't she come straight out with it? 'I think I know what you're hinting at, but I don't do it for nothing. You have to pay. I have my expenses.'

'Oh! Of course. I wouldn't expect you to. Five pounds, I understand. I'll pay in advance. Here. Look. When's the next . . . ' She gave another of her knowing winks.

'Tonight as it happens and there'll be room. Eight-thirty sharp. No parking outside.'

Venetia passed her the five-pound note with a sleight of hand movement, as though the room was full of people who mustn't know. 'Absolutely. Understood. Thank you. See you then.'

Maggie tucked the note into the jug Dave had won for her at a fair. He'd had the choice of two jugs and to her annoyance he'd chosen the one she thought the least attractive of the two, but sentiment made her keep it when she'd moved. It seemed right to keep the money in there too. After all, it was Dave who'd got her into this lark in the beginning. It felt like a lucky charm. That made five for tonight. Perfect.

By eight minutes past eight the room was ready. A fire was burning in the grate, black plastic tulips in a black vase stood on the round table – it had to be round, couldn't be square – and incense sticks burned on the mantelpiece, the hearth and the sideboard. She switched off the main light so the room was illuminated by the flames of the fire and a small table lamp with an almost transparent red cloth laid over the shade to create a mystical, fiery glow.

Maggie sat down to wait, getting herself in the mood. This old house did more for the atmosphere than that ghastly flat had done. Old memories, which the house had stored over the centuries, seemed to swirl around the room, and the flickering flames sometimes made her guests shudder with fear, for, once she'd got them going, the shadows they made appeared like people moving around the room. Ghostly, really.

At twenty-five past eight, the first of the guests arrived. It was the Senior twins, dressed in black from head to foot. They left their woolly hats at home when they came to one of Maggie's meetings and wore black headscarves instead. They each put their five-pound notes into the jug in the centre of the table and sat down next to each other. Then came Venetia, very obviously hyped up about the meeting, who took her place opposite the Senior sisters and next to Maggie herself. Conversation was never encouraged at the start so they sat in silence. Next to come was Greta Jones, then one of the weekenders dressed in what she considered was appropriate clothing for the

41

country; namely cords, and a woolly rustic embroidered sweater, which disguised her bulges very effectively. She never gave her name, even though she'd been a member of the group since its initiation.

Once all the five-pound notes had been put in the jug, it was removed along with the black tulips, and Maggie placed her hands, fingers widespread, on the polished table.

'I feel the spirits very strongly tonight. They're all around, I know,' she said. Her guests followed suit and their fingertips made a complete linking circle. Total silence fell.

The only movements in the dark were the shadows made by the flames on the walls. The corners of the room were eerie and threatening and the atmosphere was supercharged with anticipation. On occasion, Maggie went straight into a trance, other times it took a while for the spirits to move her. When Maggie's head began rolling from side to side and a low moaning came from her throat, they knew she was almost away with the spirits. Slowly, her head began circling motions, dropping on to her chest and then backwards over the back of her seat, with such increasing violence it seemed it might drop off, and the moaning grew louder.

Then, in a voice totally unlike her own, she called out as though in agony, 'Who's there? Who's there?'

The fire sparked, momentarily flooding the room with light. Only Maggie's eyes were closed, her heavy lids pressed tight together, her dark purple lips twisted tortuously as though trying to frame words that would not come. Venetia coughed; Greta Jones shuddered; the

Senior sisters pressed closer to each other; the eyes of the weekender darted hither and thither with fear.

'Who's there?' came the shuddering cry of Maggie Dobbs.

Then she shrieked and her voice became unearthly. 'It's me. I've a message for one of you. I see jars and jars and . . . labels and . . , jam, that's right . . .'

Greta Jones's eyes grew large. 'Oh God!'

'A message. Yes. You have trouble where you work. Someone doesn't like you. Take care. There's trouble with . . .'

'Yes?' croaked Greta Jones.

There was a long, shuddering sigh and then silence.

Whispering more to herself than anyone, Greta Jones said, 'That's Linda, I bet. It'll be her, no doubt. She's been sparring for a fight for weeks.'

The spirit's voice continued. 'Where are the twins?'

The Senior sisters jerked in unison.

'They're both well,' answered Maggie in her own voice. 'They're here. Do you have a message for them?'

Silence. And then a voice spoke through Maggie as though from the depths of the grave. 'They are not well. They're full of sin. I know. I keep a constant watch. My heart bleeds. Bleeds. Si–i–i–n–n–n.'

The Senior sisters shook with terror.

'What is their sin? What have they done? Tell us if you can.'

'Thieves! Thieves, I say.' Again the unearthly tones filtered through every shadow. 'Shame on you. I saw, I saw. I've kept watch since the first day I came here. I know my twins' every move.'

43

The sisters' faces drained to dead white, horror paralysing them.

The voice from the grave continued. 'There'll be a punishment to come for what they've done. A punishment more terrible than anything they've ever known.'

The sister seated next to Greta Jones collapsed against her and it was all Greta could do to stop her falling to the floor. The circle was broken. Maggie gave a great cry. The cat jumped on Venetia's knee and she screamed and screamed with shock. Alarmed, it jumped off, knocked over the table lamp, and the bulb shattered on the hearth, leaving them in darkness except for the light of the flames.

The weekender leapt to her feet to flick the switch for the centre light. Greta Jones shrieked, 'No! No! Maggie's not come out of her trance, it could kill her.'

There were five hearts beating far too fast and five people wishing the light could be turned on. Maggie snapped her fingers twice and came back to life.

'Dear God! What was the message? It must have been terrible. I got such vibrations! More like shock waves. What happened?' Maggie lay back in her chair exhausted, apparently drained of life. She always said the sprirts were something separate from herself and that she knew nothing when she 'awoke'.

Greta Jones was the first to find her voice. 'It was the twins' mother. She says, well, she says they've been stealing and they can expect a terrible punishment.' Greta choked on her last words, hardly daring to say what they'd heard.

Maggie, visibly shaking, went in the kitchen and got herself a drink of water, then came back to sit down. 'Well, have you?'

Speaking as one, the two sisters whispered, 'We have! We have!'

'Then you'd better put it to rights, hadn't you?'

They both got out their handkerchiefs and wiped their eyes.

'Mother always knows best.'

'She said so when she was here.'

'We can't give it back though.'

Maggie enquired what it was they'd stolen.

'F-f-food from the w-w-wedding p-p-arty.'

'But we've eaten it.'

'Except there's still some wedding cake in the tin.'

'We could put that back.'

Maggie shrugged. 'That's it for tonight. I can't do no more. Not tonight. I'm shattered.'

Greta's hand clutched Maggie's. 'Of course, we understand. Same time next week?'

Maggie nodded and lay back, her eyes closed.

Greta got to her feet. 'That's it then. We'd better go. What a night! The best for a while.'

'Don't you always hear voices from the other side then?' Venetia asked of Greta, disappointed no one from the other side had had a message for her.

'Sometimes it's all jumbled and we can't tell who it is. But tonight! We couldn't have had a clearer message, could we? Come on, you two, we'll walk home together seeing as I pass your house. Take my arm.'

The Senior sisters each took an arm and they went home, weak at the knees, desperate to figure out how they could make amends. For their mother to know they were still stealing . . . it really was too terrible to contemplate! And the punishment, what would that be? Their mother was a past master at punishments. They'd been glad when she died, but apparently after seven years of silence, she'd returned from the grave to watch over them.

Maggie sat back in her chair, sipping from the glass of water. Talk about getting what they paid for. She needed more than water tonight. From the sideboard cupboard she took a bottle of whisky and tipped a sturdy measure into what remained of the water. When she sat down again, her cat climbed up on to her knee, kneading its claws into her leg, purring like a kettle on the hob, glad they were on their own again. Maggie sipped the whisky and water, and smiled to herself.

Next morning Maggie found a parcel waiting on the doorstep of the main door of the school. It was very neatly put together and closely bound with Sellotape. It was about the size of four bars of toilet soap and was addressed to Mrs Fitch.

With all the instructions about bombs nowadays she did wonder whether she should call the bomb squad. It was kind of the right size for such a thing, but she guessed what it was; the wedding cake the Senior sisters had stolen. She placed it on Mrs Fitch's desk with a malevolent smile. She supposed it could be a bomb. How could she know? She hadn't got X-ray eyes, had she?

She was inspecting the boys' toilets when Mrs Fitch called out, 'Mrs Dobbs, where did you find this parcel?'

'On the doorstep, Mrs Fitch. When I came in at eight.'

'How strange. I wonder what it is?'

'One way to find out.'

'Yes. Of course.'

And as Maggie had anticipated, it was wedding cake.

How they'd got a piece that size in their bag without being noticed Maggie couldn't work out. She'd seen them stuffing rolls and tiny Scotch eggs in, and pieces of salmon carefully inched into plastic bags and then put in their huge handbags. But they must must have taken a whole quarter of the cake's top tier.

Kate looked at it, puzzled. Why should anyone want to send her a piece of her own wedding cake? It was ridiculous. She shrugged and put it by the side of her handbag ready for going home. Home, where she would find Beano and Dandy waiting with Craddock. At first, he hadn't taken kindly to her two cats, and had almost decided to say no to them, but at the last minute they'd been reprieved. Living at the Big House, they were closer than ever to their favourite hunting grounds and were really only seen in the evenings when, worn out by hunting all day, they curled up straight after their supper and were no trouble to anyone. But going home to Craddock was the best bit. He wanted to hear all her news and if his attention did wander after a while, who could blame him? To eat an evening meal with someone almost every night of the week, and no housework to do was bliss. And her career remained intact, too.

She glanced at the clock and saw it was time for the bell. Kate had had a perfectly splendid day teaching her top class. As the school was so small, she taught two age groups together, Years Six and Seven, and loved every moment. The Bliss boys were clever. She knew that from the first day. In fact, they were very clever. It was a pity their clothes were so dreadful. There was apparently no question of them wearing school uniform, and it irritated

47

her that no effort had been made to kit them out. She held them back after school that day to ask.

'Sorry, miss, this is all we have.' Philip spoke as though that was that and there was no point in any further discussion.

Paul added, 'Sorry, miss.' And looked acutely embarrassed.

'I see. Tell your mother to come to see me one day soon and we'll have a talk.'

'Right, miss.'

Very gently Kate replied, 'And my name is Mrs Fitch, not miss.'

'Yes, Mrs Fitch,' they said in unison.

'Be sharp, or the bus will have gone.'

And it had. Leaving two small girls crying by the gate, not daring to get on the minibus without their brothers for protection.

Philip came back in. 'Miss! It's gone.'

'Gone? But they know you get on with the girls. The silly man. Don't worry, I'll take you home.'

'No. We'll walk.' He hurried out.

Kate called after him, 'Wait! I'll take you.'

She grabbed her handbag, shouted, 'Good night, Mrs Dobbs,' and caught up with them as they rounded the corner into Church Hill. 'Come back and get in the car.' When she saw Philip about to open his mouth to object, she said, 'That's an order.' She stood half smiling, arms folded, looking stern.

She saw the struggle in Philip's face, the embarrassment in Paul's and the delight in the girls' faces when they realized they wouldn't have to walk all that way home to Little Derehams.

'I shall drop you off wherever you say. Come along.'

The two boys looked relieved and followed her back into the schoolyard.

When she'd finally got the four of them belted up, she turned the ignition key and set off. As she was driving down Church Hill, it occurred to her that the parcel of wedding cake had not been beside her bag when she picked it up. That was odd.

It was only two miles and a bit to Little Derehams and it was quite a relief to get there. Whatever topic of conversation she brought up elicited no response from the children. They might just as well have been mutes.

She knew exactly where they lived and smiled to herself when, five doors past it, Philip shouted, 'Stop here!'

Della had a child's battered rucksack, which Kate had put in the boot. When she lifted it out, there was a distinct rustle of greaseproof paper, and it felt heavier than she would have expected.

'Bye, children. See you tomorrow.' They stood on the pavement waving while she reversed into a driveway to turn round. Kate purposely drove slowly and watched in her rear-view mirror to see where they went. The two girls couldn't wait to get home and dashed off immediately to Simone Paradise's old cottage; the boys waited another minute and then followed. The poor things. They were terrified she might go in with them and see the squalor. If it was anything like it used to be when Simone lived there, squalor would be a polite word for the condition of the house.

'Craddock!'

He looked up from *The Economist* and peered at her

over the top of his reading glasses. 'Darling?'

'Are you feeling full of good advice?'

Craddock stopped reading and took off his glasses. 'Yes. What is it you want?'

'Well, it's not something I want, it's—'

'Yes? Spit it out.'

'I have four children at school in dire poverty and quite unable to buy school uniform. For whatever reason, their mother is bringing them up alone and they are poorer than the proverbial church mouse. They are obviously un-accustomed to poverty, because they're well mannered, dignified, proud. You know.'

'I hope you're not saying that children living in desperate conditions must therefore be ill-mannered and common.'

Kate was puzzled by his remark. 'No, of course not. What I mean is . . . well, I don't know what I mean, but they are in a bad way and stealing to feed themselves. Jimbo had a word on Sunday and he says the mother is in the Store most days stealing food, and that she almost fainted in there one day. He hasn't said anything yet, but of course it can't go on. The children are bone thin. Today they stole a large piece of wedding cake, which someone left in a parcel on the school door-step.'

Craddock straightened up in his chair and said, 'I'm losing the plot here. Are you saying that you found a piece of *our* wedding cake in a ·parcel on the school doorstep? Whatever for, for Christ's sake?'

'I haven't the faintest idea. But there it was. Carefully wrapped in greaseproof paper and in a cardboard box. But

I'm very sure that it was in one of the little girls' rucksacks when I drove them home.'

'Why did you drive them home? What's happened to the bus?'

'I was having a talk with the two boys, only for a moment, but the driver left the two girls standing waiting because they daren't get on without their brothers.'

'The blithering idiot! I'll see about this.' He got out his electronic diary and made a note. 'They're given a task, all spelt out and well paid for it too, and still they can't manage to do it right. I'll sack the lot and get someone else.'

'That's not the point.'

'It is to me. I'm paying for the damn buses and they've to go on time but, most especially, not leave little girls standing on their own. Anything could have happened. I'll fire the lot of 'em.'

'Please, Craddock, I'm not talking about minibus drivers, I'm talking about poverty.'

'So am I! That's what they'll be suffering from, when I've done with them. Poverty in capital letters. The damn fools.' He got to his feet and marched about the sitting room in a fuming temper. 'Only what they deserve. How did he suppose those little girls would get home? I mean, did he give it a thought? Oh no. Do we have the idiot's name?'

'No. But I shall find out for you tomorrow. Now, could we please talk about poverty?'

'You promise? Ring me first thing.'

'Right. Now—'

'You said to me that throwing money at a problem was

51

earning me no Brownie points, so what would you like me to do?'

'That's what I'm asking. What can we do?'

'Money is my answer, that's all I know. Money. It's the answer to everything in one way or another, and it's the only one in these circumstances, believe me.'

'Yes, Craddock, I know. What I'm saying is while you've given me complete access to your money by making a joint account for us both, would you object to me buying them school uniforms and pretending they came from the council?'

'It's my experience that you might as well be honest with the woman and tell her you're buying them because somehow, as sure as the sun rises each morning, she's going to find out and then she'll be even more mortified. What did the girl want with the wedding cake?'

Kate smiled wryly at him. 'To eat, of course, because they're hungry. Like I said, their mother is stealing from the Store to feed them.'

'Maybe she's a poor manager.'

'Oh, come on! Would she take the risk of being charged with theft because she's spending what money she has on cigarettes and gin? She's not the type.'

The following lunchtime Kate popped into the Store to post a parcel to a friend for her birthday. In front of her in the queue was Mrs Bliss, clutching a very new-looking allowance book.

'Mrs Bliss. Can I have a word before you leave?'

Mrs Bliss turned to see who had spoken. 'Yes, of course.' But she collected her money and before Kate had paid for her parcel and stuck on the stamps, she had left. Kate raced out after her and was just in time to see her disappearing into the wood on the spare land. 'Mrs Bliss!'

She stopped and waited.

'Mrs Bliss. I've been wanting a word. I hope you won't be offended, but I feel very concerned that your children don't have school uniform. I think it's making them feel like outsiders and it's not fair. I realize school uniform is out of the question for you, but I do have access to council funds, which I can use entirely at my discretion. It helps with funding parties and little extra things we need, you know. The children, in particular Philip and Paul, feel embarrassed that they don't have uniforms. If I can get permission, would you allow the school to buy uniforms for them? No one but you and I shall know you've had help.'

Mrs Bliss, for the first time, looked Kate straight in the eye. 'I would very much appreciate that. I don't like them being different. Like you said, it's not fair on them. They don't ask for it, you see, because they know,' her head went down and she muttered, 'we can't afford it.'

'I understand. That's why I'm telling you about this discretionary fund. Can I go ahead, then? All you'll need to do is take a letter from me to the school outfitters in Culworth and you can buy whatever is necessary.'

'Thank you, for their sakes.'

'They're very bright. But then you know that, don't you?'

Mrs Bliss nodded.

'Well, I've got to get back. I'll give the letter to Philip to bring home to you and you can go on Saturday.'

When Kate returned to school, she found Maggie

Dobbs searching for her, complaining loudly. 'Them dinner women, I've caught 'em good and proper. Taking food home. This time I saw it with my own eyes.' She stabbed a finger at Kate. 'A den of thieves, they are. Small portions for the kids and take home what's left. Disgusting. Stealing food from His little ones. "Suffer the little children to come unto Me for of such is the Kingdom of heaven." ' Maggie's dark brown eyes looked piously heavenwards.

'Mrs Dobbs! My office, if you please. Now.'

Standing in front of Kate's desk, Maggie outlined her evidence. 'So, she couldn't find her keys and I said they'll have dropped in your bag, and when she opened it, there it was for all to see – a basin full of food with clingfilm over it. I never said no word to her that I'd noticed, none of my business, of course. She perhaps thinks I never saw, but I did. It'll be for her old man for his supper, you can bet.' Maggie folded her arms self-righteously.

'Mrs Dobbs, thank you. I shall deal with this.'

'She's gone now, so yer can't.'

'I shall tomorrow. Please do not take matters into your own hands. I am the headteacher here.'

'I know, that's why I told you. It's to be done proper, sacking her. I've been suspicious for months, but now I've caught 'em red-handed.'

Mrs Dobbs flounced out, a look of triumph on her face. At last. The occasional bottle of cream cleaner she used for the school basins found its way from school into the cupboard under her sink, but that was her due. Taking food from children was different. She wondered about inviting the dinner ladies to one of her seances and frightening them to death like she had the Senior sisters. After all, she'd be doing everyone a good turn if it stopped them thieving, wouldn't she?

Chapter 4

Muriel, to her dismay, had been asked to play the piano for the Maypole dancing practice at the school. Kate had asked her, having seen her name in an old school log book as the Maypole pianist. The children did it on the Green each year on 1 May and the day would be here before they knew where they were. Would she? Please? Hetty's class was a very difficult one this year with several turbulent souls in it and Hetty felt she couldn't give her mind to it. Could she?

Muriel found it hard to refuse, for she'd loved the Maypole and the ribbons and all the jolly tunes ever since she'd been at the village school herself. She consulted Ralph and he'd said, 'Why not, my dear? You must.'

'I'm very rusty. I haven't played for years, not since Hetty Hardaker started at the school and took over all the music. I would have to practise.' Muriel wrung her hands. 'I hate making a fool of myself. No, I won't. I'll say no. Yes, I'll say no. Going away, I shall say. No, that would be telling fibs, because we'd have to go away when I don't want to. Too rusty, too old, lost my confidence and that's the truth.'

Ralph had taken her writhing hands in his and held them close to his cheek, then kissed them. 'My dear, if it's going to make you ill, then don't do it. But may I make a suggestion?' Muriel nodded. 'Sleep on it and see how you feel tomorrow morning.'

'Oh Ralph, of course, you're quite right. You always are. You know me inside out, don't you?' She stood on tiptoe and placed a kiss on his forehead, admired his distinguished good looks of which she never tired, and asked, 'Tea before we go to bed?'

'I fancy whisky tonight. And you?'

Muriel nodded. 'With water, as always.'

So, having taken Ralph's advice, she'd agreed and the day had come for their first practice. Two or three nights prior to the big day, she'd asked permission to borrow the school keys from Mrs Dobbs and had gone into school secretly. She found the rustiness she'd feared had melted away as soon as her fingers caught the rhythm of 'The Spider's Web', which was one of her favourites. She loved the tune and the idea of the interwoven ribbons forming the web to catch the fly. Oh yes, she was going to enjoy this. The second night she'd gone to practise, she took the keys home with her by mistake, though how she could have done that she couldn't understand because the key to the main door was huge.

So, having got home, Muriel had to set out again to take it to Mrs Dobbs, who would need it early the next day. Outside Mrs Dobbs's door, however, Muriel stood still, appalled by the terrible moaning going on inside. Being a cottage, the front door opened straight into the living room and it appeared to be coming directly from there. She tried knocking but there was no reply. Still the moaning continued and then there was a piercing shriek.

57

Unnerved, Muriel thrust the key through the letterbox and fled, trembling in every limb.

But the next morning, there was Maggie Dobbs, her usual chirpy self and apparently none the worse for the agony of the night before.

'Good morning, Lady Templeton! Nice to have you on board.'

'Good morning, Mrs Dobbs. Are you quite well?'

'Bloomin'. Thanks.' She dashed away to get on with her morning duties and left Muriel standing alone in the hall. Whatever it was, she thought, it couldn't have been serious.

Muriel enjoyed assembly and couldn't resist peeping from behind her fingers to watch the children saying their prayers. Rows of quite delightful children, from the tiny ones at the front to the bigger ones, almost ready for leaving, at the back. Such dear, dear children, with their little hands held to their faces in prayer. What a joy. Such innocence.

Then she spotted one of the bigger boys holding his nose and pointing at the new twins and laughing. The twin nearest to him was trying his best to ignore the taunting but finally erupted, giving his torturer the most enormous swipe across his face, and then pushing him so that he almost overbalanced into the next boy sitting cross-legged beside him. A wholesale fight then broke out and Kate Pascoe, or rather Kate Fitch, had to stop her prayers.

'Children!' Kate exclaimed in her most headmistressy voice. 'Please.' When the boys had settled down again, she said, with extreme disappointment in her voice, 'A fight in the middle of our prayers? That is not the example I expect from the top class. I am ashamed of you. Prayers are not to be interrupted by unseemly behaviour. Paul, come out here. You may read out the rest of the prayer I have prepared for this morning. Robert! You can hold the book for him. Come forward quietly, please.'

And they did, to Muriel's surprise. When they'd finished reading the prayer and had returned to their places, Muriel thought the dear boy must feel terribly excluded. So thin and badly dressed. Really! Why couldn't parents blessed with children take better care of them? It was so unkind. His mother needed taking in hand. And by the looks of it, those two little girls near the front were his sisters. A tear came into her eye at the thought of the humiliation they must feel with everyone else in school uniform and their clothes not even remotely decent. How unfair!

Kate's voice cut across her indignation. 'Robert, will you come to my office at breaktime? I need a word. Lady Templeton has kindly come to play the piano for us for our Maypole practice. Isn't that a lovely surprise? Shall we give Lady Templeton a clap for being so kind?' Much to Muriel's embarrassment, they clapped her and made her blush. Kate held up her hand. 'Thank you, that was lovely. So the first class to begin is Miss Booth's. Then Mrs Hardaker's and after break my class. We shall all have to put our backs into it and if you're not chosen to do the actual dancing, then you will be in the choir to do the singing before and afterwards. We need everyone to help. So each one of you will be either a singer or a dancer. To your classes, children, except for Miss Booth's.'

Kate gave Muriel an encouraging wave and before she knew it, Muriel was playing for the babies. Well, at least that was how she thought of them. The newest little girl, whom she later found was called Una, looked too frail to dance a single step, but there was something magical about her; she was light-footed, kept good time, and held her head high and with such grace, Muriel was convinced that if she'd begun playing *Swan Lake*, the child would have been the best and most elegant swan. Quite amazing, thought Muriel, for such a little girl.

She commented on it to Kate when they were having coffee at breaktime in Kate's office. 'You should see her! She's quite spectacular. A delight to watch. Such a pity her mother doesn't take better care of her.'

'I'm taking that in hand, Muriel. She takes the best care of her that she can, that's all I can say for the moment. They've big financial problems, I'm afraid.'

'There must have been a father at some time.'

'There must, but . . .'

There was a knock at the door. It was Robert Nightingale.

'You wanted to see me, Mrs Fitch?'

'Thank you, Robert.'

Muriel decided to leave. If he was going to get a telling-off, she didn't want to witness it, although he had been naughty. 'If you'll excuse me.' She slipped out of the door and left the two of them alone.

'Now, Robert, I saw what happened.'

'Their clothes stink.'

'That does not give you licence to be unkind. You have a mum and a dad at home, and your mother doesn't have to work. Mind you, with seven children I doubt she could find the time. By comparison you are very lucky indeed. I'd like you to make an effort to be friendly with both Paul

60

and Phil. They need someone popular on their side, and you are that very person. Are you not?'

Robert shuffled his feet and blushed, not liking to agree with her that he was one of the most popular boys in the school. 'But why should I?'

'Three reasons. Because you're a kind person really, because there is someone in need of your help and because I asked you to. How about it? Their problems are going to get resolved, believe me, in time, but they need help.'

'All right, but only because you told me to.'

'Robert Nightingale, you are a star. Thank you.'

'May I go?'

'Of course.'

Robert turned back from the door to say, 'They steal. Did you know?'

Kate looked up, her face expressionless. 'They do?'

'Yes.'

'Such as?'

'People's sweets, money. That was why Karen hadn't any dinner money yesterday, they'd stolen it.'

'Why haven't you told me before?'

'Because they haven't got much, and I'm not a snitch.'

'You're not, but sometimes the truth has to be told for everyone's good. Thank you for telling me, Robert. I suppose they spend it in the Store?'

'Yes. Before the bus goes. But sometimes they steal from him, in the shop, I mean. Mr Charter-Plackett knows, I think.'

Kate nodded. 'I'll have a word. Don't tell anyone else.'

'We all know.'

'I see. Leave me to deal with it. Thank you. Remember what I said.'

But the stealing problem worsened. By half past three, ten pounds had been stolen from Margaret Booth's handbag.

'I know it was there, Kate. I remember thinking I'd have to get money for the weekend at the supermarket when I paid for my groceries tonight. It was definitely there. I could stand up in court and testify.'

'Not spent it in the Store at lunchtime?'

'Never left the school premises all day.'

'I hate it when we have stealing. Really hate it, and now the minibuses have gone and whoever's taken it has got away with it. Where has your bag been all day?'

'In your office to begin with, then after lunch I had it with me in the classroom. They must be very quick, whoever it is. Fast as the speed of light for me not to notice. I'm really fed up about it. I hate the feeling of distrust in the air.'

Kate said she was going to the Store to ask if any of the children had been in before the buses left.

Tom Nicholls was behind the cash till.

'Yes, several of them.'

'Remember who they were and what they spent?'

Linda called out from the Post Office, her face pressed to the grille, squashing her nose in a distinctly unflattering manner. 'The Bliss children came in and that big Karen, young Holly Whatsits and a girl called Marie or Maria or something, but she only wanted a birthday card for her mum and I helped her choose it.'

'What did the others buy, Tom?'

'I know Karen bought an ice cream because I remember Holly telling her they wouldn't let her on the bus if she hadn't eaten it before it left. The Bliss children didn't buy anything—'

'No!' shouted Linda. 'I bet they didn't. They'd be shoplifting again!'

Kate was aghast at the venom in her voice. 'Linda! You really must be more careful what you say. Did you *see* them shoplifting?'

'Well, no, not this time, I had a queue, but they do. We know they do.'

'Then if you didn't see them shoplifting today you have no evidence to back up your story. Talk about giving a dog a bad name.'

'But they do, Mrs Fitch. If I didn't see them, it doesn't mean they haven't, does it?'

Kate took a deep breath. 'Yes, but I do wish you wouldn't shout it out for all and sundry to hear. It's not right. They have enough problems without this kind of scandal-mongering.'

Jimbo heard the raised voices and came quietly into the front of the Store. Inwardly he groaned. Not Linda again.

'Scandal-mongering! It's a fact. They've been seen.'

'You could have some compassion for them, Linda.'

Linda stood up, unlocked her Post Office 'cage' and came out firing on all cylinders. 'I'm not one of your school kids. You're not ruling me with a rod of iron. You'll apologize to me for saying scandal-mongering, I won't have it. I'm not making it up. It is true, even if it is gossip.'

Jimbo patiently intervened. 'Excuse me, ladies, if you please.'

But Linda hadn't heard him. 'I've half a mind not to let my Lewis come to your school in September. The way

63

you treat people is nothing short of . . . well . . . scandalous. It's disgraceful.'

Kate gave an exasperated sigh and said, 'I only asked you to show compassion. If your Lewis was going through a difficult patch, would you want someone shouting the odds about it all over the village?'

'It wasn't all over the village, it was in here, and you were the only customer.'

'No, she wasn't,' said Tom. From behind the tinned soups two customers appeared; Angie Turner and a confederate of hers from the bottom of Church Hill. Angie, ever bristling for a scrap, said, 'We heard every word. It's shameful shouting out loud like that about some poor kids who can't help being poor. You should wash your mouth out with soap, you should. Don't you ever dare say anything like that about my kids. Just you mind you don't. See.'

'You've some room to talk. What about when your Colin killed poor Bryn Fields because of his loud mouth? And don't tell me he didn't because I was there.'

A shocked silence followed her outburst. Everyone froze at this unforgivable accusation.

Finally Jimbo bellowed, 'Linda! That is enough. For the very last time, the *very last time*, I am telling you to leave my employment and I don't care if I have to shut the Post Office. You are not coming back in here as one of my employees. And that is final.' He walked to the door and flung it wide open, seething with passion, not knowing at that moment whether what he was doing was right or wrong; the bell jangled hysterically as though sensing the enormity of the drama.

Linda was appalled. She realized that this time he really,

truly meant it. He'd said it before, but there was something very different in his attitude today. Heavens! What would Alan say? They needed her money like a drowning man a lifebelt, and would never have that second kid she wanted if she wasn't working.

Well, she wasn't going without saying her piece. Confronting her critics, she said, 'I've slaved in that dratted cage for more years than I care to remember, locked in day in, day out. Am I glad to be rid of it! Taskmaster, you are, Jimbo, and I'm glad I'm no longer beholden to you. It wouldn't matter if you came *crawling*,' she relished the word, '*crawling* on your hands and knees, and offered me *twice* what you pay me now, which you wouldn't because you're a skinflint, I wouldn't come back, not if we were starving. It's a blessed release, believe me. And I shall take you to a tribunal for unfair dismissal, Alan knows all about 'em. Believe me, I mean every word.'

Jimbo answered her in clipped tones, keeping the tightest of control on his temper, and it showed in the cruel pleasure he took in saying, 'Do as you wish, Linda, it is entirely up to you. Take me to twenty tribunals if you want, but go, *now!*' He opened the door as wide as possible and briefly raised his boater to her. Linda flounced out, livid, speechless and defeated.

Tom was the only one to move. He entered the 'cage', retrieved Linda's handbag, and went to stand opposite Jimbo, who was still holding the door wide open. In a moment during which not a word had been spoken, Linda charged back in, spotted Tom at the door holding her handbag at arm's length by the tips of his fingers, impatiently snatched it from him and strode away without even so much as a thank you.

'Well . . .' said Angie Turner, 'she's cooked her goose and not half. Wait till I tell Colin about this. He didn't, you know, kill him.' Then she collapsed on her friend's shoulder and burst into tears.

Jimbo cleared his throat rather loudly, Tom went back to the till grinning and Kate caught Jimbo's eye. They both began to laugh, but sobered up when they realized how hurt Angie Turner had been by Linda's statement. Kate put an arm around her and said, 'We all know it wasn't your Colin. He's the last man on earth to deliberately take an action that would result in someone's death.'

'He's a big fella but he's s–s–so gentle.'

'I know he is. I know. Don't take it to heart. She'll come round and be apologizing all over the place, you wait and see.'

Jimbo shook his head. 'I've sacked her and taken her back time and again but I'm afraid this is her Waterloo. Finito. Finish. Done.' He took off his boater and smoothed his hand over his bald head, a sure sign he was agitated. He huffed and puffed a bit, then looked at Tom and said, 'Well, Tom, there's only you.'

Startled, Tom said, 'Only me?'

Jimbo nodded towards the Post Office.

Tom braced himself to spring into the breach. 'Of course. Soon have that sorted. Not much to it, I reckon. She made a lot of fuss over nothing.'

'Half a day, one to one instruction? Sunday? At two?'

'Agreed.'

'Fine. That's solved then.' Jimbo walked off into the

66

back, leaving Tom pleased with himself and Kate dazzled by Jimbo's decisiveness.

'Will you be able to do it, Tom? There'll be a lot to learn, won't there?' Kate asked.

'It'll be a pleasure. Something to get my teeth into. And I can assure all here present that there'll be no more gossiping like old fishwives.'

'Well, that'll make a refreshing change.'

Angie said through her tears, 'Not before time. I'm sorry.'

Kate patted her arm. 'Nothing to be sorry about, Mrs Turner. It was very hurtful. I fear she wasn't thinking what she was saying. Must be off. I left my desk covered in paperwork. Teaching would be all right if I didn't have so many forms to fill in. They arrive by the vanload sometimes, well, at least it feels like that. Oh for the good old days when all they kept was the register and the school log book.'

Back at school, Kate opened up the secure cupboard though how safe it would be if someone was determined to get in it was debatable, and took out the very first volume of the school log book with the intention of reading it after she and Craddock had eaten their evening meal. The sweetest smile came over her face when she thought about Craddock and she revelled in her thoughts about him for a while, only pulling herself together when she heard Mrs Dobbs whizzing round the hall with her sweeping brush. If she didn't keep a guard on herself she'd be drooling over him like a teenage schoolgirl, but why not? They'd only been married weeks and she acknowledged already they were the best weeks of her life so far.

Because they were having fun, the two of them, which she'd promised him they would.

Mrs Dobbs thrust her head round the door. 'Going yet? I've got your office to do next. Got to keep to my working plan, or I'll lose the thread of what I've done and not done, if you get my meaning.'

'Five minutes.'

'OK! I'll water the plants while I wait.'

Kate smiled at the fact that Mrs Dobbs couldn't help but mention her working plan. It was a methodical way of cleaning the school, which Kate had set up a fortnight after Mrs Dobbs had started the job, mainly because she left some jobs entirely undone and cleaned other things every day, which really only needed attention once a week. But it was a thorn in Mrs Dobbs's flesh, and she never ceased letting her know it.

When Kate emerged from her office, Mrs Dobbs was leaning on her brush handle looking injured. 'About time. I've something better to do than stand here waiting for you. School's finished and I expect to be able to get on with my work straight away. I've done the classrooms and, according to your list, the hall and your office are next.'

Kate smiled graciously and said, 'And a very good job you do too, Mrs Dobbs. When Bel Tutt left I thought we'd be in a real mess but, lo and behold, you move into the village and come to our rescue. I've nothing but praise for your standards. Goodnight. See you tomorrow.'

Ashamed of her very obvious bootlicking, Kate started up her car, realized she'd left the school log book behind and decided to go back to get it, rather than leave it out all night. Walking lightly back down the corridor in her flat shoes, Kate saw the office door was ajar; Mrs Dobbs was obviously still in there. With her back to the door, Maggie was blithely flicking through a file, which Kate knew had been in the filing cabinet when she left. Kate tiptoed back a few paces and then coughed, paused and then walked into the office. 'I've left a school log book out somewhere. Ah! There it is! Goodnight!'

Mrs Dobbs had been starting to clean the washbasin when she'd walked in, but Kate knew differently. Good cleaners, like good teachers, were hard to come by and she'd no intention of losing Mrs Dobbs, because, despite her faults, she did clean well and was reliable. She'd just have to remember to lock the filing cabinet as well as her secure cupboard, every single night.

That evening she became so engrossed in the log book she quite forgot Craddock until he surprised her by asking, 'What's so interesting in that old book?'

Kate looked up at him. 'It's fascinating,' she said. 'Listen to this: "*Five strokes of the cane on the hand for Jim Glover for idleness* – 27 May 1854." I can't believe I can read about the ancestors of people still living in the village today. It feels as if it happened only yesterday. It's so real.'

'Mmm. I expect it definitely felt real to Jim Glover. I wonder how many times our Jimmy Glover got whacked for idleness when he was at school? Some of the young horrors today could do with a dose of the cane. Smarten their ideas up no end.'

'Darling!'

'They have no moral strength!'

'Haven't they? I wonder if it made him work harder or even more disinclined to pay attention. I'd hate to have to cane anybody.' Kate shuddered at the prospect.

Craddock smiled indulgently. 'If you could, who would you cane?'

Kate laid the log book down beside her on the sofa, leaned back with her hands behind her head and said, 'Mrs Dobbs.'

'Mrs Dobbs! Whatever for?'

'Opening my filing cabinet and reading a confidential file.'

'How do you know?'

'I saw her. She didn't realize I was there.'

'Oops! Poor Mrs Dobbs.'

'I'd like to cane whoever is stealing, except I know who's doing it but haven't any evidence, and they're already far too vulnerable.'

'You're not duped by psychology, are you? Bad childhood so everything unacceptable they do ever after is excusable? Some day one has to take responsibility for oneself. I did.'

'Did you have a bad childhood, then?'

Those thin lips of his snapped shut, tight. Kate watched him debating, saw him dithering on the brink of a revelation, then decide he couldn't speak out. 'Of course not. Best of childhoods. Even if I hadn't I'd have taken responsibility like I said and got on with life.'

Holding her arms wide, Kate said, 'Craddock, my dear.' He came across to her, put the log book on a side table and sat beside her on the sofa. She held him in her arms like she did the children when they were deeply distressed. 'Don't tell me if you don't want me to know. We don't have to know everything about each other in order to love one another.'

Craddock squeezed her tightly. 'We don't. But we

should, and one day . . .' He drew back from her and looked at her intently. 'Are there things you haven't told me?'

'Yes, but a bad childhood isn't one of them.'

'What then?'

She kissed him instead of answering, and the moment passed.

After a while he asked her if she wanted a drink before going to bed.

'Vodka and tonic, please.'

He roused himself from the sofa, looked down at her still holding his hand and said, 'Best day's work I ever did marrying you. I hope you feel the same?'

Kate nodded. 'I do. I've got the best of everything. Career I can't live without, beautiful home, a husband whom I love very much. What more can a woman ask?'

'Nothing.' As he poured her vodka he asked, 'Will you sack Mrs Dobbs?'

'Absolutely not. It's for me to make it so she can't get at confidential files. Even though she speaks her mind too often, she's too good to lose as a cleaner.'

'I hope she appreciates your goodwill. Here you are.'

'Thanks.' Kate sipped her vodka and added, 'There's so much goodwill for the school among the villagers. Evie Nicholls has promised to come in to make an embroidered banner with my class, which puts them in touch with a skill I couldn't even begin to impart. Also, Muriel's coming in twice a week to play for the Maypole dancing practice, did you know?'

'No, I didn't. I'm very fond of Muriel. Wouldn't hurt her if I could possibly help it. She's a rare spirit, always full to the brim with kindness.'

'She was a bit sharp with me about the Bliss children. If she only knew . . .'

'What?'

Kate said, 'Well, I've a very good idea they are the school thieves. Ten pounds today from Margaret's handbag. She found out after the buses had gone. But don't say a word outside this room, please.'

'I shan't.' He raised his glass to her and asked, 'Kate, am I making you happy?' He looked hesitantly at her as though he desperately wanted an affirmative answer, but hardly dared hope it would be.

She smiled the same sweet smile as when she'd been thinking about him earlier in the day. 'Blissfully. More than I had ever dared hope.'

'Good. Me too.'

Chapter 5

On the Monday morning Kate found herself reading a
letter from Mrs Bliss, which she wished she hadn't
received. As she read it her face creased with disappointment, for it told her that Mrs Bliss and her little Blisses
were pleased for the offer of free uniforms but regrettably
were unable to accept charity. The children had discussed
it with her and agreed that accepting her offer was quite
out of the question, but they thanked her for her kindness.

When she went to take prayers Kate saw it was only too
true. Although they looked cleaner than usual, they were
still wearing the dreadful clothes they'd worn since they
came. It really was exasperating. On the other hand she
couldn't help feeling admiration for them, although the
children may have agreed simply because they didn't want
to upset their mother. Still, such pride! Free school lunches
appeared to be having an effect, however, because they
were looking rather healthier than when they'd first
arrived. But as they stood to sing their first hymn, the Bliss
children were only too obviously outsiders. What on earth
had happened in their lives to bring this about? The letter
had been written in an educated hand, so it was clear that
they were not accustomed to such poverty. A job for Mrs

Bliss! That was what was needed. Perhaps at the school so she could be at home in the school holidays. But what?

At lunchtime Kate was on playground duty and was busy taking netball practice with some girls in her class when she spied Mrs Bliss coming through the school gate. 'Karen! You're in charge. I won't be a moment. Play fair.'

Mrs Bliss sidled rather than walked into school, followed by Kate. 'Mrs Bliss! Come into my office.' She led the way and seated herself behind her desk, inviting Mrs Bliss to take a chair.

'It's your lunch hour, but I didn't see how I could get a chance to talk to you otherwise.'

'Not at all. I don't mind.'

Mrs Bliss's thin hand dipped into her pocket and came out clutching a ten-pound note which she laid on the desk. 'Una came home with this on Friday. I apologize. I've explained to her she shouldn't and she's sorry.'

'I'm sorry too. But I'm grateful that you've come to explain. We've had small amounts of money missing before, but the ten pounds was making the matter very grave.'

'It was my birthday on Saturday and she wanted so much to give me a present.' Her head went down and Kate thought she heard a sob escape. Her thin hands were twisting and turning on her lap, obviously in an agony of despair. They were gloveless and blue with the cold.

'I'm so very sorry you're in such dire straits. Why won't you let the school help you? Give the children some pride in . . . Sorry, that was the wrong word to use. But they must feel so different from everyone else with no uniform. They are the only ones without. Surely a helping hand can't be wrong in your circumstances?'

Mrs Bliss's head came up. 'My circumstances are my affair. The children have a home, and a mother. They're all four of them bright and they'll all make their way in the world without charity, thank you all the same. I don't know what punishment you'll hand out, but she understands you will think it necessary. Thank you for your time. I'm sorry Una did it, very sorry.'

Mrs Bliss stood up, gave Kate one last long look and departed. But despite the show of dignity, Kate had noticed her lips trembling and her voice shaking as she spoke. Damn and blast, thought Kate, what can one do in the face of such pride?

Hetty Hardaker took Kate's class and her own for singing first thing on Monday afternoons, so Kate asked to see Una in her office while she had the chance. She was deliberately eating a biscuit when Una came in and she offered her one.

Kate waited until the child had stuffed it into her mouth and was sitting there looking remarkably like a hamster. Una had her mother's dark brown eyes and the same sweet mouth and thin, wispy brown hair. There was a poise and beauty about her though, which her downtrodden mother lacked.

'Well, Una, about this ten-pound note.'

Una's eyes shifted away from Kate's face.

'You know it was wrong, don't you?'

'Yes.'

'Where did you get it from?'

'Miss Booth's purse.'

'I thought so. But it was Miss Booth's, wasn't it, not yours?'

'I know.'

'So tell me how you felt when you opened her purse and took it out.'

Una thought about the question and then answered in a most adult way. 'I needed the money for Mummy's birthday. We all did, and we'd no pocket money and I thought it would be a good idea. Miss Booth is so kind, you see, I guessed she wouldn't mind.'

'Well, I like your thoughtfulness, and the way you love your mummy enough to steal for her, but it wasn't right, was it?'

'No. But—'

'Yes?'

'We'd no money, and like I said, Miss Booth is so kind I was sure she wouldn't mind.' It clearly seemed logical to Una. They'd no money. The situation was desperate so she did something about it, and Miss Booth was so kind, she wouldn't mind. Which Miss Booth was. Kind to the point of insanity sometimes.

'It is never right to take money or anything belonging to someone else. It's the same in the Store, isn't it?'

Una hung her head, appalled that Kate appeared to be all-seeing-all-knowing. How had she found out about the chocolate? The smooth, rich, tasty feeling of the chocolate on her tongue and the enjoyment she'd experienced as it slid down her throat came back to Una, and she remembered how she'd enjoyed cleansing her teeth with her tongue to rid them of the cloying texture when she'd finished. And somehow, she couldn't feel guilty. 'We needed it. Mummy was cross when she found out, but it was too late as we'd eaten it on the bus.'

Kate recognized the yearning in Una's face and in her heart couldn't be angry. 'Well, Una, taking things must stop. It isn't right and it makes Mummy feel upset and you wouldn't want that. She's brought me the ten-pound note, I'm giving it back to Miss Booth and we shan't say another thing about it. Right?'

'Right.' Her eyes were on the biscuit tin, and Kate couldn't refuse her.

'Would you like another biscuit? Eat it here, because I haven't enough for all your class.'

Una took the biscuit she was offered with a polite thank you and then proceeded to stuff the whole thing in her mouth as though it might run away half-eaten if she didn't. Kate recognized need, not greed, in her actions. Poor child! Her arms and legs were so thin, more like sticks, whereas at the age of five she should still have the slight chubbiness of the very young. How unfair life was. How frustrating not being able to help.

Una slid off the chair as soon as the last crumb had gone down. 'Thank you, Mrs Fitch.'

'Thank you, Una. Bye-bye.'

Kate put on the kettle for tea for Miss Booth and Hetty Hardaker, and thought about who she could ask for help. Caroline! Yes! The rector's wife had two children who'd always had plenty of clothes and possibly still had some school uniforms in a cupboard somewhere . . . Yes, that was it. Straight after school. She'd pop round.

Kate was delighted when Caroline answered the Rectory door.

'I've come for some help.'

'Come in, Kate. How nice to see you. We'll go in the kitchen if you don't mind – I'm just in the middle of things. Sylvia doesn't come on Mondays any more so I fend for myself.'

Kate seated herself at the kitchen table while Caroline cleared the worktops of dishes and bowls.

'Can I get you anything? Cup of tea, perhaps?'

Kate shook her head. 'No, thanks. I've had enough tea today to float a battleship. No, I've come about the Bliss children. You might not have heard but they've moved into Little Derehams, you know, into Simone Paradise's old house.' Kate felt a certain amount of embarrassment as old memories surfaced and she noticed the flash of anger on Caroline's face. 'Well, anyway, they are extremely poor. I've volunteered to pay for them to have uniform out of my fictitious discretionary fund but the mother has refused. Doesn't want charity.'

Caroline came to sit at the table opposite Kate. 'I see, so how can I help?'

'Well, I thought that she might take help from the Rector's wife and village doctor instead. Do you have any uniform or clothes of any kind belonging to the twins, which might do for the Blisses? Things they've outgrown, you know.'

'Very possibly. They've kept their uniforms since they left, for sentiment's sake, but perhaps if there was a worthy cause . . .'

'I'd be so grateful, and you're so tactful she'd probably accept it from you. And as the twins have left, it wouldn't matter if the Bliss children were wearing their clothes, would it?'

'I suppose not. You say she's living in Simone's old house? The last time I passed there it looked as though it was falling apart.'

78

'It is. Stood empty ever since—'

'Since Simone died. Yes. Then they must be poor. I'll look some things out and talk to the children about whether or not they want to keep their uniforms.'

Kate stood up. 'I'll leave it with you, then.'

'You may.'

When she'd seen Kate out of the house Caroline went into the sitting room and stood at the window, watching Kate get into her car. She recollected how she'd hated Kate, who had started up the black magic trouble when she'd first come to the village, and for a moment her heart bled for the loss of poor old Mimi, her beloved Siamese, who had been *sacrificed* to appease the devil, or some such misguided kind of an idea. How hard it had been to like Kate after that! She still felt a frisson of distaste whenever she saw her, but that mustn't get in the way of helping the Bliss children. Caroline glanced at the clock and saw that the children would be home in about half an hour, and her heart lifted.

Overnight it seemed they had grown up. They had bags for their school books now, and Beth had insisted on having her beautiful long platinum blonde hair cropped so that it now fell neatly into a short bob. As for Alex, he'd always been older than his years and took on knowledge like a sponge soaking up water. Beth didn't make it quite so obvious but she too absorbed everything she heard with a deep, silent concentration.

How she loved them. Caroline went to put the kettle on. It wasn't milk and a biscuit they wanted now when they came home from school, but tea and a slice of toast. That seemed to be the most significant indication to Caroline that they were growing up.

In the loft were endless boxes of things she had kept, even their smallest bootees and sleeping suits. God! How small they'd been when they first arrived. What patience she'd needed, what energy, how she'd longed for a full night's sleep!

She heard Alex's key in the door. She knew it was him because he did it with such precision, whereas Beth had to fiddle about for a moment getting the key in the slot properly.

They burst in through the door, flung their belongings on to the hall floor and arrived in the kitchen in a flurry.

'I'd forgotten it was Monday and you'd be home.' Beth flung her arms around Caroline as though she hadn't seen her for at least a month. Caroline hugged her and then glanced over Beth's head towards Alex and gave him a grin. He smiled back, Peter's smile all over again. His devoted love shone from his eyes quietly, but nonetheless, just as powerfully as Beth's.

'Tea? Need I ask?'

When they'd drunk their tea and eaten their toast and peanut butter, she asked, 'Can I have a word before you disappear?'

They both nodded.

'Kate has a family of children at school, just started, and they are very poor, so poor their mother can't buy uniform or weekend clothes for them. I wondered, would you mind if I gave them a load of clothes you've grown out of?'

'I don't mind, but not our baby things. I'm keeping those for babies of mine.' Beth, now no longer able to swing her legs as she sat on the kitchen chair, spoke vehemently. 'They're not having those. Why are they so poor?'

'I'm not sure, but there seems to be no daddy around—'

'He's left them. How could he?' This from Alex who always found desertion by parents a hard thing to understand.

'Maybe he died.'

Alex thought about that for a moment and then answered, 'Maybe. You can give them anything of mine.'

'Thank you, Alex. And you, Beth?'

'Same here, but not my baby things.'

'They don't need baby things as they're all at school. Don't panic.'

'Oh well, that's all right then. But they'll need our old uniforms, won't they?'

Caroline nodded.

'OK then. We can't ever wear them again; we're much too big now.'

And indeed they were. As they got off their chairs and by chance stood side by side, Caroline saw how Alex had shot up and was taller than Beth, but she had lost her chubbiness and was beginning to look almost adolescent. It wouldn't be long before she'd have two teenagers in the house. Help! 'Daddy has a meeting tonight so we're being prompt with our meal. OK?'

'OK!'

The two of them retrieved their school bags from the hall floor and disappeared up the stairs, chattering about their homework. Just before they reached the top step, Beth called out, 'What are their names?'

'Their surname is Bliss, but I don't know their first names.'

Caroline heard an explosion of laughter. 'Bliss? Huh! What a name.'

The following day, having spent part of the morning in the loft sorting out clothes for the Bliss children, Caroline set off after lunch with her car boot stuffed with everything she could find. Some things she'd particularly loved she didn't include, those cornflower-blue shorts of Beth's with the T-shirt Willie and Sylvia had bought her, or the red shorts and red-and-white T-shirt Alex had worn every single day one summer and she'd had to wash and dry them overnight so he wouldn't get upset.

Pulling up outside Simone Paradise's old cottage brought back memories of the last time she'd been there. From where she sat in her car she could almost smell the unkempt cottage as it had been that night when they'd found Simone's children alone in there, brutally orphaned.

Bracing herself, Caroline got out of the car and headed for the back door. She gave a sharp rat-tat on the door with her knuckles because the knocker was too filthy to touch. Slowly, footsteps approached the door. A bolt was shot back and the door opened just enough for her to see a thin, haggard face with large brown eyes, deep in their sockets, staring at her.

'Mrs Bliss?'

Nod.

'I'm the Rector's wife, Caroline Harris. I've come to visit. May I come in?'

Nod.

The door was eased back and Caroline went in. It seemed as though no time had passed since she'd been here that dreadful night all those years ago. The same

82

shambolic poverty and neglect, the same unkempt smell, the same terrible need for a complete refurbishment and refurnishing. Surely that wasn't the same sofa from which one of Simone's children had arisen like a ghost when they'd forced entry into the cottage that terrible night? Caroline shuddered. God in heaven! What a ghastly mess.

'Mrs Bliss. I do hope you won't mind me coming to see you. You're new to the parish and either Peter or I always visit newcomers. May I sit down?'

Caroline found a chair, cleared it of some rags, which she hoped were not the children's underwear, and sat herself down. Mrs Bliss remained standing.

'How are you enjoying living in such an idyllic village as this?' She kept her eyes firmly on Mrs Bliss as she spoke.

'Fine. I'm sorry I can't offer you a cup of tea, but I've run out of milk.'

'I drink tea without milk.'

'Oh, I see.'

The cottage long long ago had had its two rooms made into one so Caroline was able to watch Mrs Bliss making the tea from where she sat. She noticed how frail her movements appeared, but that the cups and saucers were fine china and had seen much better homes than this. Presently the tea arrived at her end of the room and Mrs Bliss stirred the teapot to strengthen the tea and then poured it out into the cups. Caroline was under the distinct impression the tea had been made from second-hand teabags.

'Thank you. Just how I like it. You have children, I understand?'

Mrs Bliss's eyes shone. 'Yes. There's the twins, Paul and

Phil, then Della and Una's the youngest, my baby. They're all at school.'

'Oh! I have twins. A boy and a girl, but they're at secondary school now.'

'Where do they go when they leave the village school?'

'Well, they've both won places at Prince Henry's and Lady Wortley's and there is a big secondary school in Culworth with a school bus each day, so you'd have no problems getting them there, having no car.'

'Good.' A terrible listlessness came over Mrs. Bliss. Caroline decided to get on with the real business of her visit.

'Can I speak quite plainly, Mrs Bliss? Everyone calls me Caroline. What may I call you?'

'Eleanor.'

'Eleanor. I've really come to give a hand. In my car, I have a load of clothes, which used to belong to my children, and I've brought them for yours.'

Mrs Bliss got to her feet. Caroline lifted a hand to stop her protests. 'No, before you get on your high horse, I want you to think of the children. Some of it is school uniform which, as you know, they are without. Please let me bring them in. There's no room for pride when it's to do with your children being able to hold up their heads, is there? Being the Rector's wife, I am the soul of discretion, and I shall not tell a single person. And I won't take no for an answer, either. Now. Can I bring them in? They're all absolutely clean and in good repair. I wouldn't insult you by bringing rags. Believe me. The children grew so quickly some years, some of the clothes have hardly been worn. Please?' Caroline pleaded as best she could but her answer was a long time coming.

Mrs Bliss, her face covered by her outspread fingers, finally nodded.

'You clear a space on the table and I'll unload them.'

Caroline went in and out of the back door several times before the car was emptied. Eleanor Bliss was overcome. 'Such kindness. Such kindness. I can't believe it.'

As she laid the final armful of clothes on the pile Caroline said, 'I've brought loads of dry cleaner's coat-hangers; would you like them?'

Eleanor nodded. 'Thank you. You're too kind.'

When she'd brought in the coat-hangers Caroline sat down at the table again. 'Now, tell me. How else can I help?'

'After this? I can't ask for anything else.'

'Oh yes, you can. Tell me.'

'There's nothing.'

'There must be something.' Caroline looked around the cottage and her heart sank to new depths. Such dreadful poverty she hadn't encountered in a long time. She didn't know what to suggest. 'Are you renting this cottage?'

Eleanor nodded.

'From whom?'

'Someone called . . . wait while I find the letter. Here it is, Turnham House Properties.'

'Turnham House Properties! Who showed you round?'

'Just a clerk, kind of. You know, smooth-talking.'

'Have you all the utilities? Water, electricity, mains drainage, proper sanitation?'

Eleanor said, 'Water and electricity, but as for the rest . . .' She shrugged.

'Leave it to me. I shall see about this.'

Eleanor shot to her feet, looking animated for the first

time. 'No! I don't want turning out. It's the most I can afford. If I'm evicted, it'll be the street for us. I shan't get anywhere as cheap as this.'

'If I'm on the case, you most certainly won't be turned out, believe me. You must have signed a lease, surely?'

'No, not really.'

'Right.' Caroline stood up. 'Leave this with me. Don't worry about being turned out, you won't be. I'll see to that. I have good friends in the right places, so you can rest assured. Now, you enjoy sorting through those clothes I've brought. Good afternoon, Eleanor, take care. I shall be back.' Caroline held out her hand and grasped Mrs Bliss's hand to shake it. She could have been holding a bunch of dry twigs so thin and helpless was the handshake she received. She was quietly starving to death, Caroline was sure.

Full of terrible suspicions, Caroline ground her Volvo into gear and charged off to Turnham Malpas as fast as the winding, hilly lane would allow. Turnham House Properties. She'd give him Turnham House Properties! She'd always known Craddock Fitch was a sly . . . beggar. And Kate had married him! Kate! Did she know that her own husband was such a dastardly landlord? I bet she doesn't, thought Caroline. On the other hand, if she does, I'll have them both roasted alive! She was so furious about what she'd learned that she almost bumped into Gilbert Johns on a narrow piece of road where two cars couldn't pass. She reversed into a gateway and waited for him to drive by.

He rolled down his car window and shouted, 'You're in a hurry. Is there a fire?'

Caroline had to laugh. He was such a sweetheart. 'No, just angry. Been doing some parish visiting.'

'Take care, Caroline. I wouldn't fancy my chances if I had to scrape you up off the road. Peter would have my head on a pike outside the church as an example to all. Bye.'

Caroline drove more slowly after that, chanelling her anger into more constructive thought. She arrived home only just in time for the twins coming in from the school coach. They drank their tea and ate their toast with her at the kitchen table. 'Did the little Blisses like the clothes, Mum?' asked Alex.

'They were at school when I called, but I hope they will.'

'You didn't give them my blue shorts, did you? I didn't think to mention when we left this morning,' Beth asked.

'No, nor the red shorts and shirt you liked so much, Alex.'

'Good.' He then began a long story about school that day and she listened patiently. Any other day she would have been greatly interested, but today her mind was still seething with the knowledge that Craddock Fitch owned Mrs Bliss's house. How dare he, with his vast fortune, rent it to a human being in such a state? It wasn't fit for a dog.

Beth, eager to tell her adventures that day, kicked Alex's leg. 'Let me have a turn.'

'Ow! That hurt! I haven't finished yet.'

'Well, be quick.'

'So it ended with Tim telling the truth and we all got off.'

Caroline nodded her agreement. 'Good, I'm glad. I don't approve of telling fibs.'

'But I only did it to save a friend.'

'I know but you see . . .' The kitchen door opened and there stood Peter. 'Peter! How lovely! Just in time for a cup of tea.'

Caroline needed the long, loving smile he gave her and the kiss he planted on her forehead. He'd have the answer, she knew for certain.

Beth told him her story about school while sitting on his knee and feeding him pieces of a biscuit she'd chosen for him. 'Are we to take it then,' he asked, 'that you like your school or shall we ask for you to go back to the school here in the village?'

She gave him a thump on his arm. 'Of course not, Daddy, we're much too old. In any case, I love Lady Wortley's.'

'Good. I'm glad.' He tipped her off his knee. 'Now, I think Mummy is needing a word with me.'

'I haven't finished my tea yet.'

'Well, finish it and then off you go, I think she has a secret to tell me. Only for grown-ups.' Peter grinned as he said this, knowing how she would react.

'Daddy! That's mean! I'm going to stay.' Beth folded her arms and pressed her lips firmly together.

Caroline told her it was parish business, so she drank down the last of her tea and she and Alex left to start their homework. They were both resigned to parish business sometimes taking priority over their needs, and anyway, it was usually incredibly boring.

'So? What's upset you today?'

'How do you know I'm upset?'

Peter smiled. 'I can tell. We haven't been married – how long is it? – nineteen years without me knowing

88

when something is bothering you. Is it really parish business?'

'Not strictly. Kate asked me to take clothes to the new Bliss children, they're desperately poor, so I did and I was appalled at the conditions in which they are living. Even more so when I learned that Turnham House Properties own their cottage. Simone's old cottage. You know?'

'I didn't know Craddock Fitch owned property in Little Derehams.'

'Well, he does, if you can call it that. A hen hut would be better to live in than that dump. Nothing, and I mean nothing, has been done to it since Simone died, and you know what it was like then.'

'I knew he was trying to buy houses in Turnham Malpas some years ago, but I didn't know about Little Derehams. Why doesn't she find somewhere better?'

'I don't know what the rent is but obviously she's there because it's dirt cheap and it's the most she can afford. Heard of the poverty trap? Well, she's in it.'

'What will you do about it?'

'That was what I was going to ask you.'

'Ah!' Peter drank his tea while he thought. 'Does Kate know he owns it?'

'I don't know. If she does, I'm surprised she goes along with it.'

'Quite possibly she doesn't. Business is business et cetera, and he keeps it separate from his private life. After all, they haven't been married long, have they?'

'No, so quite possibly she doesn't know.'

'I'll go see for myself tomorrow morning. Parish priest calling on newcomers, you know.'

'Thank you. But when you've seen her and the house,

you'll agree something has to be done. In fact, I could alert Social Services; they'll get the wheels in motion.'

'What wheels?'

'Making Craddock Fitch bring the house up to scratch.'

'I imagine he employs an agent. Perhaps he isn't aware of the situation.'

'If he isn't then he should be. It's criminal.'

'But if he brought it up to scratch, as you call it, then quite rightly he'd want to ask for more rent and she can't afford any more you say?'

Caroline shook her head.

'Four children?'

'Yes. And they've been driven to stealing to keep food on the table. She's stolen meat from the Store several times.'

'What's Jimbo done about it?'

'Nothing, he knows she's desperate, but it can't go on, obviously.'

'I'll go round in the morning. The poor woman must be out of her mind with worry.'

'She is. You'll hate what you see.'

Peter did hate it. The condition of the house and the state of Mrs Bliss's health were both dreadful. He went straight from Little Derehams to the school to see Kate.

It was lunchtime and the children were all out playing. The dinner ladies were clearing the hall and Maggie Dobbs was keeping a weather eye on them to make sure they cleaned the floor too.

'Rector! Good afternoon. Nice to see you. Mrs Fitch is in her office.'

'Thanks, Mrs Dobbs. How are you? I haven't seen you of late.'

'Oh! Been around, you know. Busy as usual.'

'Good. I'm glad to see you're making friends. You had quite a bunch of them calling the other night.'

A light in Maggie's brain flashed on. 'Oh! Yes, plenty of comings and goings at my house, for sure. Best to keep busy.'

'Exactly. See you again soon.'

So help me! thought Maggie. He'd noticed the meetings. And as the nights became lighter as the summer approached, they would be even more noticeable. Those bright blue eyes of his saw far too much. She'd have to be careful.

Peter knocked and walked into Kate's office. She got to her feet to shake hands. 'What a lovely surprise, Rector. Can I help in any way?'

'Have I caught you when you're busy? I can always—'

'Sit down. Please. Now, how may I help?'

'I'm just back from visiting in Little Derehams.'

There wasn't so much as a flicker of any recognition in Kate's eyes.

'Been to see Mrs Bliss as she's new to the parish.'

Still no other reaction, except sorrow.

'Her house is a disgrace. It wouldn't matter if she was the most industrious housewife, which she isn't because she's so depressed, she couldn't make it look good. Leaking windows, slates off the roof and that all-pervading smell is a faulty septic tank, I'm sure. The gas fire she has must be fifty years old by the looks of it and never serviced, I imagine. There are no proper bathing facilitites apart from the old kitchen sink, the lavatory is outside the

91

back door and should have been condemned around nineteen forty. She doesn't even have a proper shorthold lease, so, in theory, she could be thrown out at any time. But what was worse was the letter heading of the landlord.'

'What could be worse than what you've just described?'

'So you've no idea, then?'

'No idea. What about? I haven't been to see her.'

Peter took in a big breath and said, 'Her landlord is a company called Turnham House Properties.'

If Peter had struck her she couldn't have been more shocked. 'You mean *Craddock* owns it?'

Peter nodded.

'I'd no idea.'

'What other explanation can there be? One must assume so, when Turnham House Properties is the name at the head of the paper.'

'One must.' Kate was gripping the edge of her desk so tightly her knuckles were white, and beads of sweat were appearing on her forehead. 'My God! I'd no idea.'

'I thought not. Can I leave it with you?'

'You certainly can.'

Peter didn't give Craddock Fitch much of a future if Kate's fury was anything to go by.

Chapter 6

'Craddock, I need some answers, although you may not like what I have to say.'

Craddock blew smoke from his cigar into the air, drew his ashtray closer and then said indulgently, as though he had no cares in the world, 'Fire away, my dear.'

'Peter came to see me this afternoon.'

Craddock sat upright. 'Was he in one of his campaigning modes? He's difficult to resist when he is. He gets those blue eyes of his looking straight into your soul and you've said yes before he even opens his mouth.'

'Oh, he opened his mouth all right.' Kate outlined their conversation, and concluded by saying, 'But the headed notepaper gave him the surprise of his life.'

'Oh?'

'You don't know?'

Craddock shook his head, took another pull on his cigar and was just expelling it when Kate said, 'Turnham House Properties.' She waited but he merely shook some ash from his cigar.

'Well?'

'If it said Turnham House Properties then it must belong to me, mustn't it? It's a subsidiary of the main company.'

'Why be so secretive? How many houses do you own in Little Derehams?'

'Almost all, a notable exception being Keepers Cottage where Louise and Gilbert Johns live.'

'You bought them one by one, you mean?'

Craddock Fitch nodded. 'I wanted to do that in Turnham Malpas but got thwarted at every turn – you know what they can be like, cussed – and the only one I managed to buy was the one Grandmama Charter-Plackett lives in.'

'I see.'

'They belong to you too.'

'Me?' Kate's eyebrows shot up. 'To me?'

'We are married and what I own you own.'

'You mean everything?'

'Every damn bit of my empire.'

'Halves?'

'Halves.' Craddock smiled at her with all the love in the world in his smile.

'But I haven't signed anything.'

'All in the pipeline. Complicated, and my solicitors didn't want me to do it, in fact they warned me against it, putting forward arguments I can't repeat to you. But I insisted. So they've dilly-dallied, till I put a rocket up their backsides a week ago.'

'But I've given you nothing.'

'You've nothing to give.'

'I know, but—'

'My dear Kate, either one marries or one doesn't, and in my view we're equal partners in everything.'

'You're saying I'm a wealthy woman?'

Craddock nodded.

94

'But I want you to know, here and now, I didn't marry you for that.'

He blew a kiss to her and grinned. 'I know that. When I married first time round I'd no money to give to the cat, never mind my wife. Well, now I have, so there you are.'

'So until I sign the papers it's not mine?'

'No, but it soon will be.'

'I'm flabbergasted.' Kate got up and poured herself another drink. 'Want one?'

'Not finished this yet.' He admired her slender figure as she stood by the drinks table and couldn't quite believe he'd captured such a wonderful creature. She was that very desirable commodity, a beautiful woman with a lively brain, and he blessed the day they married.

As she turned back to sit again in her chair Kate said, 'It still doesn't alter the fact that that cottage is a pigsty and a disgrace. You wouldn't keep a dog in it, and if you did, the RSPCA would have you in court in quick sticks.'

'You've seen it then?'

'No, but Caroline and Peter have and they are both horrified.'

He blew yet more smoke into the air and, having cleared his lungs by doing so, he said slowly and deliberately, 'You may be a wealthy woman but you have no right to dictate how I run my businesses. All, and I repeat *all* decisions are made by me. OK?'

Kate, so eager to press her case, didn't pick up on the threatening tone of his voice. 'I know nothing about business so not interfering, well, that's fine by me, but you don't appear at all fazed by the fact that you are taking rent for a house that is unfit for human habitation.'

'Kate, I've just said I make the decisions.'

'Yes, but—'

As though bestowing a great privilege on Mrs Bliss, he proclaimed, 'No buts, she's free to move anytime. There's no obligation on her part. I'm not compelling her to stay there.'

Kate had to ask. 'Have you seen it?'

'No. But I'm only asking ten pounds a week, which is nothing.'

'You should be paying her to live there.'

'I haven't had a penny rent from that cottage since Simone died. No one wanted to live in it.' His expression was inscrutable. She hated him for it; he'd never spoken to her like this. 'Time I got some return on my investment, small though it is.'

'How much did you pay for it?'

'Bought it for a song the first year I lived here. Ten thousand pounds, I think.'

'So, done up, in a beautiful village like Little Derehams, you'd get thousands upon thousands if you sold it.'

Deadpan, he stabbed a finger in the air as though it was a brilliant idea, which had never occurred to him. 'That's an idea. I might just do that very thing.'

Kate sprang to her feet. 'Please don't! The Blisses will have nowhere to live if you do. You wouldn't, would you?'

'I've said it twice and I shan't say it again: you may have half my businesses but you have no right to make decisions. Those are mine and mine alone. Another drink?'

'No.' Kate couldn't cope with this side of Craddock. She'd known it existed but it had never manifested itself in her presence before. Dear God! Had she made the blunder of a lifetime in marrying him? For the very first time since they'd married she had terrible doubts. She needed time to think, long and seriously. He had shown such utter generosity in giving her half his assets and yet he baulked at this, a minor capital outlay compared to the rest of his fortune.

She sat staring at him as all these thoughts were running through her head. He appeared now a total stranger, as though he'd invaded the sitting room uninvited and sat down in a chair of hers. The as yet slender threads by which they were bound together snapped.

Then he smiled at her. 'Have I surprised you? You look appalled.'

'I am. Totally. How can the loving man I married be so callous? So damned unfeeling? The Bliss children are suffering. Do you hear? Or are you too thick-skinned?'

'I hear, my dearest. I hear.'

'So, what are you going to do about it?'

'Nothing. If I spend money doing it up then I shall have to charge more rent, she won't be able to live there and I shall be the terrible landlord.'

'You are already. That cottage is an eyesore.'

'No one but you and the Rectory know that, and *they* won't tell. Discretion, you know, and besides I've given too much money to the church for Peter to betray me.'

Kate got to her feet again. 'Betray you? You know you're doing wrong or you wouldn't have used that word. What's more, you know Peter better than that. He wouldn't hold back from being truthful about you simply because you're a benefactor. He's honourable through and through.'

'Meaning?'

97

Kate didn't answer.

'Meaning that I'm not?'

Kate clenched her fists. 'I don't understand. You *are* honourable; giving me half of the business is more than honourable. It would be such a small matter in the grand scheme of things to have this house made habitable. Such a small thing.'

Craddock got to his feet so they were facing each other over the hearth rug. 'I shall tell you again for the last time – I make all the decisions.'

Defiantly Kate retorted, 'Then I shall wait until half the business is mine and I shall do it myself.'

He took a step forward, eyes blazing, his temper barely in check and Kate, for one terrible, frightening moment, thought he was going to hit her. If he did, then the marriage was over before it had begun. She shuddered with anger and stepped back to distance herself from his fury.

But he didn't hit her. Instead he grasped her wrist and said, 'Don't defy me, Kate, all that does is force me to take decisions I shouldn't be taking. I won't be pushed. Persuaded, possibly; pushed, definitely not. Don't make me do something that will destroy what we have for each other. There is a line over which married people must never step, because if they do, they are on the path to destruction, and in my experience married people take that step far too often, and their marriages turn to ashes in their mouths.'

As he spoke his voice became gentle and persuasive until by the time he'd finished, she was horrified how close they had come to spoiling everything they had. Kate realized he was talking about respect for one another and she wondered if perhaps in marriage that was as important as love. A huge well of emotion filled her, scrambling her thoughts, tumbling her feelings until they were topsy-turvy and more than anything in the whole wide world she wanted to put things right between them. She was in his arms apologizing and weeping before she knew it. 'I'm so sorry So sorry. I never meant us to get upset like this. I'm not used to being married, I suppose.'

He wiped away her tears and said, 'Neither am I. And I'm sorry as well Too many years having my own way, I suspect. We both need to learn how to live together.' He lifted her face from his shoulder by placing his finger under her chin. 'I love you.' And kissed her very sweetly on her mouth.

Next morning, to Kate's relief, Paul and Phil Bliss were wearing school uniform, for which she was very grateful for their sakes. Della had uniform too but not Una. She was wearing a lovely matching jumper and skirt, a bit on the big side but a massive improvement. At least Mrs Bliss had had the sense to accept Caroline's offer. The condition of the house, however, still concerned Kate. They'd had a wonderful reconciliation last night, she and Craddock, but it affected the issue not one jot.

What to do about it? She couldn't go behind his back and report the house to the housing department because she knew what that kind of deception would do to him. One thing about Craddock was that he was up front with his opinions and she'd bring the heavens down on her head if she did anything without telling him. The problem ate away at her all through the morning and she was in no mood for a deputation from the dinner ladies at the end of the lunchtime break.

'Come in!'

The knock on the door was followed by the entrance of Mrs Dobbs and the senior dinner lady, Jean.

'Yes?'

They both spoke together. 'We've come because—'

'You first.'

'No, you first.'

Maggie Dobbs moistened her lips and said, 'There's been an argument.'

'A discussion,' said Jean.

'A discussion, then, about cleaning up after dinners in the hall. Big blobs of cabbage and pudding are just left and I insist, yes, insist they clean up properly before they leave. I slave over that floor and I've got rights. Dinner isn't on my list.'

Kate looked at the two of them and thought they were worse than children. Looking at Mrs Dobbs's enemy she said, 'And what have you to say?'

'She didn't give us a chance—'

Maggie puffed herself up, full of righteous indignation. 'Don't tell fibs! You were leaving. You 'ad your coat on.'

'The others didn't.'

Kate interrupted the argument. 'If it's dinner debris then—'

Maggie Dobbs nodded. 'It is. I told you.'

'Then it's not Mrs Dobbs's concern. Out of kindness she puts out the tables for you so—'

Maggie puffed up with importance. 'Thank you, Mrs Fitch. Thank you. See, I told you, Mrs Fitch is on my side.'

100

'Strictly speaking, I'm not on either side. I'm neutral.'

'But—'

'Thank you, Mrs Dobbs, I have to get on.'

'But I—'

Kate gave her a stare, which the children knew was her final word. Mrs Dobbs knew that too and turned on her heel and left.

'You know, Mrs Fitch, she's so difficult to get on with and—'

'Mrs Dobbs is a treasure where the cleaning and caring of this school is concerned and I do not want to lose her.' By the look in Kate's eye, there was the unspoken threat that Jean herself was dispensable and the senior dinner lady left in a hurry. Wow! thought Kate. I sound more like Craddock every day. It must be catching. Moments later Kate heard Jean castigating one of her helpers about the condition of the hall floor. Kate put her head in her hands.

This business of living with someone, even a person one loved, was difficult. She thought back to last night and the row she and Craddock had had. It all amounted to nothing in the end because she hadn't moved one step forward in her self-appointed task of improving the conditions in which the Blisses were living. What could she do, though? Craddock very obviously meant what he'd said last night about all the decisions being his. Yet he was sharing his fortune with her. It was all so contradictory. She didn't even know if she wanted him to do that, but he had, despite the warnings of his solicitor. What to do with all that money if one couldn't be charitable?

Mrs Dobbs decided to call in at the Store before she went home to buy a nice piece of plaice for her supper from

Jimbo's freezer. His stuff was always as fresh as it could be. Sometimes when she'd bought fish it was so tasty it seemed as though it had by-passed the fishing trawlers and jumped out from the sea already topped, tailed and gutted straight into the freezer. She'd buy a lemon too, do the job properly.

It was true, then, what she'd heard; Linda had definitely been sacked because Tom was behind the Post Office counter. 'Hello, Tom. Enjoying your promotion?'

Tom grinned. 'You've heard?'

'Well, we've all heard that tale before, and she's usually back before you know it. But it looks permanent this time. Had another row, did they?'

Tom nodded.

The door bell jingled and in came one of the Senior sisters. Which one it was Maggie wasn't sure. No one ever knew; they were one and the same.

'Calamine lotion. And something for stomach upsets. It's my sister. She's poorly. Very poorly. And she's being sick. Sick, yes, sick. I don't know what to do. I really don't.' Miss Senior was twisting her hands together rapidly as though in a fearful frenzy of anxiety.

Tom unlocked himself from the Post Office cage and went to give her a hand. 'Not heard of anyone else having it. Is it something she's eaten, do you think?'

'Don't know. Don't know.'

Tom found the tablets he was looking for and picked up a bottle of calamine lotion on his way back to the till.

Maggie prolonged her search of the freezer a while longer to give herself time to think. Ill? With a stomach complaint? The Senior sisters were never ill. Even when everyone else was down with whatever was going around,

102

they never caught it. But here they were. Maggie's scalp prickled with alarm. Surely she hadn't done it with her tales of a punishment *more terrible than they'd ever known*? She was being daft. She wasn't a real medium, now was she? No. But maybe she'd turned into one and didn't know it. Had she really caused this illness? Maggie smiled to herself. Of course she hadn't. But it was odd all the same.

Miss Senior took an age to find the money to pay for the medicine, poking about in every corner of her purse to find the right change, and Maggie had sorted out the fish several times over before she finally left.

Tom called after her, 'If that doesn't work, get the doctor, don't forget.'

'Here we are then, Tom, while you're at the till,' said Maggie, 'plaice, lemon and two pints of milk. Nothing I like better than fish with broad beans and a drop of parsley sauce with butter in it.' She smacked her lips at the prospect.

'I've never known one of the Senior sisters to be ill. I suppose there's always a first time.'

Maggie nodded. 'I expect so. They come in every day so you'll know they're both ill if they don't.'

'Here's your change. Enjoy.'

'Thanks.' Maggie went home to put her feet up and contemplate the possibility of inviting the dinner ladies for a seance. She could have a really good time frightening them with tales she'd overheard when they were washing up in the school kitchen. It was a right hive of gossip in there at dinnertime and not half. Friendly overture, she'd call it. She'd focus on Jean, who'd caused the trouble today. She knew a few things about her she shouldn't know. Her eyes drooped and she dozed.

The next lunchtime Maggie positively grovelled to the dinner ladies for causing trouble the previous day. 'To make up for it,' she said, 'why not come for a seance one night. At my house?'

The three of them – Jean, and the two Maggie had nicknamed Mealy Mouth and Ginger Nob – looked from one to the other in surprise.

'I'm a medium, you know.' Maggie winked. 'What about tomorrow night? Half past eight?'

One by one, they agreed.

'I don't provide refreshments, which might interfere with the psychical waves, and it's five pounds each. I've got my expenses, you see.'

'Oh! All right then, half past eight. Thanks.'

'I've often fancied a go at that. Could be fun. Does it mean you can tell the future?'

'Thanks for the invite. It won't be frightening though, will it?'

'No. I want to be able to sleep at night.' Maggie laughed and twinkled her fingers at them in the friendliest way as she left them to their washing up. She found a spoon on the hall floor and as a contribution to restored relations, went back into the kitchen and gave it to them.

'Found this on the floor.'

'Oh! Thanks. That's kind of you.'

'Not at all.' Maggie left then, not wanting to over-egg the pudding.

*

'Kate? It's Caroline.'

'Hi there.'

'Just to let you know I've had a word with Social Services about the Blisses and they've promised me they'll look into it as soon as possible. Unfortunately they've staff away at that conference they've reported on TV, and some ill, so it may be a while before they're able to do anything. Just thought I'd let you know.'

Kate's heart began to race. 'I didn't ask you to do that. Why have you?'

'I thought you would want me to.'

'When you knew it belonged to Craddock. What are you thinking of?'

There was a short silence and then she heard Caroline saying, 'I felt it to be my duty to report the conditions they were living in. I thought that was what you wanted too.'

Kate took a deep breath to get herself under control. 'It's none of your business.'

'They are in Peter's parish.'

'So?'

'He has a duty of care, surely.'

'He has a duty not to interfere in what doesn't concern him. Craddock will go ballistic.'

'Craddock Fitch's temper, in the circumstances, has nothing to do with it. That cottage is a disgrace and well you know it. And there was I thinking you were a woman of high moral principles. However, it's too late now. Sorry if this has upset you, but something needed to be done.'

'I just wish you'd consulted me first.'

'Would you have told me not to do it?'

Kate had to think for a moment. Would she? Yes, she

. . . No. 'I might have asked for a little more time to work it out from my side.'

'Hmm. Well, I've done it now and I'm sure you'll agree I was right when you've had time to think about it. Sorry. Bye.'

Kate replaced the receiver and put her head in her hands while she thought about the consequences of Caroline's actions. She'd have to tell Craddock, even though it might be weeks before action was taken. Hell's bells. Had she changed sides? She fervently hoped not. But she knew, deep down, she must have done.

Chapter 7

Maggie had organized her cottage living room for the dinner ladies' seance and was sitting before the fire, readying herself for her big moment. She'd give them a thing or two to think about and not half. Then she remembered she had to shut the cat out, and got to her feet to look for her. But Tabitha was nowhere to be found. Drat. Maggie even looked under the bed but she wasn't there. Blast it. If she appeared and gave someone a fright just at the wrong moment she'd wring its neck. But a woman who dealt in the occult needed a black cat for authenticity.

There was a soft knock at the door and when Maggie answered it she saw that the woman had parked her car right outside the house.

'Move that car, we don't want people getting curious. Please.' It was Mealy Mouth and Maggie suddenly wished they hadn't turned up after all.

Eventually, when the cars were parked to her satisfaction and the curtains were drawn and the lights out except for the fire and the table lamp they joined hands, Maggie settled down and began going into a trance. With their five-pound notes carefully stuffed into Dave's fairground jug, she knew they'd expect their money's worth, so she

107

began rolling her head from side to side, and the fun began.

Mealy Mouth began to giggle. An annoying giggle, which started to put Maggie off her stroke. Then Ginger Nob gave an almighty sneeze, and it broke Maggie's concentration completely.

'Sorry. We'll have to begin again. You must be quiet, otherwise I lose the thread and the spirits won't be moved.'

'I've got cramp,' said Jean, the senior dinner lady. 'Just a minute.' She stood up and waved her leg about, then bent to rub the life back into it.

Finally Maggie asked, 'Now, are we all settled?' A deathly hush fell. Maggie closed her eyes and began again. Very slowly, bearing in mind that she needed to make it very realistic, her head began rolling back and forth and then went into circles. Then came the moaning, followed by guttural groans, then finally, 'Is anyone there? Is anyone out there?'

The tension in Maggie's sitting room was electrifying.

Not a sound.

Not a tremor.

A strange, grave tone came into Maggie's voice as she called out again, 'Who are you? Who are you? What do you want?'

'It's Dad. It's Dad.'

'Dad who?'

'I'm searching for my little girl. Is she there?'

'We don't know. Give us a clue.'

'She's the boss. I see food. I see children.'

Jean trembled. 'It must be my dad. Your little girl is here. It's Dodo, Dad.'

'Mind out, my girl. That Larry of yours, beware.'

The senior dinner lady answered, 'Beware what of?' her grammar having gone to pot in the excitement of the moment.

'That husband of yours. He's always been a wrong 'un. Remember I didn't want you to marry him?'

'I know. I know, Dad.'

'He's at it again. He's an adulterer. A liar and a cheat.'

'Oh God!'

'Beware! Beware!'

The tone of the medium's voice changed completely as she said, 'There's someone else trying to get in touch. Why, it's Evadne. You haven't spoken for a while. Welcome, Evadne. Do you have a message for us?'

In the dark, no one realized that the sound they heard of someone striving to speak was Maggie grinding her teeth.

'I can't tell,' said the spirit of Evadne.

'You must. We are prepared for your message. Have no fear.'

'Ginger. Ginger,' the spirit voice called.

Ginger Nob answered in a squeaky voice. 'Yes, I'm here.'

'Beware! You travel a dangerous path. Other women's husbands are not for you. Not for you. Take care. T-a-k-e c-a-r-e.' The voice faded away. A piece of coal fell on to the hearth. Ginger took in a shrieking breath, and the senior dinner lady moaned.

Maggie began rolling her head again and the red light from the shaded table lamp lit her features and made her wide open eyes glow like hot coals. 'Evadne's gone.

Evadne's gone.' Slowly the rolling stopped and her eyes focused.

Mealy Mouth, who hadn't spoken since the seance began, asked, 'Who the hell is Evadne?'

'I need a drink of water.' Maggie disappeared into the kitchen, leaving them to sort themselves out. Her throat wasn't half dry with all that groaning. She listened as she sipped from her glass.

But there was nothing to hear except the moaning of the senior dinner lady.

Maggie returned to her chair and waited. 'Well, that's it,' she said eventually. 'Evadne's my contact with the spirit world. Sometimes she comes, sometimes she doesn't, but when she does, boyo! Does she spill the beans!'

Mealy Mouth jumped to her feet. 'It's a load of rubbish. I'm off.'

Ginger Nob called, 'Wait for me.'

But the senior dinner lady spoke not a word. Clearly shocked to the core, she got up, tucked her handbag under her arm and stalked out.

Maggie shrugged. She'd only told them what she knew from hearing them gossiping. She'd put two and two together and decided Ginger Nob was having it off with Jean's husband Larry. She couldn't imagine what the outcome of her seance would be and as she laid her head on the pillow later, Maggie contemplated the success of the evening. It would be a while before they wanted another go! She turned over and smiled, remembering that tomorrow night it was her regulars' turn and thought about even more five-pound notes in Dave's fairground jug. It was surprising how they mounted up.

It was at that moment that she heard strange tappings

and rustlings, apparently coming from her wardrobe. Her hair almost stood on end.

She grabbed hold of the blankets and pulled them over her face but the sounds would not be shut out. 'Who's there?' she shouted. 'Who's there?'

The sound of her voice, strangled and muffled though it was, brought a 'Miaow!' from the wardrobe.

'Bloody hell! It's the cat.' Relief, what relief. She bounded out of bed to open the wardrobe door and out struggled, from among the jumble of shoes and coat-hangers idling in the bottom, poor old Tabitha. Fluffed up and indignant, the cat strode off. Maggie ran down to open the cat flap for her and then dashed back into bed and covered herself completely with the blankets. She had to face the fact that she'd frightened herself tonight. She'd have to get a grip.

The following morning each of the dinner ladies rang in to say they weren't well enough to come to school.

Kate almost exploded.

Hetty Hardaker suggested Linda Crimble. 'Jimbo's sacked her so I know she's free. Just temporarily, of course, and if she does well we could always keep her in mind for another time.'

'Good thinking. Mrs Dobbs, if I pay you for the extra hours, would you help?'

'Of course. Of course I will. We all have to rally round in times of crisis.'

Crisis indeed, thought Maggie. It had never been known before for all three of them to be off at once. At least she'd get a free dinner.

She and Linda got on famously together. They had

cleared the hall and were busy washing up when Linda declared she was at the end of her tether with Alan.

'Such a paddy he threw when I told him what had happened. All ready for going to Jimbo's last night and having it out. I persuaded him not to. I said, "Look here, Alan, he always comes crawling back because he can't find anyone else and exactly the same will happen this time, but it might take a bit longer. So please, leave it be," I said.'

'D'yer think he will?'

Linda smiled confidently. 'Of course, and it'll be different this time because I didn't half give him a piece of my mind. He'll treat me different, to say nothing of a pay rise.'

'So why's Tom in there this morning for all the world as if he'd been born to it?'

Linda dropped a plate in the sink and the water splashed all over the front of her plastic disposable apron and ran down on to her shoes, but she didn't notice. 'What? Tom? The slimeball! I'll kill him. What does he know about running a Post Office?'

'I don't know, but there he is, stamps, pensions and a registered parcel. He served me and very nice and efficient he was too.'

Linda untied her apron. 'Right! I'm off in there.'

'Eh? Just a minute, you're not leaving me with all this lot. Have a heart.'

'My career is at stake.'

'Career, my foot. You're being paid to do *this*, don't forget. In any case, you might be grateful for this job, you never know.'

'Don't think I'm going to spend the rest of my life as a dinner lady! Here, you carry on.' Linda stripped off her

112

rubber gloves and bounced out of the school kitchen with the light of battle in her eyes.

Like Maggie had said, Tom was in the 'cage' serving a customer, and Jimbo was nowhere to be seen. 'He'll be back about three,' Tom said to Linda. 'He's seeing a client about a wedding reception. Harriet's just gone home. Mrs Jones might be able to help.'

Linda lit up inside. Of course, she'd be the best one to tell her what was going on. But the mail order office was as busy as ever, and Greta Jones didn't appear all that glad to see her. 'Trying to get this lot done to catch the three o'clock post. You did yourself a good turn losing your temper like that, I don't think. He won't have you back if that's what you're hoping. The waters have closed over your head and no mistake. Get up, I want those labels you're sitting on.'

Tears welled in Linda's eyes. 'I'd rather thought—'

'Well, don't, because he taught Tom about the Post Office on Sunday and he's taken to it like a duck to water. If you want my advice you'll find another job quick.'

'Honest?'

Mrs Jones nodded.

'I wish I could get some direction about what to do. Alan is just ranting and raving, and that won't get me a job.'

'How about getting into catering? Pat Jones might need a waitress or too. She has a list of temps, just in case.'

'Waitressing?'

'The tips can be good.'

'I feel really miserable about this.'

'There's only one answer; curb your tongue. You let it run away with you from what I heard. Want cheering up?'

113

Linda nodded.

'Come with me to Maggie Dobbs's house tonight. I'll give you a knock on my way.'

'What can she do?'

Mrs Jones winked. 'She does a regular seance and tonight's the night. It's a good bit of fun.'

'Really? She's never said.'

'Well, she wouldn't, would she?'

'Will she mind?'

'Not so long as you've got five pounds.'

'I'll go straight back to the school and ask her. It's Alan's night off and he's that bad-tempered I'll be glad to be out.'

That night Maggie was well prepared. With the table polished to within an inch of its life – extreme cleanliness was a critical factor in getting the spirits to come – the fire crackling in the grate and the red scarf over the lamp, Maggie awaited her visitors. Tabitha had been put out and the cat flap locked, so there was nothing to interrupt the flow.

Maggie looked at the five pairs of hands resting on the table, little fingers touching to complete the link. Linda's were trembling in anticipation, Venetia's, with their vivid, purple nails, were steady as a rock, and Greta Jones's were relaxed. Her own, workaday hands, square and accustomed to toil, were slightly tense. The weekender's fingers were lifeless and they might as well be carrots for what good they were in helping the spirits. The fact that they were all dressed in black added a certain frisson to the atmosphere; had it been any darker they would have looked like five heads suspended around the table, like guests at some macabre feast.

When Maggie's head began rolling, Linda said, 'Ooh! Is she all right?'

'Shh!' said Greta Jones.

When Maggie started moaning Linda muttered, 'Ooh!' again and the shudder she gave was transmitted to them all through their hands. Greta thought the table shook slightly. But it couldn't have, it was a solid oak table; then again, it did have a lot of memories in it, not like something from Ikea. It was when the groaning and thrashing started that Linda really began to take fright. 'Ooh! Er.'

'Who's there? Who's there?'

Linda glanced round the room, could see no one and was grateful. But not for long. A strange, ethereal voice called out through the gloom, 'I'm here! I'm here!'

Maggie said, 'Evadne? Is that you?'

Greta Jones muttered, 'Oh God. Not Evadne.'

'It's me.'

'Welcome, Evadne. Do you have a message for one of us?'

'Yes. I need to contact Lynn.'

'We've got a Linda here.'

'Linda! Yes, Linda!'

Greta Jones said through gritted teeth, 'Answer her.'

Linda cleared her throat. 'Yes, that's me.'

'You're going through a difficult time. You need advice.'

'I do. I do,' whispered Linda.

'Alan is your strength and stay. Lean on him. Lean on him.'

'Oh! She's so right. He is. I will. I will.'

There was a long silence after this, during which

Maggie appeared to be tussling with some unseen figure. The flames, now casting huge shadows around the walls, looked more than ever before like weird figures dancing around them. The circle of five women drew closer, as if for comfort.

As though emanating from the fire, the voice said, 'I have a message for V-v-v— I can't get the name. Vera, no, not Vera.'

'Is it Venetia?' asked Maggie in a curiously guttural voice.

'No. Yes! Venetia! That's it. Yes, Venetia. Take care. Someone close to you is going to be in need of loving care. Someone very close. On the brink. Yes, on the brink. He's coming very, very close to me.' There came a ghastly scream, hands flew to mouths, and the circle was broken. Maggie went rigid. Venetia broke down in tears. 'It's Jeremy. It must be. Another heart attack.'

Maggie snapped her fingers twice and became normal again. 'I need a drink.' She went to the sideboard cupboard and got out the brandy. She'd only intended getting out a glass for herself, but looking slyly over her shoulder at the others, she decided they all needed one.

In varying degrees of shock, they sat round the table sipping their brandy.

The weekender was the least affected by the spirit of Evadne. 'Well, I come week after week and no one, but no one ever has a message for me. I shan't come any more. That's it. I was hoping for a message from my sister, who has been dead five years, as we were very close. No, that's it for me.' But the brandy warmed her inside and gradually she began to feel that it might be worthwhile for her to turn up next week.

116

Venetia stood up. 'I've got to go, see to Jeremy.' She switched on the main light. 'If it's true, then this Evadne person . . . spirit . . . thingy, must be real. When she said he was coming very close to her, did that mean . . . he's almost a spirit himself? I'd better go quickly . . .' And she left in a great flurry, muttering to herself.

'All right, Linda?' Maggie asked.

'Oh! Yes. Can I thank Evadne for her advice?'

'Next week, eh?'

Linda nodded and got to her feet, ready to leave.

Greta Jones said, 'I'll go with you.'

As they passed the Store, they saw the lights were on and Jimbo was dressing the window yet again. Linda wished deep in her heart that things were still OK between them. Still, she'd been told to lean on Alan and ask for his advice and she would.

Having arranged for Linda and Maggie Dobbs to be temporary stand-ins for a second time, Kate was delighted to find that all three of the dinner ladies were back in harness again. However, they weren't speaking to each other, and worst of all, Ginger Nob and the one Maggie called Mealy Mouth had only too obviously been *punched*, one in the eye and the other on the mouth. Kate was too polite to comment on the matter but she did say, 'If you're not speaking to each other I hope it doesn't mean you're not speaking to the children either. Whatever your problem,' she purposely eyed the two with the black and blue faces, 'they don't deserve ostracizing. I shall take particular note of your behaviour at lunchtime. Any problems and it's out.'

Kate turned on her heel and returned to her class. She'd

changed these last few weeks. At one time she would have had them in her office counselling and reassuring them, but her recent altercation with Craddock had hardened her and, like him, she wasn't prepared to stand any nonsense.

While her class did their quiet reading before school dinner, a time when she would have been marking their maths, she thought about the look on his face when she'd told him what Caroline had done.

He'd had his back to her when she'd told him and had spun round on his heel to face her. 'Done what?'

'Reported the condition of the house to Social Services. But they are understaffed at the moment and—'

'After all I've done for the church, all that money?' He began counting off on his fingers how many times he'd helped them out. 'I can't believe it.'

'I might remind you that Peter has never asked you for money for the church, it's always been you who's offered it.'

'That may be, but he's accepted it without a murmur, hasn't he?'

'Did you expect a repayment of some kind?'

'Of course not.'

'Good. For one minute I thought you were trying to buy your place in heaven.'

Craddock clenched his fists. 'That was unworthy of you.'

'Sorry, but you can't buy people's loyalty. Money isn't everything.'

Craddock paused before he answered, then said, 'Isn't it?'

'You pay for the cricket pavilion but can you let it go at

118

that? Oh no. It has to have "The Craddock Fitch Pavilion" emblazoned across the front. I wonder you didn't have your name engraved on each of the church bells you provided, then you really would have gone down in history, or even on the new church boiler on a special plate screwed to the front of it.'

'Kate!'

'It's no good looking so indignant. What is it in the Bible? "Let not your left hand know what your right hand doeth." Something like that. Well, just think about it. However, this doesn't settle the question of Caroline and the Social Services.'

'I shall do nothing. They can shout and carry on as much as they like. After what you've said, I shall do nothing. Absolutely nothing. I'll leave it all to someone else. All those overpaid, underworked do-gooders can have a birthday, at least I shall have found them something to do. But I bet I know who they'll send the bills to; *Me*.' Piqued beyond anything he'd ever known, Craddock sat down in his favourite chair, a glass of whisky in his hand and seethed inside as he picked up what Kate called his weekly Bible, namely *The Economist*, and thought to himself, at least I shall get some sense out of this.

Kate, fuming at his lack of understanding, and frustrated by not knowing how to bring him round to her way of thinking, stormed off to soak in one of her lavender oil baths to relax and think of a solution.

But Craddock kept seeing Kate's face on the page as he read, and finally he put *The Economist* down and thought about her. He'd heard the taps running and guessed she would be taking one of her scented baths.

He knew he was lucky to have found love at his age.

119

Especially love with a young woman who teased every one of his senses, and whom he loved passionately. And here he was, upsetting her when all she wanted was for a family of her children to be housed comfortably, for some paltry sum, a matter of a few thousand pounds he wouldn't notice had been spent and wasn't essential to his or his company's existence. He would do exactly as the Bible said, and sort it out quietly, without a word to anyone, least of all Kate. He'd call on Mrs Bliss while the children were at school and make her promise not to say a word.

He sensed she was coming, for the smell of the lavender oil was in his nostrils and he glanced up and saw her standing in the doorway looking at him, solemn and obviously uneasy, and his heart lurched. He mustn't do anything to harm their relationship, he couldn't lose her. Not his Kate. He held out a hand to her, inviting her to come to him and she did, kneeling in front of him, putting her arms around his waist and laying her head on his chest. He stroked her hair in greeting. They stayed there while the fire began to burn low, making amends to each other in silence.

When Craddock went to visit Mrs Bliss the following morning, his nostrils were assailed by the smell of a faulty sewage tank. His heart sank and memories of his childhood flooded suddenly into his mind.

He knocked at the door and eventually it was opened by Mrs Bliss. Over her shoulder he caught sight of the grimy, undecorated walls and the barely furnished room, and it affected him more than he could have believed. It was all there; his childhood home brought back in a flash. A home he thought he'd banished from his consciousness the day he'd walked out at the age of sixteen because he couldn't take life as it was any longer. Anything, anywhere, was bound to be better. Craddock Fitch managed a smile. Her depression registered with him immediately; it was his mother all over again. Defeated. Resigned. Filled to the brim with despair. The will to fight beaten down by lack of funds.

'Mrs Bliss?'

She nodded.

'I've come to see about repairing the roof.'

'You have?'

'Yes. Can I take a look, see what needs doing?'

'Feel free.' She closed the door and left him standing outside, feeling foolish. He went round the back and looked up at the roof. He saw where the tiles had slipped and were letting in the wet; some were lying in the overgrown garden. Craddock bent down and began collecting them together. He stacked them against the wall. The smell from the septic tank was even more noticeable round the back. God! How it brought back the memories. Well, he wasn't prepared to allow children to suffer as he had done. He turned round and saw the state of the garden, now wildly overgrown after all these years. No one could be expected to tackle this without motorized equipment. He might even find the septic tank if it all got cleared.

He rattled on the door once more. 'Mrs Bliss?' Eventually the door opened again. 'Can I come in?'

'Be my guest. Who are you anyway?'

'Been sent round to see about repairs.'

'I see.'

'I'll make a list.'

'Right.'

'May I go upstairs, see where the rain's coming in?'

She hesitated. 'Very well.' She didn't offer to accompany him so he went alone. He felt sick at heart when he saw the bedrooms. His stomach heaved at the memory of his father's voice: from all those years back, '*Get to bloody bed, the lot of yer.*' He almost retched. Could feel the weight of his father's hand. He recalled, all too easily, hiding under the blanket, trying to shut out the sound of his father arguing with his mother downstairs, waiting for the inevitable crash of their pitiable furniture as he lunged to hit her. His heart broke at the memory. He'd never gone back to see if she was all right. His neglect of her hit him with such fierceness he had to put a hand against the wall to steady himself. When he recovered a little he took out his handkerchief and wiped his hand, remembering how dirty the walls of his childhood bedroom had been. The only difference between that bedroom and the one he stood in now was that the sheets looked clean, so at least some effort was being made. But that was the only plus. The poor woman must be deeply, deeply depressed in a way he had never experienced.

He couldn't make any notes, he was too overcome. His hand trembled and his damned electronic diary just wouldn't cooperate. Damn the blasted thing. He didn't need notes anyway; it was all too familiar, embedded in his mind.

He rattled back down the stairs as fast as he could.

'Could Mr Bliss help with the work at all? Is he a handyman?'

She stared at him and turned away to look out of the window. 'There is no Mr Bliss any longer.'

'Sorry. Well, if anyone should ask you who's doing the work on your house, say anything but don't say the landlord or they'll all be wanting things done. Right?'

He didn't even know if what he had said registered with her, because she never answered. So he left, filled with a kind of missionary zeal, a feeling he couldn't remember having before. That poor woman needed help. Help to get her self-respect back, her zest for life. He wished he'd seen the children. On his way back he heard the schoolchildren out playing so he turned into Jacks Lane, pulled up and got out of the car to lean on the school wall. What fun they were having. How carefree they all appeared. Free as air.

He almost wished . . .

Hetty Hardaker was on playground duty and she came across to have a word when she spotted him. 'Hello, Mr Fitch. How're things?'

'Kate said you'd got some new children, a family of four.'

'That'll be the Blisses.' Hetty turned to search the playground. 'Those two boys standing talking by the main door and the two little girls skipping over there. Lovely children. Very bright. The smaller girl has dance in every bone in her body. A delight to watch.' She turned back to look at him, curious about his reasons for visiting the school like this. 'How are you, Mr Fitch?'

'I'm very well, thank you. Don't let me interrupt your duty.'

Hetty nodded. Obviously she wasn't going to get anything out of him this morning. For a moment she paused to wonder why Kate had married him.

★

Maggie Dobbs crossed Jacks Lane on her way to the school and saw Mr Fitch still leaning on the wall watching the children.

'Morning, Mr Fitch.'

'Good morning, Mrs—'

'Dobbs. I'm the school caretaker.'

'Of course, of course, Kate's mentioned you.'

Mrs Dobbs joined him, laying her forearms on the school wall. 'Them new kids, nice little things. That little Una, over there look skipping, you should see her dance. Smashing! Like a ballet dancer she is, so light on her feet and such, well, I think style's the word.'

'So Hetty said.' He turned to look at her. 'Kate's delighted with the way you look after the school. She thought she'd never get anyone as good as Bel Tutt, but you are.'

Maggie blushed. 'Thanks. It's all right as a job until it rains and then . . . my floors, even before prayers, are filthy. Still . . . must get started on the dinner tables. Be seeing you.'

She left him still standing there and went inside to begin.

Jean, senior dinner lady, was early and helped Maggie to put out the tables.

'You know,' she said softly, 'the other night, Dad's spirit saying what it did? Well, it was right. I challenged Larry with it when I got 'ome. Except you know that other spirit, Edna or something, warned Ginger about tempting other women's husbands? Well, it wasn't her, it was . . . ' She couldn't bring herself to say it so Maggie said it for her.

'Not her with the mealy mouth?'

124

'Yes.'

'I don't believe it. Her? That's a laugh. So what happened with your Larry? Move that table a bit closer. That's right. Is he full of apologies?'

'Oh yes! Amazed he was that I'd found out. Been going on for three months and her as sweet as a nut to me. The slut.'

'So how come Ginger was black and blue, then?'

'Well, I gave her a lift home and went with her inside and even though she'd protested it wasn't her I told her husband, and before you could say knife, he'd fetched her one. Trouble was, that night, Mealy Mouth's husband found out in the Royal Oak from a mate of his and he went home and hit her across the mouth.' She added with a disgusted look, 'Very rough they are, you know.'

'So has anyone fetched your Larry one yet?'

'No, only me and he's promised to behave himself from now on. Thank goodness, and thank you, Maggie, very much for contacting Dad, and finding out for me. I wouldn't mind another go sometime.'

Maggie surveyed the hall, satisfied the tables were in the right places, and as Jean walked off to the kitchen, she thought, behave himself? Till the next time. That Larry had a roving eye by all reports. Mealy Mouth wouldn't be the last, and certainly wasn't the first. With these approaching light nights, she wondered about changing to that Ouija thingy she'd read about. But would it be any more successful than an ordinary seance?

Chapter 8

On Saturday night the bar was filled to overflowing. Dicky had piled logs on the huge open fireplace and the flames were licking up the chimney and throwing out enormous heat. But they did need it, for it was a bitterly cold night and the refuge of the Royal Oak, with its glittering brasses and comfortable chairs, was exceedingly appealing. Seated on a chair as close to the fire as possible was Vera from the nursing home. Alone and looking worried.

'Hello, Vera. Long time no see.' It was Sylvia from the Rectory.

'Hello, Sylvia.' Vera wasn't altogether sure she wanted Sylvia's candid grey eyes focused on her, however kindly.

Sylvia found a chair, pulled it across beside Vera and sat down. 'You're not too well?'

'I've been at the hospital all day.'

'I'm so sorry.' Those sweet grey eyes of hers were filled with sympathy. 'I'd no idea you were ill.'

Vera shook her head. 'It's not me. It's Don.' She felt Sylvia's hand on her arm, stroking her with such gentleness.

'Oh, Vera. I didn't know he was sick.'

She'd be crying in a minute. It was only keeping a tight

126

grip on her emotions that was keeping her going. 'He isn't ill, well, he is . . . he had a bad fall this morning.' Vera had her handkerchief at the ready, knowing she couldn't hold out for much longer.

'Broken some bones, then?'

Vera nodded. 'Mending the gutter. One joint had slipped and when it rains, the water pours down the windows, so he'd climbed up the ladder to mend it. He was very high up near the gable end and . . .' Her sobbing was quiet but altogether painful. She felt Sylvia's arm around her shoulders.

'There, there. They're very good at the hospital. Remember when Flick Charter-Plackett was run over when she was little? They put her back together again and I'm sure they'll do the same for Don.'

Vera felt herself being hugged. She could hear the words of comfort but they meant absolutely nothing. Sylvia didn't know what she was talking about because she hadn't seen him in hospital after they'd operated. She had and it was a sight she never wanted to see ever again.

A loud, hearty voice said, 'Hello, Vera! Nice to see yer. Oh, sorry. Whatever's the matter?'

Vera couldn't answer Willie. She did hear Sylvia say, 'Just go get yourself a seat, Willie, I'll be a while.'

Between her sobs Vera told how she'd heard the crash of Don falling down. At his age he shouldn't have been climbing but he was the odd-job man now he was retired and anything that needed doing he did. There was blood seeping from his head, and his shoulders and spine seemed awkward and she remembered someone shouting, 'Don't move him.' After that, she heard nothing because the only sound that penetrated her numbness was the ambulance siren. On and on and on, all the way to Culworth.

'You know they work miracles nowadays. They'll get him sorted, believe me. Look, why not come and sit with Willie and Jimmy like we used to, eh? It'll be like old times. How about it? Don't sit here by yourself.'

But there'd be no orange juice to order for Don, not tonight or any other night. Not with his brain . . . 'No, thanks, I wouldn't be good company tonight. We've had such happy times lately, it doesn't seem fair.'

'We can't order these things, Vera.'

Vera looked up sharply. 'You've housekept at that Rectory for far too long. Them's the sort of words the Rector would use.'

'Look, let me go get him. He'll help.'

'No.'

'Please. He's wonderful in a crisis, so reassuring.'

'No. Just go and sit with Willie and leave me alone. There's nothing anyone can do.' Vera felt Sylvia move away. Why ever had she asked Jimmy to drop her off here instead of taking her straight to the nursing home to her lovely, airy flat where she and Don were so happy? She'd come for help, that was it. The hospital had said to go home, to get a good night's sleep and come back tomorrow. How could she sleep with Don laid unconscious in intensive care, bandaged, black and blue, eyes made into slits with all the swelling, a neck brace on, and tubes and wires all over the place? The laughter and bustle of the bar passed by unheeded as she wallowed helplessly in a sea of misery.

★

Maggie Dobbs came in about half past nine. She surveyed the bar. The usual trio of Willie, Sylvia and Jimmy were sitting at their table, Mealy Mouth was with her husband, some noisy men were celebrating something or another and then, as she glanced at the fire and thought how welcome it was, she saw the Rector sitting beside Vera. He was speaking earnestly, his long back bent as he held her hand, one arm laid across the back of her chair. She paid at the bar for her favourite tipple, gin and orange, then went directly across to the settle to sit beside Sylvia and find out what was wrong with Vera.

'It's Don, he's had a serious fall off his ladder. He's in a bad way.'

'Oh, I am sorry. Poor Vera. They are good landlords to me. I wouldn't wish it on anyone. Mind you, they are putting up the rent from next month.'

Rather snappily, Sylvia retorted that she didn't think they'd be worrying much about that at the moment.

Maggie sipped her gin. 'He could die from it, you know. I expect she'd perhaps want to be back in her cottage if he did. That'd land me in a mess and not half, just when I've got a steady job and my home sorted out and friends and things . . . God, I hope not.'

Willie muttered something she didn't quite catch. 'What did you say, Willie?'

'I said, spare a thought for poor Vera.'

'Well, I am. But it affects me a lot more than you if he dies. I don't want him to die, believe me. My home's just right for me. I've landed on my feet.' Maggie looked across at Vera again and saw the Rector had got her smiling. What the blazes was there to smile about in the circumstances?

Vera had thought she wouldn't smile ever again. She was glad someone had got the Rector for her. Then all of a sudden she remembered. 'My God! I never thought about our Rhett! He doesn't know.'

'Where is he?'

'Gone for a weekend to Weston with his friends. If Don dies, he'll never forgive me. I'll have to tell him.' The smile gone, she wept again for Rhett and his hurt if his grandad, the only father figure he'd ever known, died.

'Soon solved. I'll ring the camp and leave a message.'

'But I don't know the number.' Vera moaned quietly, feeling her pain all over again, only worse for Rhett's sake.

'No worries.' Peter took his phone from his pocket and dialled enquiries.

After he'd contacted the holiday camp and left a message for Rhett, Peter offered to take Vera to see Don before she went to bed.

'But I can't visit this time of night. They won't let me.'

'They will if you're with me. I can go any time I like. Then I'll drive you back tonight or you can stay all night if you want to.'

'You're very kind. I could come back on the bus tomorrow, couldn't I?'

'Just as you wish. I'll go get the car. Wait here.'

While Peter got the car, Vera nipped to the loo and tried to get rid of the traces of her tears. If Don was conscious, she didn't want him seeing her looking like something the cat had dragged in and forgotten. Her image in the loo mirror didn't do her spirits any good whatsoever. Her hair was straggly, her eyes swollen, her skin grey with the worry and her clothes looked as though she'd been wearing them to bed. A bit of lipstick would give her a lift.

The door opened and in came Maggie Dobbs. 'All right, Vera? Sorry about Don.'

'The Rector's taking me back to the hospital.'

'I understand he's bad.'

'Oh, he is. Couldn't be worse.' Vera felt the tears coming again, but she wouldn't let 'em, not in front of Maggie Dobbs.

'Let's hope you have better news when you go back.'

'Thanks.' Vera finished putting her lipstick on, sorted her straggly hair, put her comb away, snapped her handbag shut and left without another word.

Maggie watched her leave. Something niggled at the back of Maggie's mind about Vera. As she flushed the loo, it almost came to her, then it was gone. Whatever was it? Something important, but what? Was it about Don? No, she knew nothing about Don. Nothing at all. She went back to finish her drink, still puzzling. She couldn't listen to the others, as it grew into an anxiety that jangled her nerves and ruined her evening. Then, it hit her like a thunderbolt. The seance! That was it! Evadne *had* been talking about Vera, not Venetia! Oh God! What a mistake to make! Was it all her fault? Was that it? She'd seen Jeremy only the other morning, taking his rigorously imposed daily constitutional through Home Park, so she knew he was all right.

Sylvia nudged her. 'What do you think?'

'What about?'

'About getting a card and signing it for poor Don.'

'I . . . of course. Count me in. If he lives that long.'

'Maggie! What a thing to say.'

'You don't fall on your head from a great height and then prance about like a spring lamb. You're usually in your box in no time at all. Goodnight.' Maggie left the three of them looking appalled and went home. Home? Was that what she called it? She could hardly bear to put the key in the lock and see where it had all happened. Tabitha, for some reason best known to herself, was sleeping in the middle of the carpet and Maggie stood on her tail. Tabitha gave the most horrendously agonized yowl and fled for her cat flap.

The gin and orange had had no effect on Maggie's nerves so she went straight to the sideboard, fished out the brandy and poured herself a double, for purely medicinal purposes. She sat down in her rocking chair, reached forward and poked at the fire to improve the blaze. By mistake she missed replacing the poker on her fire iron stand and it crashed on to the tiled hearth, the sound reverberating around the cottage and scaring the living daylights out of her. Was every object trying to warn her that she'd gone too far this time and meddled in things she frankly didn't understand? Or was there nothing *to* understand? She'd only meant her seances to be a bit of fun, a change from the telly.

Sitting there with her feet on the fender and the brandy glass cuddled in her hands, Maggie contemplated her position. Had she become a medium without knowing it? Had she really got influence? She recalled the seance when she'd . . . well, whatever it was, she'd felt different, more involved. She swallowed the last of the brandy. Perhaps practice made perfect? The rocking chair swung back and forth furiously. She'd pretended for so long, but now it might be for real. If that was so, then she had the kind of power she'd never possessed in her life. Old Fitch got his power through money. Was she getting hers through the spirit world? There was only one way to find out; have another seance and see if it happened again. The brandy began to take effect, the rocking chair slowed its pace and Maggie fell asleep.

She woke when Tabitha jumped on her knee.

'You stupid cat! Frightening me like that!'

Tabitha's eyes appeared unusually large and knowledgeable, far too intelligent for a normal moggie. The hairs at the back of Maggie's neck prickled slightly, and she felt goose pimples on her arms. Tabitha stared at her, purring as she kneaded her claws into Maggie's flesh. Surely Tabitha wasn't a witch's cat, was she? Her Dave had found Tabitha, extraordinarily thin and soaked to the skin, straying on Exmoor when they were on holiday, and brought her to their caravan to be looked after. Maybe it was all Tabitha's fault. Perhaps she really was a witch's cat and had been guided to Dave by the spirit world. Was Exmoor significant? No. It was just an old moor like any other. Could have been Ilkley Moor or Dartmoor or the moors where them Brontës lived and died.

Maggie sprang to her feet, put Tabitha in her basket by the fire, placed the fireguard around it and made her way up to bed. The bulb in the bathroom flashed and went out the moment she switched it on. Well, she wasn't going hunting downstairs for a new bulb at one o'clock in the morning, she'd get washed in the dark. Maggie peeped out of the bedroom window before she shut the curtains. The village was as peaceful as it always was. From her window she could see lights on in Willie Biggs's cottage. They'd be watching one of those late-night films Willie was so fond of. The Rectory's bedroom light was on too. There wasn't a sound. It was amazing how quickly she'd got used to the quiet of the countryside. Dave would have loved it here. Oh, Dave! Why did he have to die so unexpectedly, so devastatingly? It wasn't fair. She wondered if the Rector had got back yet and if he had, what news of Don he had brought.

Then a thought sprang into her head and comforted her. She never pretended to get any messages to do with the weekender who came so regularly, and that was because she knew nothing about the woman at all. When she was pretending to be a medium she used information she already had in her head about the people concerned, like with the dinner ladies, so she *couldn't* have become a real medium. The Senior sisters, for instance, had concocted their own interpretation of what she'd said. Maggie grinned at the memory of finding the wedding cake on the school doorstep.

She was on the verge of sleep when she remembered that Don's fall had had nothing to do with anything she knew about him and Evadne was made up, a figment of her imagination.

It was four o'clock before she finally fell asleep through total exhaustion, and when, at about six o'clock, Tabitha crept under the blankets and cuddled up to her, it felt comforting, like a kindred spirit . . . Kindred spirit indeed. A cat! What nonsense. But she didn't throw her out, as she normally would have.

The next morning was Sunday and the only way Maggie was likely to find out about Don was to go to church. By a quarter to eight she was dressed and ready. Checking her face in the mirror she had to laugh despite her anxiety. Fancy, her, Maggie Dobbs, lifelong sceptic, off to church! Her Dave would have laughed if he could've seen her. Deep down she wondered if she was drawn by fear, but near the top of her consciousness, she acknowledged she genuinely needed to know about Don, and that was all.

At seven fifty-five, Maggie entered the ancient doors of her parish church for the first time and crept down the aisle. There couldn't have been more than thirty people in the congregation and she felt each one of them was staring at her. She decided to sit near the back, two rows behind the worshippers sitting furthest from the altar. She knelt like she'd seen on the telly but didn't know what she was supposed to say, so she silently mouthed, 'Please help Don.' Then in case there were other seriously ill men called Don she added, 'Don Wright, that is.'

Maggie sat up and settled to listening to Mrs Peel on the organ. She glanced down and read the words embroidered on her kneeler. 'Forgive our sins.' Had she sinned? At this moment, contacting the dead didn't seem like pretence.

The Rector arrived with the choir and the whole panoply of the Church at its most majestic held her attention. During prayers, Peter made a special mention of Don and prayed for his quick recovery. Maggie sighed with relief. At least he was still alive. She felt better until the closing prayer, which was delivered almost poetically by Peter, like an actor on a stage: 'Keep us from falling into sin, or running into danger . . .' Danger. What a word to choose. Maggie got that creepy-crawly feeling in her insides, and by the time the service concluded, she was a bag of nerves all over again.

She hadn't realized that Peter would be shaking hands

135

with everyone at the door; there was no escape for her. Those intense blue eyes of his looked straight into hers and she felt this overwhelming need to ask him if she was consorting with the devil by holding seances. He gripped her hand and said how pleased he was to see her, that Kate Fitch had said what a good job she did at the school and how delighted he was that she was so quickly becoming a valued part of village life.

Confronted by such crystal-clear Christian affection, Maggie scuttled off to the safety of her home, completely nonplussed.

Her regular seance night came around all too quickly. Maggie followed the same routine except that, having shaded the light on the low table by the fire and placed the chairs around her table, she got out a wine glass that had once belonged to her grandmother, gave it an extra special wash and polished it until it shone, placed it upside down in the middle of the table and then around it, in a large circle, she placed in order the twenty-six letters of the alphabet, written out in her own hand, bold and unmistakable.

This was the same but different. She might not get any results, but as it would take much longer than the trance, they'd get their money's worth.

They all expressed surprise at the changes.

Maggie explained. 'Thought we needed something a little extra.'

'But what do we do?' asked Linda.

'I know.' Greta Jones placed a finger on the upturned wine glass. 'We all do this and ask a question and it spells out the answer.'

'How can it? It can't speak,' Linda replied scornfully.

'It moves to each letter and spells it out.' Maggie said this with a smile.

Venetia was scornful. 'Who pushes it?'

'The spirits guide it.'

Linda, still unemployed, had reached new depths of scepticism. 'I bet. You'll just push it.'

Maggie looked shocked. 'I most certainly will not.'

'Well, I'm not paying five pounds for a load of cheating,' stated Linda, arms folded and lips pursed.

The Senior twins said together, 'We will! It could be interesting.'

'Go on, Linda,' said Greta Jones. 'Give it a whirl. You might hear something about a job.'

Linda brightened and nodded her head. 'All right, then.'

The weekender hadn't come this time, something about staying at home to do the decorating. Instead, Angie Turner accompanied Linda, who hadn't asked if that was all right.

Maggie was annoyed, but didn't say so. Five pounds was five pounds when your washing machine had just packed up. With their money tucked up safely in Dave's jug and put away in the cupboard, Maggie sat down with the others.

'Now. We want absolute silence when we begin or nothing will work. Everyone puts a finger on the wine glass, only a light touch remember, the glass has to have room to move. It's one hundred years old, full of history, and very sensitive. We'll sit quietly, thinking of questions and I'll ask the first one to get the ball rolling. Ready?'

There wasn't so much as a tremor in the fingertips laid gently on the base of the glass. It was another cold night and the fire was more than welcome, but Linda noticed how the flames wavered about the walls and she wished they didn't. Five minutes without speaking was beginning to take its toll on her. Just as she was thinking it was all a con, Maggie asked, 'Is Don still holding his own?'

Within seconds the glass was moving right across directly to 'Y', then 'E', then 'S'. A sigh of relief went round the group.

Angie asked the next one. 'Am I going to win the lottery?'

The wine glass hesitated, then stopped again in front of the letters 'Y', 'E' and 'S'. Angie let out a cry of delight.

Greta Jones said, 'It'll be ten pounds. Don't get too excited.'

'Then again,' snapped Angie, 'it might be ten million.'

'Oh yeah!'

Each of them in turn asked a simple question, so that only an affirmative or a negative answer was required. Maggie felt she was losing their attention. 'Is there a message for any one of us tonight?'

The glass rocked slightly and Linda became convinced the table had rocked too. The glass spelt out a sentence this time, slowly. Tantalizingly. L-i-n-d-a-m-u-s-t-a-s-k-p-a-m-f-o-r-a-j-o-b.

Maggie called out, 'Linda must ask Pam for a job! Pam. Who's Pam?'

Greta Jones said, 'Not Pam, Pat. It'll be a waitressing job. She'll be short-handed. I did say.'

Linda shivered with fright. 'Really? I'll ask her first thing in the morning. Oh God. I feel all squirmy inside.'

'Shh! Someone ask something else.'

This time a Miss Senior asked her mother if she had any

138

more advice for the two of them. But the answer was jumbled and they couldn't make head nor tail of it. Disappointed, Maggie asked the next question, prompted by she knew not what. 'Dave? Do you have a message for me?'

There was a long silence, once or twice the wine glass rocked, Linda was convinced the table had rocked again. Then hesitatingly the glass spelt out g-e-t-t-h-e-n-e-w-w-a-s-h-i-n-g-m-a-c-h-i-n-e-o-n-t-i-c-k-b-e-f-o-r-e-i-t-s-t-o-o-l-a-t-e.

Maggie was horrified. She blanched. Her finger was glued to the glass and wouldn't come away. The others took their fingers off and Linda and Venetia began to laugh.

'Honestly!' said Venetia. 'What a laugh. That's ridiculous. Who pushed it? Come on, who was it?'

Maggie stuttered. 'But it's true, it's broken down, they can't mend it. It's too old. No parts. They told me today.'

'My lord!' The Senior sisters clutched each other.

Linda muttered, 'It's real then.'

Angie cried out, 'This is dangerous.'

Maggie said, 'What did it mean "b-b before it's too late"?'

'Too late for what?' asked Greta Jones.

A deathly silence descended on them all. In the light of the lamp it was possible to see seven ashen faces, which not even the glow from the fire could colour. Eyes were wide, flicking from one to the other, seeking a grain of comfort.

Angie was the first to speak. 'Come on. Spill the beans, someone. Confess.'

But each in turn shook their heads. In fact, when Angie

139

looked into their faces she could see none of them were guilty. She swallowed hard.

Maggie stated firmly that she thought they'd done enough for tonight.

'No. No. Let's have one more turn.'

Reluctantly, Maggie nodded.

So they started again but everything was confused once more and nothing made sense. Suddenly, out of the jumble came recognizable words: t-e-r-r-y-i-s-w-e-l-l-a-n-d-h-a-p-p-y.

'Oh my God! Oh my God!' Mrs Jones shouted. 'After all this time. Wait till I tell Vince! Oh my God!' She was quite out of control. Mopping her face with her tissue, fanning herself with her hands, laughing hysterically, filled with happiness. 'Now that really is it for tonight.'

Venetia asked if Mrs Jones had ever heard of her two boys since they'd disappeared after all that trouble with the police.

Mrs Jones put on a brave face when she replied, 'Not a word. Not a blinking word.'

'That's wonderful for you, isn't it?' Angie said. 'I don't understand how it happens.'

'It's connecting with the spirits, that's what,' asserted Maggie.

'Well, I never,' said Linda. 'Talk about being interesting. I don't know when I've had such a good night. Better than the telly, 'cos it's real. I'll talk to Pat first thing.'

'It's made my day has this. A message from our Terry. Well, well. It's been terrible not knowing.'

Maggie said nothing. One happy customer was all that was needed to make a success of her 'evenings'. She'd try this again.

As they picked up their belongings, Maggie asked, 'Same again next week or back to the usual?'

With one voice they all said, 'Same again.'

'Goodnight, Maggie.'

'We'll make it nine o'clock next week. The nights are getting lighter and we don't want to draw attention to ourselves. In any case, it's always better in the dark.'

'Nine o'clock it is, then.'

The absolutely deliciously alarming thing about it all was that on the following Monday morning the postman knocked at Mrs Jones's door and handed her an airmail letter from New Zealand. 'Thought I'd hand it to you personally, Mrs Jones. Not often you get a letter from the other side of the world, is it? Good morning to you.'

It was from Terry. So all that terrible worry that had come to her when Vince had said that if our Terry was sending messages to her from the spirit world, logic dictated he was dead, disappeared. She'd spent a ghastly weekend after he'd said that. But all that was at an end. Joy!

On the following Saturday night, Angie and her Colin won £254.42 on the lottery with numbers they'd never used before, and Linda got a job immediately waitressing at one of Jimbo's functions in Culworth.

The secret of Maggie's seances was out.

Chapter 9

Kate stood in her classroom doorway, watching Mrs Dobbs water the plants in the hall. There was something about Maggie she couldn't quite put her finger on; a listlessness, a kind of anxiety that hadn't been there last week, or ever before come to that. 'Mrs Dobbs?'

'Yes.' Maggie turned to look at her.

'Are you well?'

'Yes, thanks.'

'Sure? Nothing worrying you?'

There was a hesitation before Maggie answered, 'Nothing at all.'

'I've got a letter addressed to you from the education office. I've an idea it's good news.'

Alarmed, Maggie said, 'Not my notice, is it?' She thought of the payments on the washing machine she'd had delivered according to Dave's instructions. She took the letter from Kate and stuffed it into her apron pocket. 'I'll read it later.'

'Of course it can't be your notice and if it is, which it isn't, I shall have a lot to say to those nincompoops in the office. Their ears will be burning and no mistake. I don't want you to leave, believe me. Open it and see.'

'No.'

Kate was puzzled, Maggie wasn't her usual self at all. The spring had gone out of her step, and she looked thinner. Added to which she was quiet. If Maggie was in school, then normally everyone knew about it.

Time after time, Maggie had told herself it was only a game. But when she heard that Angie had won on the lottery, that Linda's name was on Pat Jones's list for waitressing, and most worrying of all, apart from Dave's message, that Greta Jones had received a letter from their Terry in New Zealand on the Monday morning after the seance, she'd become completely overwrought.

She felt a great leaden weight lodged somewhere just under her ribs and it wouldn't go away. It was there when she bent over to squeeze the mop in the school bucket, when she put down Tabitha's dish and, worse, it was always present as soon as she began to eat. Frighteningly, she'd promised them another of her regular evenings, and she couldn't see how she could get out of it.

Kate always had time for the children to tell her their news, even though they were at the top of the Junior School age group, because she felt that the children who lived out on the farms needed to catch up on events which had passed them by because of the remoteness of their homes.

That morning Paul Bliss said, 'Did you know, Mrs Fitch, that Mr Turner,' he thrust out his chest and his chin and gave a very good imitation of a strong man posing for a photograph, 'you know, big Mr Turner, well, he's won loads of money on the lottery. Loads and loads.'

'Yes, we heard that,' said Karen from Year Seven. 'He's a millionaire.'

Scornfully Paul retorted, 'He isn't.'

143

'Mrs Turner got told by the spirits she would and she did,' said Phil Bliss.

Kate laughed. 'The spirits! What spirits?'

'Them what come when Mrs Dobbs does her seance,' said Karen.

'What nonsense is this?'

Karen gave a long rambling description, grossly exaggerated, about the evening when Mrs Turner had heard she was to have a win. 'They say it's all dark and scary and ghosts come to dance on the walls.'

'Well, I think you've all got it wrong. I'm glad Mrs Turner's won some money, though. Those little twins of hers go through clothes like nobody's business. Mrs Dobbs doesn't communicate with the spirits, because no one can.'

Karen stoutly declared that Kate was wrong. 'She does, Mrs Fitch, honest. You ask her. Them old Senior sisters, the ones you can't tell which is which, they go. Honest.'

'Really?'

'Oh yes. They calls up the dead people and they speak. They calls 'em up every week on Fridays.' Karen rolled her eyes and the rest of the children made spooky sounds, nudged each other and giggled in pretend fright.

Kate sat looking at her class squatting on the carpet in front of her and thought there might be some truth in what they were saying. Even Karen, with her vivid imagination, couldn't think up something like this without it being at least partly true.

Karen put up her hand again. 'And Mrs Jones from down Church Hill, she's had a letter from their Terry and she hasn't heard from him for *years*. Mrs Dobbs got a message from the spirits for Mrs Jones and they told her that their Terry was well and happy and he's a millionaire in . . . where was it? Oh yes, New Zealand.'

Another child obviously seriously attracted by the idea of communicating with the dead asked if they could get Mrs Dobbs to have a seance at school for them. 'I could have a word with my grandma. She was deaded when I was five. Mum would be pleased if I did.'

'Perhaps Paul and Phil could talk with their dad. He's dead, isn't he? That'd be nice for Mrs Bliss.'

Kate stamped on this idea immediately and channelled their thoughts into something less sensational by asking Robert Nightingale to show everyone where New Zealand was on the map on the back wall of the classroom. By posing some interesting questions about the country, she deftly drew their news time away from Mrs Dobbs and her activities.

But at the end of the school day Kate went back to thinking about Maggie Dobbs's Friday night seances and decided to have a word with her. Kate cleared her desk in her little office in good time and was sitting waiting for Maggie when she called out, 'Is it free?' and walked in.

'Oh, sorry. I'll come back.'

'No, that's fine. I just need a word. What's all this business about then?'

'What business?'

'All this that's going round the village about you and the spirits and ghosts on your walls?'

'Don't know what you're talking about.'

'You do.'

'I don't.'

'Maggie!' There was a warning note in her voice, which

145

Maggie knew meant she wasn't going to let the matter drop.

'I know nothing. Can I get on now?'

'Nothing?'

'No, nothing.'

'What you really mean is you don't want to tell me.'

Maggie shrugged. This was one secret Madame Fitch wasn't going to get out of her, no matter how hard she tried.

'The children say you hold a seance on Friday nights and call up spirits who send messages to you.' Kate put her head on one side and looked questioningly at Maggie.

'I never.'

Astutely Kate declared, 'I think you're worried about it. In fact, very worried.'

'I'm not. I'm here doing my work and earning my money and that's that. In any case, my life outside this school is nothing to do with you.'

'Quite right.' Kate stood up. 'However, if you do need someone to talk to, I'm a good listener.'

Maggie listlessly wiped the windowsill and remarked, 'Don Wright's still holding his own, they say. Though they don't know how.'

'Good, I'm glad. Nice chap.'

'Yes. I'll press on then.'

'Right.' Kate picked up her briefcase, said goodnight and left. She hadn't got far with that piece of investigation but she was damn well going to tackle Craddock about the Blisses' cottage tonight and get a result. She'd tried once or twice since that fateful evening when she'd thought everything between her and Craddock was lost, but he'd

146

stonewalled her just like Maggie had done now. However, the time had come.

The housekeeper was on her evening off, so she and Craddock dined on the same meal as the students were having and found it as tasty and well prepared as only one of Jimbo's staff could make it. 'I'll say this about Jimbo, he does know about food.'

Craddock dabbed his mouth with his napkin. 'He is excellent. He also knows how to keep the staff on their toes and they do it so willingly for him. I swear they'd poison us all quite cheerfully if he told them it was necessary. We could do with more people like Jimbo in the business, believe me.'

Kate nodded her agreement and then came out in a rush with, 'May I mention something that has been off our agenda for some time now, but can't be ignored?'

'Fire away, my dearest, there's nothing you can't discuss with me.' Craddock lit his cigar and looked at Kate. 'Well?'

'The Blisses' cottage in Little Derehams.'

Cautiously Craddock answered, 'Yes?'

'Have the Social Services been round it yet?'

'Not to my knowledge.'

'Have you done anything about it?'

'Me? Personally?'

'Yes.'

'No.'

'They're still living in that mess?'

'I haven't been to see.'

Kate flung down her napkin and got to her feet. 'You are asking me to live in luxury like this and yet you can allow those children to live in poverty? And you don't care?'

'Be careful, Kate, very careful. Don't step over the line.'

'Don't step over a line *you've* drawn. I haven't drawn any line. Where the health and welfare of my children are concerned, nothing and I repeat nothing will stop me fighting for them. It's a disgrace, Craddock, an absolute disgrace that you are giving your name to such a state of affairs. They'll all know in Little Derehams about your neglect, every man jack of them.'

He had a wry smile on his face when he answered, 'They will, I've no doubt. Everyone always knows what I'm doing.'

'And you don't care?'

'No.'

'I'm ashamed of you.'

'Are you?' A dangerous glint came in his eyes, which she noticed but ignored because she was so angry.

'Yes. Why can't you help them?'

'If, *if*, I want to help them I shall, without any pressure from you or anyone else.'

'But Craddock, why? Explain why you won't help them.' Kate sat down again and watched while he blew a ring of smoke up to the ceiling and wondered if he was aware what an incredibly sexy activity he made out of smoking his cigar.

'I've explained I won't be pushed into making decisions that are rightly mine to make. I shan't repeat myself.'

'Please, please, do it for me.'

'Wheedling will bring even less of a result. As far as I am concerned, the matter is no longer up for discussion.' He couldn't pursue it. If he did, his right hand would certainly find out what his left hand was doing and she'd said it shouldn't.

'Please, darling?' But she could see from the expression on his face that he'd finished with the whole matter. Well, she hadn't. 'I can't understand such hard-hearted cruelty. Not from you. You're not the hard villain everyone considers you to be. I know that. Look what you've given me, half your assets. Why can't that side of you be uppermost *all* of the time?'

'The difference is that I love you, like I've never loved anyone ever before. That's why.'

'It's worth nothing to me if you can't help that poor woman. She's desperate.'

Craddock appeared to ignore her but his eyes, half shut, were watching her very carefully. 'Enough is enough, my dearest. Let's go into the drawing room, and we'll raid the drinks cupboard.'

'No, thanks. I'd choke having a drink with you.'

'Kate!'

'I would. You're a viciously hard businessman and I can't think why on earth I ever thought differently. You'll have to come to your senses, Craddock. You're inhuman if you don't.'

Mr Fitch shot to his feet, his pale face flushing and his fury at her accusation all too evident in his eyes. 'I won't have this. Enough is enough. I don't wish to have the matter mentioned again' He stormed out of the dining room.

Kate stood listening and was astounded when she heard his car starting up. The wheels spun on the gravel as he let in the clutch and she heard the roar of his Rolls as it sped away down the drive at a furious pace. Craddock driving himself? No chauffeur?

Her legs turned weak and she held on to the back of her chair to steady herself. If only he'd see how right it was to put that cottage in order. Damn and blast! Whatever had made her say he was inhuman? What a fool she was. She'd never get the hang of this marriage business if she lived to be a hundred. His mobile! He never went out without it. She'd ring and apologize. No, she wouldn't. Yes, she would. No, she wouldn't. He'd have to come round to her way of thinking.

An hour later, when there'd been no sign of his return, she rang his mobile. The words on the tip of her tongue were, 'Darling, please, I'm so sorry.' But she never got the chance to say them; his mobile was switched off. She tried again an hour later, but there was still no reply.

Kate went to bed, sorrowing.

She woke early the next morning with a pain inside herself, which puzzled her for a moment until she remembered the row of the night before. She reached out her hand to feel for Craddock beside her but he wasn't there. Rolling over on to the side of the bed where he should have been sleeping, she tried to comfort herself but it wouldn't work. The sheets on his half were cold and the pillow felt harder than a rock, so she rolled back to her own half, warmed it up again and lay dwelling on her distress.

He'd been away a couple of times on business since they'd married and she'd pined then for the lack of his presence in the bed they shared, but this was ten thousand times worse because this time she didn't even know where he was and, worse, he'd cut off her line of communication with him. Once, when he'd been away in Sweden for a couple of nights, he'd rung her during the night and they'd talked and talked and he'd said how he missed her beside him and she'd said how she missed him. But this time . . . there'd been no such call.

Tears seeped slowly from under her closed eyelids and she brushed them away with the corner of the sheet. The defiant, independent, tough-minded, self-made woman called Kate was reduced to tears over a man. Hell's bells! How she'd changed.

She rose early and was in school only minutes after Maggie had arrived. She was thankful Maggie was early because at the last minute she hadn't been able to find her own set of school keys.

Maggie called out from the children's coat room, 'Who's an early bird then? Couldn't sleep?'

'Something like that.' Kate went straight to her office to sit at her desk and do some admin before the school woke up.

Laid on her desk was a single red rose and a card. She put her thumb under the flap of the envelope and pushed it open. 'My dearest, more sorry than I can say. C.' She could almost feel the tenderness with which he'd placed the rose, and the love that had triumphed over his anger and forced him to try a reconciliation. Deep down, he must be gentle and loving. He hadn't disappeared. He must have come back into the house and slept in the other bedroom without disturbing her.

Kate picked up her bag and flew out to her car. She reversed and drove like fury back to Turnham House. She skidded to a stop on the gravel by the front door, leapt out and tore up the stairs to the flat, but there was no one there. The bed in the spare bedroom had been slept in, the breakfast table, laid for two, still had the used dishes on it. So he'd even had a quick breakfast after she'd left the house. Her school keys she found on the table by the bedside in the spare bedroom.

She left the flat and went out to the garage where his car was always kept when not in use. It was already gone. Damn him for playing games with her. She'd have to be patient and wait for him.

At school that day the children found Kate preoccupied and willing to be relaxed over just about everything. She was so unlike her usual organized, enthusiastic self that the children took advantage of her mood, and by two o'clock she'd abandoned timetables and they were all painting and drawing and generally messing about as only children can. One half of Kate was angry about the lapse in discipline, the other was worrying about Craddock and whatever she would say to him when he got back from the office.

Maggie had seen the rose, taken note of Kate's obvious distraction and put entirely the wrong interpretation on it. The natural assumption for anyone who even half knew Craddock Fitch was that it couldn't possibly be him. Not in a month of Sundays, because where his heart should have been there was a lump of concrete.

Maggie was in the Store almost before the school bell rang for the beginning of the school day, behind the tinned soups, divulging this juicy piece of information to any who cared to listen.

'No! He couldn't have.' This from Mealy Mouth, who was getting her shopping done before the Store got busy. 'Not him.'

Maggie nodded in agreement. 'So what conclusion can we come to? Eh? I ask yer.'

'Why! It's disgusting. Married only a few weeks and she's started that already.' Mealy Mouth hunched her shoulders and said confidently, ''Course, I knew it was only a matter of time, there being such an age difference. It stands to reason.'

'Exactly, all I can say is think of the alimony.'

Mealy Mouth rolled her eyes and pursed her lips. 'I should say.'

They were unaware that Muriel, getting her shopping before going over to the school to play for the Maypole dancing, was standing behind the pair of them while she chose some soup for lunch.

'Mrs Dobbs! I am appalled that you can speak in that manner about something of which you know nothing. Shame on you.'

Muriel hadn't raised her voice so much as a decibel but had put just the right amount of emphasis on her words to make Maggie and Mealy Mouth feel embarrassed.

'Did you see who put the rose on her desk?'

Maggie shook her head.

'Well, then, you actually don't know, so you shouldn't gossip. We've all jumped to the wrong conclusion about Kate and Craddock. I really believe they have genuine' – she was thinking of saying love but it didn't quite equate with what she knew of Craddock Fitch so she changed it to – 'affection for each other.'

Maggie answered grudgingly, 'Maybe you're right. Shan't say another word.'

'That's good. Ah! Here it is.' Muriel popped a tin of Jimbo's specially imported chicken soup into her wire basket and went on her way. But Maggie was undeterred. Waiting until Muriel was well out of earshot, she muttered, 'Well, I shall think what I like. There's something going on. Believe me.'

'I know the housekeeper there, I'll have a word. On the right day she can be very chatty.' Mealy Mouth nudged Maggie's arm and winked.

Muriel arrived at school with her thoughts about the rose firmly pushed to the back of her mind. But it was difficult to think nothing was happening; Kate was not her usual lively self. But Muriel had a plan in mind and she was bursting to tell her.

'Kate. I've been thinking.'

'Yes?'

'We'll have to make sure I'm absolutely right but isn't it one hundred and fifty years this summer since the school was opened? I know the school house wasn't built until 1855 because it says so on the lintel, but I'm sure the school itself was built in 1853. If I'm right, shouldn't we have a celebration?'

'Is it? Of course, the first log book . . . I looked at it a few weeks ago. I'll check it again, but I'm sure you're right. What a wonderful idea. We could invite everyone we know who's been at the school.'

'Past headteachers perhaps?'

'Of course. Muriel, that's a brilliant idea. I'll give it some thought.'

'We could have an exhibition of photographs. The children could give a performance and we ought to have a plaque or something to commemorate, or a tree planting or something permanent like that. And a meal. Perhaps a buffet because there'll be lots of people there.'

'On a Saturday, of course. Muriel, I could kiss you.' Which she did.

'And a thanksgiving service in the church. Perhaps the mayor from Culworth could come?'

'Muriel! You are an inspiration. I herewith co-opt you on to the committee. Ah! Here come the children. I'll leave you to get on.'

Kate went back to her class, grateful that Muriel had thought of something to help block out her problem about Craddock. Would he or wouldn't he be in the flat this evening?

The merry strains of the Maypole dancing tunes eased the anguish bearing down on Kate's soul and she recollected the love Craddock demonstrated to her. She knew in her heart of hearts this was simply a teething problem for two people finding themselves married, much to their surprise and not quite knowing how to deal with the situation. Yes, of course, that was it. A full-hearted apology was what was needed, even if she felt none of it was her fault, which it wasn't.

The moment school was over for the day, Kate did a brisk tidying of her desk, and found Maggie Dobbs in Hetty Hardaker's classroom watching Gertie the gerbil having a mad five minutes racing round her cage. 'I'm going, Mrs Dobbs, see you in the morning.'

'This is just like us, isn't it? Racing round, not knowing where we're going, but going all the same. Life's a pig, isn't it?'

Kate had to agree with her. 'It can be. Yes. Sometimes,

you know, I feel like letting Gertie out and giving her her freedom.'

'Well, if you do, make sure she's outside and not in here. I don't fancy coming upon her while I'm cleaning. She could give me a heart attack. You feeling better?'

'Better? I'm always feeling better.'

Maggie shook her head. 'You're lucky then.' She held her hand up in salute and turned to get on with her sweeping.

Kate went back to Turnham House and the moment she was indoors she asked Craddock's secretary if he was in his office.

'Yes, he is, Mrs Fitch. If I could say he's not in the best of moods . . .'

Kate knocked on his door and went in. It was only the second time since she'd known him that she'd interrupted him during business hours. She'd forgotten the wonderful linenfold panelling and the old shelves encircling the room, filled end to end with, she was sure, books that hadn't been opened in years. It had been the library when Ralph Templeton's family had owned it and the huge fireplace was still there, now filled with gleaming brass fire irons and a wonderful display of flowers. By the fireplace were two leather chairs, the superior kind with wings, looking as though someone very ordinary had no business sitting in them.

Craddock was on the telephone and when he realized who'd come in there was a pause in his conversation. Then he picked up the thread again and she had to wait. Her heart began pounding. She was being ridiculous; he was her husband after all and he did love her.

156

Craddock replaced the receiver on its cradle and got to his feet.

Neither of them spoke.

But they looked at each other.

Long and hard.

Kate saw a flicker of a smile.

Craddock saw the anxiety in her eyes. 'My dearest.'

'I should never have said what I did. I'm so sorry.'

'Neither should I. I'm sorry too.' He opened wide his arms and she went round the desk and clung to him.

'It's hard being married. I don't quite know how to behave.'

'Neither do I. I'll ring for some tea.' Craddock let go of her and spoke to his secretary. 'Tea for Mrs Fitch and myself, please, in my office.' He invited her to sit in one of his imposing armchairs. He pulled a small side table between them and sat down.

There was silence while they waited for the tea to arrive, but they were used to that. Somehow they could communicate without words.

His eyes never left her.

She studied the strength in his features, the thick white hair, the pale blue eyes, which at times were so cold and calculating but at this moment were full of love, making the years between them matter not one jot. She started to say the words she'd been going to use when she'd rung his mobile and couldn't get a reply. 'Darling, please . . . I'm . . .'

'Hush. No more apologies. We were both in the wrong. I'll try not to lose my temper quite so ferociously.'

'Why hide from me?'

'Because I couldn't face you.'

'I see. We won't do this again.'

'No.'

Kate leapt to her feet, her hands on the arms of his chair, bent forward and kissed his lips. 'I'll try not to interfere.'

'You're right to spring to the defence of the underdog.'

'I am?'

Craddock nodded.

'Does that mean—'

'Kate! Please don't open the matter up again.'

'Sorry, but—' There came a tap at the door and in came the secretary with a tray of tea.

'You pour, my dearest.'

'The rose. Where did you get it from at that time of night?'

Craddock grinned. 'The service station on the by-pass.'

'Romantic anyway.' They both laughed.

The telephone rang and on his way to answer it he took time to kiss her. The taste of hot tea was on his lips and she could smell the strong essence of the aftershave he used, and she craved his touch. Her eyes never left him as he answered his business call. She loved the way his hands gesticulated as he spoke, the wide variety of inflections in his voice, and the very, very slight hint of a northern accent, which occasionally crept through; she wondered about his origins. But best of all she loved the desire in his eyes when he looked at her as he crossed from the desk and stood before her smiling. He studied her face for a moment, then he kissed her on the forehead. 'You'd better go. I still have things to do.'

'I'll be in the flat, taking a bath. I've a meeting of the

school anniversary committee tonight so I shall be eating early. Is that all right?'

'Of course. I shan't be long.'

They held the inaugural meeting in the school hall with Kate taking the chair, unaware that before the meeting was over she'd be wishing she'd never even started the whole idea. Tea was served at the start, along with a tasteful plate of biscuits kindly provided by Muriel. When the biscuits had all been eaten and a few voices had finished muttering about some people having only one biscuit when others had had two or three, Kate called the meeting to order and began her speech.

'Thank you all so much for coming tonight and being so kind as to volunteer your services at the anniversary weekend. I really want this to be the best kind of celebration we can possibly make it. If the programme is lacklustre, we shan't tempt people to come and the whole thing will be a flop. As far as the school is concerned, we have decided we must have the children performing something. I've spoken to Arthur Prior about photographs on the day and he has faithfully promised to be available. I also thought to ask Peter about a service on the Sunday morning. That really is as far as I've got. So if anyone has any other ideas, please tell us now.'

Pat Jones raised her hand to speak.

'Pat.'

'I'm more than willing to volunteer to organize food and the serving of it. Would you want it in the church hall or in the school? Either way, I'm not bothered. Though I do prefer—'

A confused babble of voices greeted this statement and

159

Kate had difficulty in sorting out what everyone was saying.

'I would prefer it to be in the church hall,' she said. 'I'd like to put up a big wall display of school life through the ages. If the food is in there as well then we'll have a massive concentration of visitors in the school hall and all that space going spare in the church hall.'

Someone from the second row piped up. 'Well, I disagree. It's a school, not a church event on the Saturday, so it should all be in the school.'

Pat snapped, 'Like hell it shouldn't. Sorry for speaking out but there'll be tables and chairs and trestle tables with the food on and the school hall's too cramped. In fact, the church hall could be a bit cramped, but at least you wouldn't have everyone squeezed in one place.'

'Exactly,' said Kate. 'I agree. Hands up those who agree food should be in the church hall.' She counted and found the motion carried by a narrow margin in favour of having food in the church hall.

A man from down Shepherds Hill grunted, 'Well, are you going to ask Jimbo to supply the food for free?'

There was a general shaking of heads. Muriel said, 'I don't honestly think we can ask Jimbo to provide the food for nothing. He's always being expected to do that and it's simply not fair.'

'He can afford it. That shop's a goldmine with his catering and the mail order. He's making money hand over fist. He could contribute something, greedy beggar that he is.' The speaker had forgotten Harriet was sitting further along his row.

Harriet was indignant and answered the challenge in her most haughty manner. 'I beg your pardon. Jimbo and I have discussed this very point. The only reason you have a shop in this village is because it's supported by the mail order and the catering. Without that, the Store would have to close. Jimbo and I will not be providing the food for free, but we will sell it at cost if you want it. Further than that we are not willing to go.'

There was a mild round of applause here and Kate gave her thanks to Harriet for her kindness.

'That's OK, Kate, but I don't want to hear any more about Jimbo not being generous. He is, to a fault sometimes.'

'Exactly,' said Muriel. 'Exactly. Thank you, Harriet, my dear. And thank Jimbo for us too.'

'But what about volunteers to help Pat? Are you giving your services?' said someone in the back row, who appeared all set for trouble.

Pat nodded. 'Of course I am. That's what I said. I'll search for some people to help. Leave it to me.'

There still remained a certain amount of chuntering from the back row and Kate decided she'd better find something for the awkward ones to do before matters got taken out of her hands. 'One problem we shall have is parking. Is there anyone here who has experience of organizing car parking so people don't find themselves hemmed in when they want to leave? I've arranged with Craddock that we can have Rector's Meadow for parking and Home Park if need be.'

A hand went up in the back row. 'I'll be responsible for that. I'll find some assistants too.'

Kate made a note. 'Thank you. Now about the—'

'What about bunting and flags?'

'Good idea.'

161

Willie Biggs offered his services. 'We've plenty left from the Jubilee. I'll sort it out but I'll have to have someone to help put it up. I'm not keen on climbing ladders.'

Colin Turner agreed to help Willie and then came up with an idea of his own. 'How about a cricket match? Village versus Old Boys? If we play in the early afternoon it'll be over before the kids' show.'

A babble of approval followed his suggestion, then someone said a cricket match could go on until evening.

Various ideas were tested until Colin came up with time limits and run objectives. 'Like these one-day matches except it'ud be about four hours. Start at noon.'

Kate thought that an excellent idea and said so, and the motion was carried unanimously.

Hetty Hardaker then asked where the children's show would be held, and so it went on. By nine o'clock the whole weekend had been arranged and Kate was feeling particularly pleased that there hadn't been any vicious outbreaks of dissent . . . until the question was broached about who would be sitting on the VIP platform to watch the children.

'Who are the VIPs?'

'All the committee?' someone suggested.

Rather disparagingly someone else said, 'Don't be daft; that'd be too many.'

'Are we inviting the old headteachers?'

Kate agreed. 'Who else if not them?'

She noticed then that Muriel's face flushed, that Harriet looked distinctly uncomfortable and that the faces of several others had suddenly and inexplicably shut down. 'So, yes, they'll be on the platform, which reminds me we shall need men with muscle to get the platform in place on the Friday night.'

'Right!' said Colin Turner. 'There's a few dads who'll be useful for that. I'll make sure they turn up.' The moment passed.

Margaret Booth suggested a few ideas for the display in the school hall and they were about to close the meeting when a spokesman for the annoying clique on the back row stood up to speak. 'We still haven't decided who's sitting on the platform. I suggest all the school staff. After all, they've done most of the work.'

'What about me? I'm doing the flowers in the church and a right task that will be, I can't be left off.' This from Sheila Bissett, who had been quiet for once.

'Come on, Sheila, we'll have a platform stretching from one end to the other if everyone gets on. Have some sense.'

'You'll be on then, will you, as car park organizer? I think not.' She bristled and hunched her shoulders to show her indignation. 'Don't listen to him, Kate, he's nothing but a troublemaker.' She looked round for support but found people were evading her eye.

Hetty Hardaker said she'd be too busy with the children and Margaret Booth agreed. 'We're not bothered, are we, Hetty? So that'll be two less.'

The car parking troublemaker resented Sheila's bossiness, and said so in no uncertain terms. Sheila rose to her feet and declared that some people didn't know their place, and what was more, she'd refuse to do the flowers.

Muriel braved her wrath by saying, 'But Sheila, we always have your flowers and we can't manage without them. You're so good at floristry, in fact excellent would

163

be a better word. Think of how lovely the Sunday service will be with your arrangements. I'm sure space will be found for you.'

Sheila sat down again, her pride restored by Muriel's observations. 'Very well then.'

Kate smiled broadly in relief, having visions of the entire committee resigning en masse. 'Very well then, leave the platform to me. I'll sort something out. Agreed?' She smiled in turn at everyone on the back row, one of her dazzling smiles, which were hard to resist. There was a general air of agreement.

Before Kate closed the meeting she remembered to mention the souvenir programme she was planning. 'I thought we'd charge two pounds for it, something to take home, you know, with photos and history. What do you think?'

Everyone appeared to like the idea, except the newly elected head of car parking. He snorted his disgust. 'Two pounds! That's far too much. Far too much. Seventy-five pence at the most, or even fifty pence. Who can afford two pounds? That's daft.'

Sheila Bissett took her chance to get her own back and declared, 'Two pounds will barely cover the printing expenses. Two pounds it is. Hands up all those who agree.' She looked fiercely round at everyone from her seat in the centre of the front row. 'Well?!'

A volley of hands went up and Sheila's decision was ratified.

Sylvia suggested a list of headteachers right from the beginning would be interesting.

Muriel said, 'We must have photos of them too, if that's possible. Well, the later ones.'

'Lovely. I'll make a note. I'll be in touch with each of you before the day, you can be assured of that. Goodnight. Thank you.'

Gratefully, Kate went home, wishing she'd not brought her car, because a walk home up the drive would have helped to blow away her anxiety. She'd no idea how difficult the villagers could be. Most of it was caused by old feuds, some long-forgotten insult or incident, which still rankled. As she rounded the bend in the drive and saw the old house, she thought of the tales this house could tell if only it could speak.

Chapter 10

As Kate had said, they all knew in Little Derehams what was going on in the cottage that had once belonged to that witch Simone Paradise. They'd watched gardeners from the estate tackling the wilderness that passed for a garden, seen the septic tank chaps sorting out the smell of sewage – and a right week that had been, disgusting it was. They weren't too sure about what was happening inside but someone had seen a new bathroom suite being delivered and it wasn't a cheap, second-hand one either. And another person had seen what she thought was a new cooker and new cupboards for the kitchen going in. But Greenwood Stubbs, the head gardener at Turnham House, coming down to watch over the proceedings, had definitely given the game away. No prizes for guessing who was footing the bill – high and mighty H. Craddock Fitch, no less.

When cans of paint were carried in and the odd-job man from the estate marched through the newly replaced garden gate, wearing white overalls and carrying a ladder, then they knew for certain that a complete facelift was going on. Lucky Mrs Bliss. Lucky, silent Mrs Bliss, who never exchanged a word with her neighbours beyond good morning. What had she done to deserve all this special treatment? Well, it wouldn't do, they could all manage very nicely with a new bathroom suite, to say nothing of the double glazing she'd had installed.

Turnham House Properties had a very busy week fending off demands from the other cottagers. They were sorry Mrs Bliss didn't speak to any of them because they'd have had an opportunity to give her the sharp edge of their tongues. Talk about favouritism. As it was, the property office didn't give a toss about their requests, and instead it was they who received the sharp edge of the land agent's tongue.

The build-up of resentment carried further afield than Little Derehams. Having no public house of their own (the Monk's Hood Arms had been converted into a house thirty years ago), drinkers used the Royal Oak as their hostelry.

Consequently, one night when Vera Wright had gone in there in an attempt to alleviate her dread of the fact that Don was still hovering between life and death in Culworth Hospital, the matter of the renovations at the Bliss cottage was the subject of conversation. Opinions varied. The attitude of the Turnham Malpas residents was, why not? Little Derehams residents came down on the side of injustice.

'We've got some damn great holes in our winda frames. Don't matter how big yer fire, the wind don't harf blow some blasted great draughts round yer ear'ole in the winter. We've told the agent but o' course he's under strict instructions.'

Vera asked, 'Instructions? From who?'

'That bug—'

Vera interrupted swiftly. 'Mind your language in here. You know how strict Dicky is.'

'Mmm. Fitch. Lives in luxury up there with his fancy piece and leaves us to get rheumatics 'cos he's such a skinflint.'

'How long is it then since you sold out to him?'

'Old Fitch bought it from us ten years back.'

Vera leaned forward and tapped the table. 'And you've paid only a moderate rent this last ten years, I'm told. You were glad enough to accept his money when it suited. In Turnham Malpas we didn't sell, well, one person did but she was in dire straits at the time. The rest of us decided to keep our independence. Every one of you daft lot sold out to him. More fool you. If you've any sense you'll fit your own double glazing in with the money he paid you for the cottage.'

'Eh? Yer what?'

'You heard.'

'Why should I? He owns it, not me.'

'I know he does. But if you want a bad draught round the back of your neck, well . . . it's up to you.'

'Of course you're on his side, stands to reason, you're an owner same as 'im.'

Surprised it was common knowledge that she owned Maggie Dobbs's cottage, Vera retorted sharply, 'Whatever. Yer can't have both the bun and the ha'penny in this life.'

Similar arguments were being conducted on the much coveted table next to the settle, on the tables close to the log fire and especially in the wider part where several tables were close enough to allow eavesdropping on other conversations. The bar hummed with the topic and soon everyone had taken sides. In the main, Turnham Malpas residents were in sympathy with Mrs Bliss, and the Little Derehams people were against.

After closing time came, the argument was carried on outside in the road. Eventually people living in the village went home shaking their heads over the stupidity of the Little Derehams people selling their homes to someone like Mr Fitch, and they felt smug in their wisdom. While they had houses worth thousands now that property prices had risen so steeply, those in Little Derehams had nothing. Not a few chuckled to themselves as they snuggled down in bed under their very own roofs.

But the resentment against Mr Fitch festered and bubbled until it burst forth in a protest. A crowd of about thirty villagers from Little Derehams collected quietly outside Turnham House main door early one evening, knowing for sure that Mr Fitch was there – they had friends among the domestic staff at the Big House – and they unfurled their banners, waved their placards and chanted a song they'd made up at a meeting earlier in the week.

The land agent came out first to listen to their demands but he made no progress at all. 'We want Mr Fitch! We want Mr Fitch!' they all chanted.

So the agent returned inside and went to ask Mr Fitch to come out to speak to them. Boiling with temper – he had feared this might happen – Craddock stalked outside, in no mood to be placatory.

Holding up a hand to hush the chants, he began by saying, 'I hear what you ask. If I do the improvements to your houses that you demand, then your rents will have to go up to pay for them. I'm not a charitable institution, I'm running a business, and the rents you pay now will nowhere near cover the costs of double glazing or anything else. So, what shall we do? It's up to you. You could of course always buy back your houses from me, but you'll get a shock when you hear how much they have increased in value since you sold them to me.'

'How much then? Go on, how much?'

'At the very least double what I gave you for them. Could be more.'

A gasp of horror went round the crowd. Jaws dropped, fists were raised, and Kate, who was watching from an upstairs window, became anxious.

'You're bloody well off then!'

'You're doing it for that Bliss woman, why not us?'

Kate couldn't believe her ears. Doing it for that Bliss woman?

'You're a thief. You bought 'em for a song then.'

'I paid the fair market price at the time, which you agreed to.'

'Forced our hands more likely.'

'I didn't make you sell your houses to me. On the contrary, you couldn't wait to get your hands on the money.'

Grumblings rumbled around the crowd. Someone shouted, 'But why's that Mrs Bliss getting everything done for *her*? Tell us that, if you can.'

'What favours has she done you, eh?'

A loud guffaw went up, and there was much elbow-nudging, smirking and knowing winks.

Craddock almost boiled over. He could have taken a whip to them all. It was what they needed; a whipping, handcuffed to a wall, until the blood ran and they'd no thought for anything else but their own pain. All the pleasure he'd taken at owning practically the entire village, improving the footpaths, placing flower tubs at strategic points, improving the lighting with decorative lamps, restoring the tiny medieval prison cell still standing in their high street, and renovating their market cross, turned sour in his mouth. And Kate was listening to this! And the students here for a week's training! So much for not letting his right hand know what his left hand was doing. So much for trying to keep, albeit secretly, in Kate's good books. Damn them all to everlasting hell. A plague on their houses.

Then he said the one thing that played straight into their hands. Because it occurred to him that they might take the initiative to get back at him through Mrs Bliss he shouted, 'Don't anyone here dare take out their anger at me on Mrs Bliss. This,' he made a sweeping gesture with his arm, 'is not her fault. *I* chose to improve her house, at my own expense. She's not to be threatened in any way. You understand?'

A roar went up, a great roar of mocking laughter, which made his blood run cold. He spun on his heel and went inside, slamming and bolting the door behind him. The crowd stood angrily arguing among themselves, not knowing what to do next. But within minutes they retired down the drive to plan their next move.

Craddock stood behind the door, shaking with emotion. For Kate to even think . . . The students were standing at every available window at the front of the house, watching and commenting. A hush fell over them when Kate brushed past and ran down the stairs to meet Craddock, who was now standing, fists clenched, red-faced and quietly swearing in the middle of the hall.

When he saw Kate coming towards him Craddock drew in a deep breath.

'Craddock! Come up to the flat. Please.'

'My office.'

'OK.'

He unlocked the door, went straight to the drinks cupboard and poured himself and Kate a glass of brandy. 'I don't like brandy, Craddock.'

'Drink it. Drink it.'

'But I . . .' She felt his hand shake as he handed it to her and decided not to cross him. It tasted foul to her, but at the same time she welcomed its warmth and hoped it might settle the queasiness that had afflicted her when she'd heard that mocking laughter. Too terrible to describe was the appalling sensation of unease that had almost overcome her when they'd mocked him. It was a kind of concerted, primeval bellow, which boded nothing but ill. Perhaps if she'd gone down and stood beside him that might have diffused the anger. But hindsight was all well and good, she hadn't.

Craddock went to sit in one of his big leather chairs, cradling his glass in his hand. 'My God! I seem to be doing a lot of apologizing lately and it's not in my blood to do so. You listened?' Kate nodded. 'Of course you did.'

'You're repairing her house then?'

'Every stick and stone of it. Look where it's got me. Threatened on my own doorstep.'

'They'll calm down. You'll see.'

'It's been like this before but with our villagers. That lot tonight seem evil to me.'

'They'll have calmed down by tomorrow, you wait and see.'

172

Kate watched the unnatural colour in his face settle to its usual pallor.

'I don't need to say this to you, but there is *nothing* between Mrs Bliss and me. All I wanted to do was to please you.'

'I feel ashamed that you feel the need to reassure me. Of course I know there isn't, it never crossed my mind. But I'm grateful that you are attending to her house. It will make such a difference and I love you for it.'

'I didn't mean you to know until it was finished. You see, when I went to the house and saw . . . Anyway, that's for another time. If there's something you'd rather be doing, I'll sit here a while longer.'

'If it's all right, I'll stay with you.'

There was nothing more to say on the matter without repeating herself so she sat silently, thinking. That he'd done as she asked amused her. Secretly repairing the house without telling her was, in its own way, an acknowledgement that he had heeded her good sense and her compassion. But there was something more behind it, a further reason to do with his past perhaps, the past he didn't feel able to tell her about.

Peter learned on the village grapevine of the incident up at Turnham House and was seriously worried. He'd had to deal with stone-throwing and threats when those two crazy sisters, Gwen and Beryl Baxter, had locked Flick Charter-Plackett in the cupboard under their stairs. Windows broken, threats, an unparalled outbreak of community anger. And here they were again, except this time it was people from Little Derehams. Since, pastorally, they were under his care, he decided to take steps.

'Caroline! If I'm not back for lunch, send out a search party.'

'Why? Where are you going?'

'To Little Derehams.'

'Whoops! You make it sound as though you are going to Outer Mongolia.'

'Feels like it after their protest march. What can they be thinking of?'

'They're jealous, that's why.'

'Jealous of Mrs Bliss? For heaven's sakes, the woman's very existence is in jeopardy.'

'Greedy?'

'Yes, you're right. Greedy. They were only too glad to sell to Craddock when he wanted to buy.'

'Exactly. You'll need the patience of Job and the wisdom of Solomon.'

'Can't believe that old Fitch has set about improving her house. I wonder what made him do it?'

Caroline grinned at him. 'The threat of Social Services knocking at his door? More likely marriage has made him soft in the head.'

Peter looked doleful. 'I can sympathize.'

'Peter!'

'I can. I've been soft in the head ever since I met you.'

'I can't say I've noticed.'

'No. But I do things I wouldn't previously have done.'

'What, for instance?'

'You're the only person who can distract me when I'm taking a service. I catch your eye and my concentration goes into a spin. Anyone else's eye and I have no reaction at all.'

Caroline laughed. 'I don't believe that. Off you go. Good luck.'

He stepped close to her, took her in his arms and kissed her, gripping her so tightly she could scarcely breathe.

'Peter! Please! Not this time in the morning. Sylvia's here.'

'I'd forgotten.' Peter listened and heard the vacuum cleaner running upstairs. 'We're all right for a moment.' He kissed her again, a kiss that set her pulse racing.

When he released her, Caroline said. 'Ooh, Rector! You've made me quite breathless.'

They both laughed.

'I'll be back tonight then.' Peter took hold of her hands and pulled her to him again. He hugged her. 'And that's a promise.'

'Rector! You are a one!'

He left through the back door to go to the garage at the end of Pipe and Nook Lane. As he shut the garden gate behind him he waved to his wife and she waved back, wondering if it wasn't only Peter who'd gone soft in the head; she loved him so much and was capable of forgiving him anything at all to have him beside her every day.

Peter drove to Little Derehams, thinking about what he was going to say to his parishioners. He'd begin by talking to Louise Johns, as she and Gilbert owned the only house in the village not bought by Mr Fitch. Perhaps she'd have a clear idea of exactly what was behind the protest last night.

Louise appeared to be knee-deep in babies. What a contrast to the Louise he'd known when she was Village Show secretary and had fallen, as she thought, in love with him.

175

'Good morning, Louise. Called at the wrong moment, haven't I?'

'Come in. It's always the wrong moment in our home. We really need a house twice the size. Come in, mind where you step.'

She did right to warn him of the dangers underfoot. There were toys strewn all over the living-room floor, to say nothing of pieces of archaelogical specimens belonging to Gilbert's work. Their newest baby lay in a Moses basket on a low table, two toddlers were trotting about holding toys the other wanted, and someone who looked almost ready for the village playgroup was playing a xylophone quite tunefully.

Above the noise, Peter said, nodding towards the musician, 'He sounds quite musical. Takes after his father?'

Louise, slimmer and more outgoing than before her marriage, nodded. 'You're right. Gilbert is delighted. To what do I owe this visit? Is it about the one hundred and fifty year celebrations at the school? Gilbert's terribly keen to get stuck in.'

'No. I don't know anything about any celebrations.'

'Big party, I understand, and a special church service, with your permission, of course, and there is a whisper that the mayor from Culworth will be invited.'

'No one's said anything to me at all. I'll have to see Kate about it. No, what I came to see you about was the protest at Turnham House the other night. I wondered if you had some inside information and could enlighten me, seeing as you and Gilbert are the only ones not to be involved.'

Louise separated the two toddlers arguing over the toys by diverting their attention to a Noah's ark lying abandoned on the table. 'All I know is that they are angry because Fitch is repairing the Blisses' cottage. It desperately needed it, it wasn't fit to live in quite frankly, and of course everyone else is asking why not theirs. But their cottages are not in the same desperate state. It is, or rather was, appalling, but now they all fancy double glazing and new bathrooms and quite a few would like a new kitchen too.'

'So, basically, it's envy and greed.'

'Put bluntly, yes it is.'

'It got quite nasty, I understand.'

'I don't know. I've been so busy and Gilbert took his namesake to nursery this morning so I didn't get a chance to chat.'

Peter said, 'I'll leave you to it, Louise. Thanks for the help. I'm going to see as many as I can this morning. Hopefully I might be able to cool matters a little.'

'It'll be an uphill struggle, I'm afraid. They're very determined.'

It was indeed an uphill struggle.

Reason had flown out of the window so far as the other villagers were concerned, no matter how Peter argued that of course they couldn't expect to have work done on improving their houses without the rent going up and that Mr Fitch had offered to sell them back their houses.

'But look how the market's changed. These houses are worth at least twice what he paid us, and none of us has that kind of money. It's not fair. No, not fair at all. But we'll get our own back. We have plans.' Their plans involved a lot of tapping of the sides of noses with their mouths clamped tightly shut.

Peter made no headway at all, and he left Little Derehams sick to the heart at their intransigence. His next call was to the school. He often popped in and always tried to make it at a time when Kate was free from teaching, but this morning he'd misjudged it entirely. She was deeply involved so he went to sit in her small office to wait for her.

Eventually the bell rang for break and she came bursting in, apologizing. 'So sorry to have kept you waiting. Just so busy. What can I do for you?'

'I came to hear your version of what happened the other night.'

'The protest, you mean? It was frightening, really alarming. They meant business. They were very angry and of course it suited them to go away with completely the wrong idea about Craddock and Mrs Bliss.'

Peter looked surprised.

'They assume that there is something going on between them and that's why he's improving the house. In fact, he's doing it up because I asked him to, after what you and Caroline had said. We were both shocked.'

'I'm not surprised you were. I'd no idea . . . I've been to see those who are at home this morning and they're all saying just wait and see what happens next. Louise says it's sheer greed motivating them.'

'It is. Since he bought all their houses he's done lots of things to improve their village but of course none of that counts, does it? It's very soul-destroying.'

Peter asked about the celebrations.

'Have I not told you? I'm so sorry, I seem to have had such a lot on my mind these last few weeks. Yes, we're planning big celebrations. I'm working on a souvenir brochure, and we're trying to contact all the people who've been pupils here in the past. The mayor has promised to come, and Muriel suggested a service in the church. She thought of loudspeakers relaying it to the church hall because there'll be so many people there. Yes, it's going to be very exciting.'

'Sounds marvellous. Let me in on your plans, what weekend and such, and certainly it would be great to have a service on the Sunday. In general, I expect the bulk of the people will come on the Saturday.'

'I would think so. And do you know, Muriel has the address of the old man who was headmaster before the headmaster before Michael.' She clicked her fingers trying to remember his surname. 'Michael Palmer, yes, that's right. The old man's name is Godfrey Browning, he's ninety-five and has all his onions at home. His wife's still alive and she's coming too, and his grandson is bringing them. Isn't that lovely? We're going to invite Michael Palmer and his wife too, of course, though he won't see that much change, will he, having left only recently? But old Mr Browning certainly will. I'm very excited about it.'

Happily reeling off all her plans for the celebrations, Kate didn't notice that Peter was not responding in the slightest. If anything, he was distinctly withdrawn.

Margaret Booth came in with coffee for them both but he refused it. 'Got to be in Penny Fawcett in twenty minutes for a meeting, so mustn't stop. Thanks all the same.'

Kate said, 'When I've finalized everything, you'll be the first to know. It'll be the last weekend of the summer term.'

Peter opened the door, intent on leaving quickly, then turned back to say, 'Take care, Kate. Don't let Craddock take the protest lightly.'

'No, I won't.'

Peter crossed the school yard, fighting to control his inner turmoil and thinking how blithely Kate had mentioned Michael Palmer and his wife coming back to the village. He couldn't expect Kate to know that so far as he and Caroline were concerned, the last thing they wanted was Suzy Meadows, or rather Palmer, as she was now, coming back to the village and meeting the twins.

He stood beside his car, lost in thought. Dear God, he prayed, let them be booked to go on holiday. Don't let them come. I can't face it. Surely she won't want to come, will she?

He drove to Penny Fawcett and the meeting about the future of their community hall with a heavy heart. It passed by in a whirl, and when he left to go home for lunch, he was glad someone had taken the minutes, because he remembered very little of what had been said.

His beloved Caroline being put through the mill yet again all because he, her husband, hadn't been able to resist a wild moment of temptation, was more than she should be asked to bear. But he'd have to tell her. It was no good waiting till the day. But he wouldn't mention it straight away. He'd pray about it and get it sorted in his own mind first.

But then Peter realized he wouldn't be the first person Kate had told, not by a long chalk. Perhaps the whole village had already tumbled to the situation that would arise that weekend: his two children meeting their real mother for the first time. If he had his life to live all over again, would he have done what he did had he known the consequences?

Chapter 11

The wine glass, which was washed and polished to within an inch of its life, was standing upside down in the middle of Maggie's gleaming old oak table, waiting for the arrival of her guests. There was no fire tonight, only the light from the small reading lamp with the red cloth placed over it to make the room more . . . intriguing. She was huddled in the chair beside the fireplace, sipping vodka, which she'd been told wouldn't leave the smell of drink on her breath. Did she need that vodka? Yes, indeed she did.

Nothing had felt right since that night when she'd had that message from her Dave. Bless his little cotton socks. When Kate had said there was a letter from the office for her, she was sure it was to say she was being sacked, and that it was yet another punishment for doing the Ouija board. But, it was to tell her about a pay rise, and to an extent, her confidence in herself and her ability to be in charge of her own life returned. That was until she recollected Dave's words again about getting the washing machine before it was too late. What had that meant?

A discreet tap at the door made her hide her vodka glass in the cupboard beside the fireplace. With her face wreathed in smiles, she opened the door and let the Senior sisters in. They gave her their money, which they could ill afford, and chose their favourite seats at the table.

'No fire tonight?'

'You've not lit the fire.'

'No, thought it was warm enough. Five of you in here, and the room's only small.'

'There'll be six coming.'

'Six tonight.'

'Who's that then? No one's said anything to me.'

'Her ladyship.'

'Lady Muck.'

Maggie shivered in horror at the prospect of Muriel being present. 'Who?'

'You know, Lady Sheila.'

'Lady Bissett.'

Maggie sweated with relief. 'Oh! Sheila Bissett! What's she coming for?'

'No idea.'

'No idea.'

There was a loud rat-a-tat at the door.

Maggie went to answer it. It was Sheila.

'I'm not late, am I? The Misses Senior said nine o'clock, but Ronald would keep talking. Oh, there you are.' She nodded a greeting to the two sisters.

'No, you're not late. You know it's five pounds?'

'Yes. Here you are.' She handed over a five-pound note, which was so dirty it looked as though it had spent most of its life down a mine. 'Sorry it's a bit of a mess, I found it in an old purse. Where shall I sit?'

She sat down and began to chatter. Maggie had to interrupt. 'Please, no talking, it upsets the spirits.'

Sheila's hand flew to her mouth. 'Oh! Sorry.'

When everyone had arrived, Maggie began. It felt more difficult to get the atmosphere conducive to calling the spirits when there was no fire to make dancing patterns on the walls, but eventually the right feeling was established and Maggie solemnly put a forefinger on the base of the wine glass and nodded to them to join her. Seven was a mite too many for a small wine glass but they all managed to find space for their fingers.

Now what?

The glass rocked and flirted about a little, but when Maggie asked if there was anyone out there with a message it began to move with purpose: b-e-w-a-r-e-h-e-w-h-o- m-a-k-e-s-t-h-i-n-g-s-b-e-t-t-e-r-m-a-k-e-s-t-h-i-n g-s- w-o-r-s-e-.

Venetia whispered, 'What does that mean? Who makes things better and then worse?'

'I don't know,' Maggie replied.

Venetia clapped her hands as the meaning dawned on her. 'I do. That's Mr Fitch. He's made the Blisses' cottage better and it's making things worse. Think of the protest the other night. That's it, I'm sure.'

'S-hh.' Maggie replaced her finger on the glass and so did the rest of them. E-v-i-l-e-v-i-l-e-v-i-l- . . .

Sheila giggled. 'Its needle's got stuck!'

'S-hh,' Maggie repeated.

The glass moved again, then it began spelling out jumble, which no one could piece together to make sense. Next it said b-i-g-h-o u-s-e-t-r-o-u-b-l-e-h-c-f-h-c-f t- r-o-u-b-l-e . . .

Venetia became very agitated. 'Oh, my good Lord. H.C.F. That's Mr Fitch.'

They tried again. The glass was almost bucking as it

sped along spelling out d-e-a-t-h-d-e-a-t-h-d-e-a-t-h-t-o-h-c-f.

Maggie picked up the glass, and flung it into the empty fireplace, where it should have smashed into a thousand pieces, but didn't. It simply bumped against the logs she'd put there so the fireplace didn't look so empty, and rolled to the edge of the grate, balancing precariously, as though making up its mind whether or not to smash itself to death on the tiled hearth. All eyes were on the glass, waiting for it to crash.

Maggie was trembling. Venetia was horrified. The others tried to come to terms with what the wine glass had spelt out for them.

'*Is* HCF Mr Fitch?' asked Sheila in a frightened voice, her usual ability for vacuous social chit-chat entirely deserting her.

Venetia nodded her head. 'Yes, he's Henry Craddock Fitch.'

'You seem to know a lot about him,' commented Greta Jones.

'I've worked long enough for him.'

'But in what capacity?' Greta asked slyly.

Venetia blushed. 'In charge of leisure activities for the students.'

Sheila Bissett laughed. 'Oh! Yes.'

None of them noticed that Maggie was almost hysterical.

'Shall we rescue the glass and start again? See what it says next?' asked Linda, always eager for a bit of drama.

Maggie was rigid with fear and didn't offer to pick up the glass, so Sheila, being the nearest, got up to get it. As her fingers touched it, the bulb in the table lamp flashed and went out. She screamed, the others followed suit and pandemonium reigned.

None of them gave a thought to Maggie.

Pitch black though it was, they managed to grab their belongings and flee helter-skelter out of the house and down Church Lane, as though the very devil himself was after them.

Maggie began to sob. Deep, searing sobs, which tore at her lungs, and made her shriek as she drew in her breath.

It must have been fully five minutes before Maggie remembered her glass of vodka. She switched on the main light, opened the cupboard and knocked back the remains of her drink in one go. Filled the glass again and drank it down neat. Things swam a little as it hit her stomach, but she poured another one and downed that too. She went to sit in her easy chair by the fireplace, frightened to death.

Just what had happened? She could swear on the Bible that she hadn't pushed the glass. It had moved of its own volition and spelt out d-e-a-t-h. She allowed her eyes to slide around to look at the glass, now lying so innocently on the edge of the grate. Grandmother or no grand-mother, that glass had to go. But where? She couldn't face looking at it in her bin, it would be a week before the bin men came again. Should she bury it in the garden? No, not on her own property. Definitely not. Then she remembered the litter bin on the spare land behind Linda Crimble's house. Of course, she'd put it in there and be rid of it. Now? In the dark? She couldn't sleep with it in the house, but in her present state she didn't fancy crossing the little footbridge to reach the bin. It was dark outside, the wind was getting up and the trees on the spare land would be rustling and stirring, and it was blasted dark

185

among the trees with no lamps. No, the dark *and* rustlings wouldn't do.

Then she thought of the big wheelie bins at the school. Of course. One of them was already half-full. That was it. She'd go now, right now and put it in there. Her legs felt like jelly at the thought of going out in the dark, but she put her rubber gloves on – she couldn't bear to touch the damn thing with her own skin – found a newspaper, picked up the glass by her fingertips and hurriedly wrapped it in the paper, with lots of Sellotape so it couldn't escape.

Without pausing to lock her door, she dashed down Church Lane, round into Jacks Lane, crossed the school yard, heaved up the lid of the half-full wheelie bin, and flung it in. By the sound of it, it still hadn't broken.

'Maggie?'

Sweat broke out all over Maggie's body.

A light shone on the wheelie bin.

Her legs went to jelly again.

'Maggie! What are you doing?'

What a relief. She knew that voice. Her mouth was so dry her tongue was sticking to the roof of it.

'Are you all right?'

'Kate!'

'Yes?'

She wet her lips again. 'Tell him. Warn him.'

'Who?'

'They've said he's going to die.' Maggie grabbed Kate's arm to steady herself, and in the light of Kate's torch she was surprised to see she was still wearing her pink rubber gloves.

'Maggie! You've not been holding a seance again, have you? Honestly!'

Maggie nodded.

'In the school? Surely not? Not in my school.'

Maggie shook her head. Still clutching Kate's arm, she said, 'I mean it, he isn't safe.'

'Who isn't safe?'

'Your hubby. Mr Fitch. The spirits said so, tonight. They spoke of death.' An unearthly groan came involuntarily from her lips.

Kate began to laugh. 'Honestly, Maggie, I've never heard such nonsense. It's absolutely ridiculous. You can't possibly think it's true.' But in the light of her torch she saw how frightened Maggie looked, felt the intense grip of Maggie's hand and knew she meant it.

'Look here, I'll walk you home.'

'Thank you.' Maggie tottered by the side of her, now overcome not only by fear, but by the vodka she'd drunk so rapidly.

The door was wide open, just as she'd left it. Kate suggested she'd wait until Maggie was safely in bed and then she'd leave.

'No, no, I'll be all right.'

'I insist. I shall worry if I don't know you're safely in bed. I'll sit here and wait. Take as long as you like.'

She sat in Maggie's favourite chair beside the fireplace and looked around, expecting to see something strange after the seance. But there was nothing. The room looked perfectly normal. Couldn't have been more normal, in fact, except for the odd collection of chairs around the dining table, and the letters of the alphabet scattered across the table. Seven chairs. Maggie had had a busy night. Kate heard footsteps in the room above her head and the thump as Maggie flung herself into bed.

From the foot of the stairs she called out, 'OK, Maggie? I'll go now.'

She heard a muffled, 'Right. Thanks,' from the bedroom.

'We'll talk in the morning at school. God bless. I'll lock the door. Sleep tight and don't worry. It's all nonsense and you know it is.'

Maggie put her head under the blankets and longed for Dave to be there to give her a cuddle, and soothe her fears. But he wasn't and he wouldn't be, ever. Great tears rolled down her cheeks, crept over her jawline, trickled down her neck and settled on the pillow. There was one thing for certain: she wasn't holding another seance meeting as long as she lived. Like Angie had said the other night, it was dangerous.

Kate had gone home after leaving Maggie's to find Craddock pacing the floor.

'Where have you been? I was just about to come to find you.'

Kate flung down her bag and keys, and flopped down in a chair. 'I was at the school catching up, that's all.'

'It's half past ten. Surely you don't need to work until then?'

'I've been doing the brochure for the celebrations. It's beginning to look quite good. I'm rather pleased with it.'

'I've a perfectly good computer in my office. You could work there and then I would know you're safe.'

'Craddock! You should have rung me if you were worried.'

'I did and there was no reply. I didn't want to appear a fussy husband, even though I am. Give you space, you know.'

'Thank you. I do need my space. What possible harm could come to me, though, sitting in good old Turnham Malpas School on a spring evening? None at all. I fancy tea. Want some?'

'Yes, we'll both make it.'

He followed her into the kitchen and while she put the kettle on, he got out the tray and put cups on it.

'Do you know, darling, I loved that school house when I lived there. Still do. There's something very historical about it.'

'One hundred and fifty-some years later I expect it is.' He smiled at her. 'But Turnham House is even older.'

'I know. Many births, marriages and deaths will have happened here, but there's something special about the school house. When I finished work tonight I went in there and stood in the bedroom looking out, thinking.'

'What?'

'Oh! I don't know, just thinking. I felt . . . this sounds stupid, but just for once I thought it would be good to sleep there. I nearly rang you and told you.'

'Then the tongues would start wagging.'

'It would be a kind of closure on my life there. To sleep there, married.'

Craddock, inclined to indulge her in his relief that she'd come to no harm, said, 'Well, why don't you? There's nothing to stop you.'

Kate almost told him about Maggie, but changed her mind. As she poured the tea she said, 'Indulge me even

189

further. How long is it since you slept in a tiny place like the school house?'

'Longer than I care to remember.'

'Then let's both do it. For fun. Just this once. Please? I shan't ask again. I just want to do it. You and me. In that tiny house like ordinary people.'

It was even longer since he'd done anything quite as downright giddy as this, but it felt right to indulge her, to have a silly experience with this woman he loved. 'But what about a bed?'

'There's one there with clean sheets. I put them on while I was mooning about tonight. It's a double, big enough. We could even use my car to be less conspicuous. What do you say? Please?'

'Drink your tea and just this once we will.'

'I love you so very much.' Kate picked up her cup, but before she drank from it she kissed him. 'I know I'm being sentimental and I probably won't ever want to do it again. It'll be like camping out, won't it?'

'And just as uncomfortable.' He smiled to show he didn't mean it.

They put their cups and saucers in the dishwasher, Craddock turned out the lights and hand in hand they set off.

At the school house they stood together, by the bedroom window where Kate had looked out earlier that evening.

'Think, Craddock, of all those children who've been through this school, spread out now all over the world, busy living their lives. Lives that people sleeping in this room had the opportunity to influence. Some will never have come home again. They'll have been buried in shell

190

holes, sunk to the bottom of the sea, died in far-off lands. Others came home to Turnham Malpas to die. But it's right that they should come home, isn't it? Where they belong.'

'Bit morbid, my dearest. But I should like to die here where at last I'm beginning to feel I belong, with a service in the church and laid to rest under one of those big, leafy beech trees.'

Kate shivered. She placed a finger on his lips and forbade him to mention it again. It sounded too much like an echo of what Maggie had said to her earlier.

She put her arms about him. 'I'm so glad we fell in love. We're just right for each other, aren't we, Craddock? Just right. I have come home.'

He held her tightly to him. 'Time for bed.'

The next morning, by half past six, they were back home in the flat after their night camping. They showered, dressed and were ready for breakfast at seven-thirty as though they'd never been away.

As Craddock left for London, en route for a couple of nights in Sweden, Kate said thank you again for indulging her whim.

'I could quite get to enjoy it. It was good. Bye, my dearest, take care.'

'And you.'

The chauffeur was holding open the car door for him, so they parted formally. She waved as they swept past her and wished she was going with him. Niggling at the back of her mind was Maggie's warning. Then she realized how little credence Craddock would give Maggie's tales of death and had to laugh.

★

Maggie went shopping after she'd opened up the school, with the intention of scurrying home and not emerging again until it was time for putting out the tables for school dinners. She had planned to use the time to thoroughly clean her own living room, to rid it of any nasty aftertaste of last night's events. She would scrub every corner, every shelf, as clean as she could make it, to rid it once and for all of anything to do with spirits, good or bad, that might still be lurking. She'd rearrange the furniture too, so as to disturb the remaining spirits. It was the only way she could think of to make the house feel right again.

During the night she'd consulted Dave and told him, wherever he was, that she was doing no more of this seance business. 'You see, Dave,' she'd said, 'it's getting dangerous. Too real for words. I began to think I really was a medium. Which I'm not, you know that. I'm going to go to church to make a clean start. Wipe the slate clean, as you might say. I shall miss the money but there you are. Goodnight, love, God bless.'

So when the first person she met when she was in the Store choosing some packet soup, just right for a woman alone, was Mrs Jones, she was at a loss to know what to say.

'Hello, Maggie. All right? By heck! We had a bad scare last night, didn't we? It was ages before I got to sleep. Tell yer something I bet you don't know, my Vince came home late last night from the Legion and he says, and I've no reason to disbelieve him, that the light was on in the bedroom in the house and there was someone in there.'

This piece of news brought Maggie to life. 'Did he? Was he sure?'

'Absolutely. The curtains weren't drawn and the light

192

was on. He could see a man and a woman standing at the window.'

As Maggie's mind tussled with the dilemma of not letting on she'd seen Kate that night at the school, she remembered the rose on Kate's desk and the whole situation became clear as crystal. She was having an affair, she must be. Married only weeks and having an affair! She'd come out of the *school house* with her torch, and not from the direction of the school building. My God! So, who was in the school house with her?

'Maggie?'

'I've not gone deaf.' Maggie flattened herself against the tinned soups, as someone struggled to get by. 'This is strictly between you and me, right? She had a rose put on her desk the other week. A single red rose with a card. First thing. It was there when I opened up.'

Mrs Jones's brown eyes widened.

'Now it wouldn't be old Fitch, would it?'

'From what we know of him, no.'

'Heart of stone.'

Mrs Jones nodded. 'Can't imagine him as a romantic husband. So who was it in the school house with her?'

'It stands to sense it wouldn't be old Fitch.'

'Exactly.'

Mrs Jones heard Jimbo cough significantly and had to leave this interesting piece of speculation. 'Coming, Mr Charter-Plackett, coming. It's not quite nine. You didn't read the card then?'

'Of course not. What do you take me for?' Maggie grinned. 'In any case, it was stuck down so I couldn't even if I'd wanted to.'

Mrs Jones nudged her and laughed and they parted

friends, but Maggie knew she should have said she wasn't having another seance, thank you very much and sorry like. But she hadn't, so she still had that hurdle to jump.

The rumour circulated the village in no time at all and reached Kate by the end of the school day.

A mother who freely admitted that each of her three children had different fathers, and who openly declared she was always on the lookout for a new stud to warm her bed, told Kate what she'd heard, while searching for her son's coat in the coat room. 'You're a dark horse! Mind, I'm not surprised, it can't be any fun married to someone as ancient as Craddock Fitch! God help us! Still, you do right, get it where you can I say. Eureka!' She triumphantly held up the missing coat and raced out to catch up with her boy, leaving Kate in a devastated state of shock.

How she managed to drive home after school she had no idea. Common sense told her it was quite simply malicious gossip, which in another day or two would be supplanted by some other piece of juicy speculation, but it hurt and frightened her just the same. What was it based on? A rose on her desk? Bedroom lights noticed when they'd slept together in the school house? Who knew about both those incidents? Maggie Dobbs. So now one couldn't even sleep where one wanted with one's own husband without tongues wagging. Things had come to a pretty pass.

With Craddock in Sweden, she ate her evening meal alone, and half an hour afterwards fetched it all up, kneeling sweating and distressed beside the lavatory in her bathroom. Finally, her stomach raw with retching and the foul taste of bile in her mouth, Kate crumpled down against the bathroom wall, hammered her clenched fists on the floor and wept.

Chapter 12

If Craddock Fitch thought that two nights away in Sweden would allow the situation with Mrs Bliss and the improvements to her home to blow away with the wind he was quite mistaken. In his absence every single householder in Little Derehams wrote to him asking for work to be done on their own houses, mentioning minute details such as 'loose brick on path to bin in back garden' or large improvements such as 'new bathroom', installation of 'gas pipes' and 'connection to main sewage system'. His land agent dreaded his return but no more than Kate, who knew she had to tell him about the gossip and hated the thought of upsetting him.

But to her surprise, he roared with laughter. 'What will they come up with next?'

'It was the rose on my desk and the lights in the school house bedroom that night. They can't believe that you'd be so romantic, thus it couldn't possibly be you.'

'Heart of stone and all that?'

Kate nodded. 'Exactly. But then they don't know you like I do.'

'No, they don't. It's so good to be back. Lovely to think about coming home to you.'

'You've no idea how glad I am to see you back.'

He picked up on the odd tone in her voice. 'What do you mean? Is there something you haven't told me?'

Kate hesitated and then admitted her momentary fears for his safety. 'It's just Maggie's seances. I know it's all ridiculous, but what with her saying that and then finding out about the rumours, I was at a very low ebb. It all kind of mushroomed.'

'Kate, it is a pathetic attempt to gain some notoriety. It's all rubbish and anyone who believes it is a fool.'

'I know that, but she's been right once or twice apparently, and people believe it now.'

'Well, we've no need to, so don't worry yourself about it any more.'

Kate sighed. 'I won't then, if you say so.'

'I do. My main problem is all these idiots in Little Derehams wanting huge improvements to their houses.'

'Let's face it, Craddock. They know they've made the most tremendous mistake selling their houses to you and paying a nominal rent during their lifetimes. But looked at another way, any improvement is bound to improve their value to you.'

Craddock blew a smoke ring into the air and with eyes half closed he muttered, 'You've got a point there. I could make a token gesture to shut them up, couldn't I?'

'They'll never be off your back if you don't.'

'Wise. That's what you are, wise. I might well do just that.' He began to think of improvements he could make without massive financial outlay.

Kate watched the way he smoked his cigar. There was such style about the way he did it. 'What made you start smoking cigars?'

'My father smoked them.'

'Do you know that's the first time you've ever mentioned your father.'

'Is it?'

'Yes. Are you like him?'

'In looks, you mean?'

'No, well, in anything.'

'Not a bit.'

'You *are* allowed to talk about him to me.'

He looked angry and got to his feet. 'I'm for bed.'

'I'll be up in a while. Thank you for laughing.'

'What about?'

'Those rumours. You know I haven't done anything like that, don't you? If I did, which I wouldn't, I'd tell you.'

'You'd tell me?'

'Of course. You'd need to know.'

'That's frank to say the least.'

Kate shrugged. 'That's how I am.'

'I see. Thank you for letting me know, anyway.' He'd said on his wedding night that she was full of surprises and apparently he was right.

The next morning Craddock was in Little Derehams the very first thing. He went armed with a hammer and was to be seen apparently testing walls and tapping concrete paths, knowing full well he'd be enticing an irate tenant out before too long. Sure enough, out came the tenant who'd complained of dampness in the side wall of his house.

'What are you doing banging on my wall at this time in the morning?'

'Just testing for the damp you say you have.' Mr Fitch

straightened his back and made a note on a piece of paper. 'Needs fresh mortar.'

'And what about that loose brick in the path to the bin, eh? Going to wait till I break my ankle on it?'

'Certainly not. While the chap's here he can take a bit of mortar round and fix it.' He ostentatiously made another note on his paper. 'Right. Gas you were thinking of? That right?'

Taken aback, the tenant could only nod.

Another note was added to his list. 'Gas. I'll look into that.' He smiled and took his leave.

A similar procedure was acted out at each house until he came to Mrs Bliss's. She was gardening out at the front and he leaned on her new gate. 'Good morning, Mrs Bliss!'

'Good morning.' She walked slowly towards him, giving him time to notice the improvement in her.

'The garden's beginning to shape up.'

Her thin, angular face almost broke into a smile. 'Yes. I enjoy gardening.'

'Can I see the work that's been done? I like to know my orders have been carried out.'

'Of course.' Mrs Bliss opened the gate for him and he followed her into the house. He admired the new kitchen, took notice of the redecoration, sniffed the air and found it clean and sweet, so the septic tank must have been attended to satisfactorily, went upstairs to check the damp patches in the bedrooms, inspected the new bathroom and came downstairs beaming. 'Are you pleased with what's been done?'

'Of course. Who wouldn't be? Thank you.'

He also wanted to talk about the paucity of furniture in the place, and searched for the right words. 'I'm pleased. I now feel as if I've done my bit for this cottage. Now, this is very personal, Mrs Bliss and you mustn't take offence, but it appears to me that a few more sticks of furniture wouldn't go amiss.'

Mrs Bliss spread her hands. 'I'm more than grateful for what you've done, but no money means no furniture.'

'I see. He isn't giving you maintenance, then? Wherever he is.'

'He can't. He's . . . dead.'

Mr Fitch put out a hand to touch hers as it lay on the table. 'I'm so sorry, I'd no idea. But if you're in such deep financial water, are you not qualified to take a job of some kind?'

Mrs Bliss stared at him blankly.

'There must be something in the village you could do, surely?'

'Before I married I was in IT support. Degree, that kind of thing. But now I've no clothes to wear, even to go for an interview. It takes me all my time to feed the children and they're always growing, so they always come first where clothes are concerned.'

Mr Fitch tapped on the table with his fingers, beating a kind of tattoo while he thought. 'You know, it costs me a small fortune to get someone up from London to see to our computers at Turnham House. Fees for this, expenses for that. You would be doing me a good turn if you did it for me. It wouldn't be full-time, only a couple of days here and there, but if we could call on you at a moment's notice, that would be worth a packet to me. What do you think? It might be a start.'

Tears trickled, then ran down her cheeks. She pulled out a tissue from her skirt pocket and dabbed at her eyes.

Shaking her head she muttered, 'I don't think so. My confidence has completely gone. I've taken on board everything life's thrown at me, kept going for the sake of the children, dragging myself up by my shoelaces day after day, month after month, stealing to feed them. How low can one sink? You're kind, but no thanks.'

'What did your husband do?'

'He was an explorer.'

Mr Fitch delved into his memory. 'He wasn't! What was his name . . . not . . . Oliver Broakes-Bliss? *The* Oliver Broakes-Bliss?'

When Mrs Bliss nodded, he replied, 'I so admired him. That trek across the North Pole went so wrong but he did do it, against all the odds. Truly magnificent! Such courage. You must have been so proud of him.'

A gleam of satisfaction came into Mrs Bliss's eyes, but they soon clouded over. She blew her nose, tucked her tissue away and said, 'I was, but at what cost?'

'Surely he got sponsorship?'

'He did for that expedition, but his next one . . . at the South Pole . . . when he froze to death . . .'

'Of course, so sad.'

'Catastrophic. For us all.'

'But I seem to recall that a clothing firm financed him?'

'They made a lot of ballyhoo about it, but it no way covered anything like the costs and unknown to me, he took out a second mortgage. When he died, we lost the house. So not only had we no home but we had massive debts.' Mrs Bliss tried to steady herself by taking in an enormous breath, but it didn't work and she broke down in tears again.

'But he was such a brave man, so dedicated, so

200

imaginative in what he tried to do. I can't believe his widow was left destitute. The media were round him like flies. He appeared very successful. And his book! Surely that brought in some money?'

'It didn't sell very well, and he'd spent the advance before he left on that last expedition.' Cynically she added, 'Even his death didn't boost the sales.'

'Look, you must take this job I'm offering. Think about it and ring me. OK? I mean it.'

'I'm sorry for telling you my life story. I'd made up my mind when we moved here that I was leaving Oliver behind and here I am . . .' She wiped her face again and got to her feet. 'I'll see you out.'

Mr Fitch tapped her arm. 'Think seriously about that job. I need someone like you.'

'I don't know who you are. Where do I ring?'

He handed her his business card. 'Ring Turnham House, I'll get the message even if I'm not there.'

Mr Fitch left her cottage glad at heart. At least he was making a difference in a place where his own finances were not at the core of his intention. Though it would be good if she'd do the IT work.

He sat in the car outside her house studying the list of repairs he'd made for the other cottages. He stood to make, at the very least, double or even triple the money he'd paid to buy them, and he was getting modest rent for them all in addition, so anything spent on maintenance would be money well used. For once, his land agent might actually have a smile on his face. Fancy Oliver Broakes-Bliss! How he'd admired him. Though he did seem to have been a fool with money, and that was never a good idea.

201

He was about to set off back to Turnham Malpas when Peter drew up in his car and got out.

'Good morning, Craddock. How's things?'

On a weekday, Peter in full cassock with that whacking great silver cross tucked into his broad leather belt always unnerved Mr Fitch. He felt that gear was best kept for Sundays. Feeling at a disadvantage, he got out of his car. But that didn't do much good either for he was almost a head shorter than Peter and still had to look up at him.

'Things are fine, thank you. Just been visiting my tenants. They're a grand lot.'

Hearing such sentiments from Mr Fitch astounded Peter. 'They are?'

'Yes. They are. Seen Mrs Bliss's improvements?'

'Not yet.'

'You'll be surprised. She's beginning to look better herself, too. Which is all to the good. Sad life she's had. Needs helping along the way. Nice to see you, Peter.' He made to get back into his car, then remembered some-thing else. 'Kate's working away at the anniversary celebrations for the school, you'll be glad to hear. She's getting a lot of support from old pupils and previous headteachers. Two previous heads and their wives are coming. Remember Michael Palmer, nice chap, but lacked guts? He's coming with his wife and daughters. It's going to be a good weekend.'

'Indeed, I expect it is. Kate's good at that kind of thing.'

It was as he put his car into third gear and was charging down the High Street that the terrible recollection struck Craddock. My God! Mrs Palmer, the wife of the headmaster, was that Suzy Meadows. He wondered if Kate knew the story.

Peter made up his mind on the spot that he wouldn't go to sleep that night until he'd told Caroline about Suzy. Obviously the entire village must know but they'd had the discretion not to mention it to Caroline, knowing the hurt it would cause. Well, he couldn't shirk his responsibilities any longer. Tell her he must.

He knocked on Mrs Bliss's door, opened it and called out, 'It's Peter, from the Rectory.'

It was time for bed before Peter had plucked up the courage to tell Caroline. 'Darling, you know this anniversary for the school?'

'People talk about nothing else, apart from Kate's romance with an unknown man and Mr Fitch visiting Mrs Bliss far too often.'

Peter frowned. 'No one's mentioned that to me.'

'That's what they're saying. But it's not true.'

'I'm glad. There is something that *is* true though.'

'Oh? What's that?'

'Kate has invited previous headmasters to the Saturday celebrations.'

For a long moment there was no reaction from Caroline and she continued flicking through the church magazine as if searching for the article he knew she'd contributed. But it didn't fool Peter. She looked up at him. 'She hasn't accepted?'

'I haven't asked, but it sounds like it.'

Caroline flung the magazine across the sitting-room floor. It shot under the television and they both sat watching it, as though waiting for it to make the next move. Neither of them had mentioned her name but they both knew to whom she referred.

Teeth clenched, Caroline ground out, 'I can't believe it of her.'

'She might not come.'

'She will. She wants to see them.'

'I don't think she'll be that thoughtless.'

Caroline looked him straight in the eye. 'You know that for certain, do you?'

'No, of course not.'

'Having sex with her doesn't mean you know her mind. Her *mind*, at the time, was the last thing you thought of.'

'Caroline!'

'You don't like the truth about this matter, do you, Peter?'

Peter didn't answer immediately. He tried to pick his words very carefully, striving not to distress her any more than need be. 'I'm sorry. Of course I don't know her mind, but I would imagine that at the last moment she will decide not to come.'

'You told me she begged to see them that time when she thought we were on holiday and you were saying prayers in the church and she came across you by chance. Remember? It's only natural. Any mother would. *I* would. But then, I wouldn't have given my own children away. *Never*. Understand? *Never*.'

Caroline lay back in her chair, her eyes shut, trying to bear the pain without flinching. Peter leaned forward, rested his elbows on his knees and clasped his hands in front of him. 'You've always valued the generosity of her spirit, giving us the children. It was what we both wanted, don't forget that. Both of us. We've had twelve years of happiness caring for them. Surely we owe her something for that? One glimpse. That's all. In twelve years.'

Caroline leapt to her feet. 'Just whose side are you on?'

'Yours, of course, it goes without saying.'

'Her own girls will be leaving home shortly. Maybe she needs to fill the gap? She's not having them. She's not.'

'No way. She can't have them. In any case, they won't want her.'

'We don't know what their reaction might be.'

'I do. They'll be staying here. Believe me.'

Caroline went to the window. She stood staring out at the darkening sky, daring herself to think of Peter and that woman making Alex and Beth. 'How could you do it to me? Have sex with *her* on a whim?'

'I can never find the words to apologize. There are no words big enough.' He went up to stand behind her, his arms around her waist. 'Shall I write and ask her not to come?'

Caroline asked, 'Do you have her address, then? You haven't been in touch all this time, have you?' He felt shocked by the accusative tone in her voice.

'No, of course not.'

'I hope not.'

'Kate will know it. Obviously.'

Caroline studied his suggestion and dismissed it. 'No. That would be pathetic. We can't do that. Hold me tight. Tighter than that.' They stood there for quite a while, each lost in thought, watching the sky darken to night.

It was Peter who broke the silence. 'Time for bed.' He released her. 'The two of us, together, can cope, you know.'

'I'm so damned jealous.'

'Of what?'

'That in one wild moment, she was able to give you

205

children and I, who love you so, can never. And,' she added, so softly he could scarcely hear her, 'I'm jealous of the passion you shared.'

This statement humbled Peter more than anything she'd ever said before about this situation. All he could think to say was, 'But *we* share passion, you and I.'

She was standing so close to him that he could feel her slight nod. 'Yes, we do.'

Caroline made no offer to move so they stood, his hands on her shoulders, staring out at the night sky. 'Don't write. She can come. I'm not saying I shall be able to manage to speak to her, because I can't even say her name out loud, but the twins should see her. After all, I'm so lucky. Not only do I have the children, I have you, so by comparison I am doubly more blessed than she. But it still *hurts*. Very badly indeed. I'm dreading the day. Should we tell the children of the possibility?'

Peter shook his head. 'Nearer the time, maybe.'

'Alex will be angry. Beth will be curious about her.'

'Perhaps. We just don't know.' He bent his head and kissed the nape of her neck. 'Love you.'

'She won't want them, of course she won't, I'm being ridiculous.'

'She can't anyway. They're ours by law.'

'You're right, I'm not being ridiculous, just normal.' She caressed his hand where it lay on her shoulder.

'Absolutely.' Peter went to bed, leaving Caroline to follow when she was ready.

Was there never to be an end to this problem? She rather thought not. The children didn't appear to be any different since they'd known about their natural mother, seen her photograph, talked about her, but that was seeing

206

an image. What might happen when they saw the real thing? In flesh and blood, moving, speaking, smiling, and heard her, watched her, touched her? Caroline shuddered. If it had never happened, if they'd never come here, if he'd never seen her, their lives would be so . . . barren now. And that was the crux of the matter. She was barren. Caroline clutched at her stomach and could have torn the offending organ out with her bare hands she was so angry; this place where babies should grow.

Taking in a deep breath and determining not to rail against something that couldn't be changed, she turned her thoughts to Alex and Beth. For their sakes she had to be brave about this situation, to appear in control of herself and to sound pleased they were having this opportunity to meet their mother, even if she was writhing with anguish inside.

She stayed by the window, looking out at the village, loving every cottage, every tree, every blade of grass and wondering when they might have to leave. They couldn't stay here for ever, that wasn't the course Peter's calling would follow. One day they'd have to go, and she might be able to put all this behind her. If he did get a call to go elsewhere, she would welcome it. He'd spoken briefly about leading a church project in Africa. She'd go with him willingly if he got the chance, but for the moment she still had her problems in Turnham Malpas to face. And Peter to face too.

Caroline sighed, turned from the window, checked Peter had closed windows, locked doors, and went up to look at the children before she went into the bathroom. Alex was laid on his back, arms outflung, fast asleep. She bent to kiss him and thought for the millionth time how like Peter he was. In Beth's room she stumbled over some books flung on the floor by her just before she fell asleep. Beth was curled foetus-like, her fair hair tousled, eyelids fluttering as though she dreamed. So like Suzy.

When she entered their own bedroom she looked straight at Peter. He was fast asleep. He was lying on his front, his head turned to the right, both his arms straight down by his sides, the duvet pushed down around his waist. She slipped quietly into bed and rested a hand on his bare back to enjoy feeling him breathing. She smoothed her hand across his shoulders, ran her finger down his spine, sensed him stir slightly, and loved the strength of him, physical and spiritual. His skin felt chilled so she pulled the duvet up over his back and tucked herself in at the side of him. Close up, warm and safe. Nothing and no one could take this away from her. Whatever storms life might throw at her, she was secure with him, and just for a moment she felt triumphant. Suzy might have given birth to his children but she hadn't got them – or him. They all belonged to Caroline Harris, who hadn't enough words in her vocabulary to describe how much she loved them.

In Turnham House Kate and Craddock were discussing the situation at the Rectory.

'I am so glad you told me. I'd no idea. Absolutely no one has even hinted at it.'

Craddock put down his glass of whisky. 'They've all been tight as clams about it once they all knew.'

'Amazing how they can keep secrets when they want to. But Peter, falling to temptation like that? It's hard to believe.'

'How about poor Caroline?'

'She must be . . . well . . . I don't know what to say. She must be so lovely in her heart, so totally Christian to have forgiven him.'

'One assumes she has. But then, when we did that play, "Dark Rapture", she very nearly ran off with someone else.' He related the whole story to Kate and she was shocked.

'Well, well, is there anything else I ought to know?'

Craddock smiled. 'No, that's enough for tonight, except to say Mrs Bliss's cottage is finished and she's out gardening, which is good. And,' he puffed a cloud of smoke into the air, 'I've given my land agent a long list of repairs for Little Derehams.'

Kate leapt to her feet and went to kneel in front of him. 'That's wonderful news. I'm so pleased you've decided to listen to them. That protest the other night frightened me to death.' She kissed him. 'You taste disgustingly of whisky and smoke.'

'Would you rather I didn't smoke? I'll stop if you wish.'

'No, don't. You smoke with such style, it's really very sexy.'

'Sexy? My God! How do you make that out?'

Kate had to laugh, he seemed so horrified. 'I don't know, it just is.'

'Well, I never. Time for bed. I've an early start. Am I earning respect, do you think, by doing all these repairs and whatnot in Little Derehams? Is that what you want?'

'It will go a long way towards changing their attitude to you, believe me. Bed, now, before you get carried away with self-satisfaction.'

'Me? Self-satisfied? Never!'

Chapter 13

Maggie Dobbs left school by five o'clock, went home, made herself a cup of tea and sat with her feet up on her little coffee table to contemplate the school anniversary weekend. When she thought of the work entailed she could have cried. All them feet tramping across her clean floors and people leaving rubbish. It simply wasn't fair. She wondered if she should ask for extra money for working overtime. After all, she wasn't a charity, was she? By the time it was all finished she guessed she'd have put in ten hours and then some.

Tonight they'd all be expecting a seance and she hadn't yet plucked up the courage to tell them she wasn't doing it any more. Her plan was to lock up, something she rarely did, and keep quiet upstairs till they'd all knocked and given up and gone home. Then she'd have to say sorry, she'd forgotten all about it and wouldn't be doing it again. Wild horses couldn't make her.

Tabitha leapt on to her knee and settled down to sleep, purring like a coffee mill. She was a good friend was Tabitha. In fact, when she thought about it, she was the best friend any woman could have. Not counting Dave. Maggie rubbed behind Tabitha's ears, ran her hand all the way down her back from her head to the very end of her tail, gave some time to thinking about Dave and then lifted Tabitha on to the floor and, springing to her feet, said to herself that she'd have to tell them.

But leaping up from her rocking chair, intending to go, was as far as she got. After all, old Fitch was still here. He hadn't died. She wasn't a real medium; Angie Turner happened to win on the lottery by chance and it was a happy coincidence that Mrs Jones had had a letter from their Terry. She'd let anyone come, half the village if they wanted to, and she'd give them the night of their lives. She cleaned her living room at the speed of light, wiped the black vase with the dishcloth, blew the dust from the black tulips, put them in the vase and placed it in the middle of her gleaming oak table, collected the chairs together from the bedroom and the kitchen, rushed upstairs and washed her face, and in a rush of enthusiasm her hair too, and changed her dress. Her resolve wobbled while using the hairdryer but she pulled herself together when she thought about the money in Dave's fairground jug.

She'd do her trance rather than the Ouija because she had control over that. She burned the last incense stick from a bundle her cousin Joanne had given her years ago and wafted her arms about to spread the smell, ate a hasty sandwich in the kitchen because she didn't want any nasty food smells spoiling the incense, and finally sat down at five minutes to nine to await her guests.

She wasn't disappointed. It was a good thing she wasn't doing the Ouija wine glass because there wouldn't have been a glass big enough to accommodate all their fingers.

'Not the Ouija board? We had such a good time with

211

that. My heart didn't stop beating for ages after last week,' said Greta Jones.

Maggie replied, 'I should hope it didn't or you'd be dead.'

'You know what I mean.' Mrs Jones sat down on her favourite chair.

Every seat was occupied. The Senior sisters arrived, eager with anticipation, plumped themselves side by side at the table, stuffed their five-pound notes into Dave's jug and waited breathlessly for the seance to begin. Venetia arrived in a whirl, spreading waves of cloying perfume that almost drowned the incense. Sheila Bissett also came, in what she thought was an appropriate gypsy-type outfit more suited to the occasion than her usual glitzy clothes. But the paisley scarf she wore on her head only made her look as though she was about to clean the house from top to bottom. Maggie suppressed a giggle.

Angie Turner arrived last. 'Oh no! I thought it might be the Ouija board.'

'Well, it isn't. I'm giving it a rest. Sorry.'

'My friend's just coming.'

'I didn't know you were bringing someone.'

'I knew you wouldn't mind. It's Linda Crimble; she's been before.'

'Oh, that's all right.'

Finally they were all seated. Maggie settled her mind, closed her eyes and waited just long enough to make them impatient.

Linda said then, 'Just a minute, we've forgotten to draw the curtains.' Being the nearest she got up to close them. Just as Maggie got going again, Sheila remembered she hadn't got her handkerchief with her and got up to dig in her handbag for one. Maggie began again and this time there was a knock at the door. Everyone jumped. Thinking it would be another person for the seance, Maggie shouted, 'Come in,' before remembering the door was locked, so Sheila got up again to open it. There, on the doorstep, was Muriel Templeton, chirpy and happy as usual, with that special look of innocence she always wore.

'Oh hello, Sheila. I've called to collect Maggie's charity envelope. I left it last week.' She had her charity badge secured to her cardigan, and a leather bag into which she was putting the envelopes.

'Lady Templeton! Right, I'll ask Maggie.' She half closed the door so Muriel couldn't quite see in, whispering, 'Where is it, Maggie?'

'Behind the clock.'

But before Sheila could find it in the dark, Muriel pushed the door open again and came in. Reassuringly she said, 'If you can't find it I do have some spare ones in my bag.' Through the gloom she spotted faces she knew. 'Oh! I'm so sorry. I didn't know you were having a meeting. Is this something I should be attending? I've completely forgotten if it is. But I could always collect the envelopes another evening.'

She stood in the doorway smiling brightly while Sheila shuffled through the various pieces of paper Maggie had stored behind her clock. 'Ah! Here it is. All ready for you, Muriel.'

Apart from Sheila, none of them uttered a word. Maggie was dumbstruck, sitting foolishly with her head resting against the back of her chair, her mouth as wide open as her eyes. The others were paralysed with embarrassment. Muriel looked smilingly from one to the other, waiting for a reply, but none answered her and Sheila was obviously anxious to close the door again. So she stepped out on to the road and left them to it.

Maggie came back to life and said firmly, 'Lock it! Lock it! If anyone else knocks, we'll take no notice.'

A sigh of relief went around the table. Maggie strove to recapture her mood but found it hard. God! They'd all be wanting their five-pound notes back. She dropped her head forward and tried once again.

Slowly, she began moving her head, first right back, then circling round so her head dropped on her chest, then round and round. The groaning began, the howling started and she was away. 'Who's there?' she called. 'Who's there?'

Apart from the small reading lamp on the table by the hearth with the red cover over the shade, there was no other light, not even from the grate still piled with the logs Maggie had put there at the start of the warm weather. If anything, the strange reddish light was more spooky than the flames, and several guests shivered.

Maggie said 'Evadne?' Her voice rose almost an octave and they all thought she really was away this time and it was going to be a good night.

'Oh God!' Mrs Jones whispered to herself. 'Not Evadne.'

In Evadne's sepulchural voice Maggie said, 'Whose mind is troubled tonight? There's someone here afraid and anxious. No? Then it's someone close by. Very troubled. Ve . . . Ve . . .'

Venetia whispered, 'It's not me.'

'It'll be Vera,' said Sheila.

'Evadne' continued to moan. 'He dices with death. He's so very close. Welcome! Welcome to you!'

Linda trembled. 'Does that mean Don's just died?'

'Oh God! I hope not.'

Then Maggie's voice changed again. 'Is that all you have to tell us?'

Back in Evadne's voice she replied, 'I'm going now to welcome him. Au revoir!' Her voice floated up half an octave and Maggie waved goodbye, her white hand glowing pink in the red light from the lamp.

Linda smothered a shriek.

The Senior sisters held hands.

Angie Turner's face went a strange shade of greenish white. 'Do you suppose Don really *has* just died? Is that what it means?'

Sheila Bissett asked in a high-pitched voice if she should get Ron to get the car out and go to the nursing home to tell Vera?

One of the Senior sisters said, 'No, no. We mustn't. It may not be true.'

Angry that they doubted Maggie's word, Angie said, 'Of course we must tell her. It's only right. It'll be true. What about my win on the lottery?'

They couldn't deny that.

They all looked at Maggie for guidance, but she was still away with the spirits.

Maggie spoke again with yet another message. 'Linda, are you there? Linda?'

'I'm here.'

'Take care, there's trouble brewing. Work. Work. Take care.'

'Oh! No! Why? What trouble?'

'Jim . . . Jim . . .'

Linda squeaked, 'She means Jimbo. He's found out I'm on the payroll again.' She began to cry noisily, which completely broke Maggie's concentration and she gradually wound down from her highly emotional state, rocking and moaning, shaking and groaning, until they thought she was losing her mind. But gradually she came to, looking blankly at them all.

'All right?'

They nodded.

'I need a drink!' She got out the brandy from her sideboard cupboard and poured them each a tot into one of her tiny vodka glasses. It was scarcely a mouthful but served its purpose.

No one spoke until they'd given the brandy time to reach the parts that needed it.

The first to speak was Sheila. 'I still think we should go down and tell Vera.'

Maggie asked, 'Tell Vera what?'

They all looked horrified. If they'd wanted proof that Maggie was genuine, this was it; she really had been possessed by the spirits if she didn't know what had been said.

Greta Jones cleared her throat and took the plunge. 'While you were under the . . . influence, as you might say, you said that Evadne was going to welcome Don to . . . well, wherever Evadne is.'

It was Maggie's turn to go a strange colour. She flushed bright red and gripped her glass so tightly they thought she would break it. 'You mean Don's . . . you know. . . . gone to glory?'

They all nodded.

Maggie's face drained of colour and she fell off her chair on to the floor, in a dead faint.

'Doctor Harris!' shouted Linda. 'Go get her.'

The Senior sisters shook their heads and whispered hoarsely, 'No. No. We'd have to tell her.'

'You're right, the Rector wouldn't take kindly.'

'But what can we do?' Terrified that another death in the village might be laid at the Turners' door, Angie knelt down beside Maggie and patted her cheeks. 'Maggie. Maggie. Come on, love. Maggie. Wake up!'

But Maggie didn't respond.

'Now what can we do?'

Venetia dashed for the kitchen, coming back with a jug of water in her hand, which, without further ado, she emptied over Maggie's face. The effect was instantaneous. Maggie sat up with a jerk, shaking her head and spluttering. Linda found a teatowel and gave it to her to wipe herself.

Maggie shouted, 'What the hell?' Then she remembered their conversation and began to whimper. 'What have we done? Oh God! What have we done?'

'We haven't done anything,' protested Angie. 'But I tell you one thing, I'm not coming any more. Here, let's get you up, Maggie.' Being tall and having two exceptionally lively twin boys to deal with, she was able to heave Maggie up on to a chair with the greatest of ease. 'There, that's you sorted, and don't take on about this. You didn't make Don die, now did you? That's if he *is* dead.'

Maggie shuddered. 'Don't come no more, any of you. That's it. Final. No more. I've done with it.' She glared round the group, then buried her head in her hands.

They all crept out, in one way disappointed but in

another glad, because things were getting far too dangerous. They were dabbling where they shouldn't.

Not one of them slept properly that night, least of all Maggie. She was so distraught she allowed Tabitha to sleep in her bed, glad of something warm and comforting and normal to hold on to. If only she'd told them all not to come! Well, she hadn't and now this had happened. Poor Don. Poor Vera. Maybe Vera wouldn't want to live in that flat any more and she'd want her house back. Then where would she go? Maggie covered her face with her hands.

Tabitha took her chance, slid quietly out of bed and headed off downstairs to her cat flap, hoping to get a bit of peace and quiet out in the garden under the shed because she certainly wasn't getting any sleep where she was, with Maggie squeezing her tightly all the time. But the slap of the cat flap as it shut on Tabitha's tail alerted Maggie. Her only connection with normality had gone off into the night. She was in such confusion in her mind that she raced downstairs and went out through the front door calling, 'Tabitha! Tabitha!' That blasted cat; she was never there when you needed her.

Then she forgot the cat and began looking to escape the evening's events; anywhere would be better than being in bed alone, and she ran, utterly confused, calling out, seeking sanctuary.

Bedroom lights turned on, windows were opened, people shouted, 'What's up? Who is it?'

But they got no reply and more than one imagined they were seeing a ghost, something white in the pitch black.

In her panic, Maggie remembered the Rector. He'd know what to do. She'd seen him talking to Vera the day of Don's accident, he'd known what to say then. It took a while of knocking on the Rectory door before the lights went on and she heard someone running down the stairs. 'Rector! Rector!'

She was still banging on the door and shouting when it opened and she almost fell into his arms. 'Oh, Rector, help me, please.' The relief of finding another human being whom she knew could help her was too much and Maggie collapsed in a heap on the hall carpet.

'I'll put the kettle on.' Caroline headed for the kitchen. Peter helped Maggie to stand up and followed Caroline into the kitchen, supporting Maggie, who was by now almost legless with fear.

Seated at the kitchen table with her arms resting on it to keep herself upright, Maggie said, 'It's Don. He's dead, isn't he?'

'Is he? Well, he regained consciousness this morning, I saw him about five o'clock this afternoon and was delighted with his progress. Vera sat with him this evening and rang me when she got back to say he's improving by the hour. Have you heard differently?'

Maggie's eyes slid from one to the other of them, wondering how much she could tell them and what she should keep to herself. That cup of tea was a long time coming. She felt she'd been here hours. 'No, well, yes, in a way. Well, no, I haven't actually but . . .'

Caroline came straight out with it. 'You've been holding a seance again? Is that it?'

Maggie looked up at Caroline and decided that Peter was a better bet. Looking him in the eye across the kitchen table, she said, 'Doctor Harris is right. The spirit I pretend to be in touch with said she was going to welcome him in.

219

Whoever it was. So someone was on the brink of death but it wasn't Don.' She reached into her nightie sleeve and pulled out a tissue and wiped the sweat and tears from her face. 'I'm never holding another one as long as I live. It started as a joke, kind of, but now it's getting serious and I'm frightened and the blasted cat ran out and left me alone and I couldn't bear it.'

Peter asked, 'What were you using, a Ouija board?'

Maggie shook her head. Then she nodded, laid her head on her arms and wept.

'Here's your tea, Maggie. Sit up and have a sip, it might do you good.'

The cup clattered in the saucer when Maggie picked it up and the tea spilled down her chin as she sipped. Caroline handed her a piece of kitchen towel and she caught the drops before they fell off her chin.

'You see, being a widow I have to watch the money a bit careful like and doing the seance helps out. I never meant no harm, but all of a sudden I seem to be doing it proper and I'm frightened to death. They've all gone home thinking I'm genuine but I don't believe I am. Am I? What can I do? I'm terrified about what might happen next. At least if Don's OK, that's something.'

Peter took her hand and held it comfortingly. 'So you can't really be doing it if you thought Don was dead and he isn't.'

Maggie said, 'Of course I can't, can I?' But she began shivering uncontrollably.

Caroline, who was not best pleased at being woken up just two hours after having gone to bed, offered her a bed for the night. 'It's in Sylvia's old room. I always keep it made up, just in case. No one will harm you here. Believe me.'

'I'll never sleep. Never again.'

'You will when I've given you a sleeping tablet.'

Maggie looked up gratefully. 'Would you really give me one?'

'Just this once. Emergency and all that. Have you locked your door?'

Maggie thought for a moment. 'No, but that don't matter. I've nothing to steal.' She opened her mouth to speak, daren't, changed her mind, tried again. There was a silence while they waited for whatever it was that was on the tip of Maggie's tongue. Eventually, in the smallest of voices, she asked Peter, 'Am I damned?'

Peter smiled at her. 'If you are truly sorry for what you've done, no, you are not damned. But it's a matter between you and God. I'm not an intermediary.'

'He'll,' Maggie pointed to the ceiling, 'forgive me, then? Fresh start like?'

'I'm certain. You've actually done no harm, have you, apart from venturing where you shouldn't?'

'That's right. But I feel desperate inside. Black and ugly. It was the money, you see. I've still got the washing machine to pay for. That's the worry.'

Peter advised her to find more work. 'A casual job, Saturdays or something, until you're straightened out.'

Maggie's face brightened. 'I could, couldn't I?'

Caroline said rather firmly, 'I'll show you the bedroom. You've got your nightgown on so I don't need to lend you one, do I?'

Surprised to find herself sitting in the Rectory wearing her nightie, Maggie shook her head.

'Get into bed and I'll bring you a glass of water and the sleeping tablet. There's a bathroom next to the bedroom if you need to use it.'

They climbed the stairs together, Caroline's arm around her waist, and Maggie felt grateful for the caring touch of another human being. She could hear Peter rinsing her cup under the tap and she envied the two of them passionately. Her Dave, lovely as he was, never rinsed a cup out for her in his life. These two had something special and she wished, how she wished she had a share of it. At least he'd promised her she wasn't damned to hell. The big lump of fear in her chest was beginning to dissolve, at last.

Caroline came in with a glass of water and a tablet in a small plastic cup. 'Here we are.' She stood watching. 'Who else was there tonight? Are they frightened too?'

'Not as much as me. If Don's all right, who did we get the message about?'

'Look, you and I know it isn't true, don't we? You haven't really been in touch with spirits.'

'Well, I don't know about that. I was right about Angie Turner and the lottery, wasn't I?'

'Considering how many times Angie and Colin put money on the lottery I suppose they're bound to win some time, aren't they?'

Maggie agreed.

'That's the only thing you've actually got right, isn't it? You haven't actually *made* anything happen, have you?'

Maggie shook her head.

'Then lie down and go to sleep.'

Caroline pulled the duvet up for her and impulsively bent to kiss her goodnight.

Maggie caught hold of Caroline's hand. 'Thank you for being so kind. I'm beginning to feel better.'

'Good. I'm glad.'

'Just got scared.'

Sleep caught up with Maggie in no time at all but as she was finally dropping off, a thought crossed her mind. They'd been wrong once and got the wrong man. If it wasn't Don then it might be someone else. Maggie tried to work it out, but fell asleep thinking how quickly the tablet had worked. She could do with a few more of these.

It was left to Kate to open up the school next morning because Maggie, still sleeping in the Rectory attic, couldn't be roused. On her way to the surgery, Caroline had rung Kate on her mobile to explain.

'She won't be in until lunchtime, I imagine. Got herself thoroughly scared so I gave her a sleeping tablet and it's knocked her out.'

'Well, we had our bit of drama too, last night. About half nine Jeremy Mayer had another heart attack and had to be rushed to hospital. He was so determined to keep fit he overdid the swimming and collapsed as he got out of the pool. Craddock drove him and Venetia to the hospital. We all feared the worst, but he's still holding his own this morning. Thank goodness.'

'It all happens here, doesn't it?'

'Absolutely.'

While she waited at the main traffic lights in Culworth, it struck Caroline that Maggie might have got the wrong man but she had got the right idea and at about the right time too . . .

There was a loud impatient toot from behind and she

realized the lights had changed to green. As she sped on she told herself off for being gullible. Heaven help her. What on earth the village would make of this she dreaded to think.

Chapter 14

That morning in the Store, Jimbo was fuming. They were all keeping their heads down. Mrs Jones in the mail order office hadn't even emerged for her morning cup of tea and the staff working in the kitchens dreaded the thought of him coming in to find fault. They all knew the reason and realized that the axe could fall anywhere today.

Jimbo was unaware they knew he was angry, because he was making strenuous efforts to disguise it. But he most definitely was. He'd been studying his overheads last night and had discovered that Linda Crimble was on his payroll again, quite regularly too. She was only waitressing, but just the same, he was paying her good money when he'd vowed he would never employ her ever again, no matter how tight the staffing. Tom had slipped seamlessly into the Post Office work and didn't make one quarter of the song and dance about it that Linda had.

He glanced at his watch. Pat Jones was coming in for their weekly discussion and he couldn't wait for the moment. Ten minutes and she'd be here.

'Coffee, Tom?'

'Thanks, yes, I will.'

After Jimbo had given Tom his coffee he went into the back office to brood. Seated in front of his computer he checked out how many times Linda Crimble had worked since he'd sacked her: ten times. He'd give that Pat Jones something to think about when she came. He couldn't believe it. Ten times she'd worked for him and he hadn't realized. His accounts person wasn't to blame; all he did was pay their wages each month. So finally Pat Jones was the one to blame. He heard her voice in the Store, as she passed the time of day with Tom.

She came through and he knew the instant he saw her face that something was wrong.

'Pat? How're things?'

'Sounds serious about Jeremy, doesn't it? Don't like Venetia but you can't help feeling sorry. Apparently Maggie Dobbs at the school said the spirits had told her. Scared to death she was, running about like a headless chicken at midnight in her nightie, and the Rector took her in.'

'I know, they've all been on about it this morning. But that's not what you're worried about, is it?'

'How do you know I'm worried?'

'Your face gives you away.'

Pat nodded. 'Remember the night of the party for the rugby club in Culworth?'

Jimbo nodded.

'Well, I was that short-handed for staff you wouldn't believe. All planned for and then one by one they began ringing up, saying they couldn't make it. I was desperate. In fact I was on the verge of ringing you to say we couldn't do it. First time ever I'd have let you down and I couldn't stand it. In the nick of time, Linda Crimble rang and said she was wanting some work and did I have anything. It sounded like an answer to a prayer. So . . . I

226

took her on. I knew I shouldn't, but things were getting to the catastrophe stage. I almost rang you up about it but didn't and thought it would just be the once. Well, she proved to be excellent. Polite, eager to help, remembered what people had asked her for, didn't get fussed. Couldn't have asked for better. And she could handle the rowdy ones. You know what those rugby reunions can get like, but she fended them off as polite as you please. So . . I gave her some more work when Bet went sick.'

'But you knew—'

'I know I did. But I didn't want to let you down. However, she's flouting your rules about the staff taking home leftover food right left and centre. I suspected she was taking food home and I caught her last night at the Royal Naval Association do, putting a whole dish of Jubilee Chicken aside and then telling the clients there was none left. I whisked it out on to the buffet and saw her looking for it when we'd finished, but I never said a word.'

'I see.'

'So, I've got to sack her.' Pat looked up at him, dreading his agreement.

'Just how good is she?'

'Excellent. She's kind of found her niche. Very reliable and pleasant, and she looks immaculate. Hair always tidy and make-up well done. I've no complaints about the way she works, except she's stealing. It's not just leftover bits you see, like a couple of individual desserts or something, which you don't mind, them being no use to anyone.'

'Has it been explained to her?'

Pat nodded. 'Of course. It's so difficult when she's a

friend, kind of, 'cos she lives in the village and we all know her.'

'Send her in to see me. Now, let's get down to the catering diary for next month. Ready?'

They sorted out the engagements for the following month amicably enough, but Pat left feeling like a traitor.

When Pat rang to say Jimbo wanted to speak to her, Linda felt sick at heart, and her voice shook as she agreed to see him that morning. She guessed what it was about – the Jubilee Chicken that had mysteriously found its way back on to the buffet table. It would have been just right for those friends of hers coming for a buffet lunch the following day and would have saved her a mint of money. But she hadn't taken it, had she? Only tried to. But then there was that big dish of cold roast beef, which had done them for dinner three times. Then, as she brushed her hair, she remembered the sherry trifle, which had been the most beautiful she'd ever tasted. Her Alan had loved it. If only she could cook like that. Her hand shook so much when she was putting her lipstick on that she had to wipe it off. Maybe she would look better without it today, more serious.

Jimbo was at the front of the Store talking to a rep when she went in. He nodded to her and said, 'See you in the back office.'

It was a full ten minutes before he put in an appearance, by which time Linda's mouth was so dry she couldn't even run her tongue over her front teeth to unstick them from the insides of her mouth.

'You wanted to see me, Pat said.'

'That's right.'

She braced herself for the biggest ticking off of her life. Instead Jimbo said, 'Pat tells me you're making a really good fist of waitressing. Smart, bright, polite, keen. I'm happy to hear it. She says it seems as though you've found your niche.'

Linda flushed bright red, and sweat began to run down between her shoulder blades. 'Oh! Yes, well, I love it. You really see life when you're waitressing. The tales you hear; I could write a book!'

'I'm glad you're enjoying it. She wonders if you'd like to be taken on permanently?' Jimbo couldn't believe he'd said that.

Linda's eyes opened wide. Why was the conversation not going the way she'd expected? Obviously Pat hadn't noticed her taking things. Mentally Linda rubbed her hands together with glee. 'Well, yes, I would like to be permanent.'

'Good.' Jimbo offered his hand to seal the deal. 'I'll tell Pat. Be seeing you.'

Linda said good morning and thank you and turned to leave, filled with relief. As her hand closed on the door handle, Jimbo added, 'Of course, it all depends on you not thieving from me.'

Linda felt as though she'd been cast from stone. Still holding the door handle, she became aware again of the sweat running down between her shoulder blades and yet now she was chilled to the marrow. 'Oh!'

'I don't mind a couple of leftover salmon mousses, or a few mushroom vol-au-vents, or some bread rolls that wouldn't be any use the following day, but a whole Jubilee Chicken, I classify that as theft.'

'I didn't take it.'

'I know. Pat knows her job, Linda. She has eyes at the back of her head; that's why I employ her. She only has to catch you once more and I shall prosecute.'

Linda swung away from the door, more angry with him than she could ever remember. 'Prosecute? Me?'

'Oh yes. Definitely.'

'You'd be laughed out of court.'

'Would I indeed?'

'All over *one dish*?'

'All over one *huge*, catering-size dish, completely untouched. I might not win, but you'd be discredited and rightly so. Still want the job?'

She did. She'd no alternative. 'Yes, and I shan't take anything, anything at all. Never again. I promise.'

Jimbo smiled. 'Good. Then we both know where we stand. You're very lucky I've taken you on. You've Pat to thank for that. So mind your Ps and Qs.'

'Right. Thanks. Good morning.' Her legs were trembling as she walked back into the Store. There was a lively babble of conversation going on but Linda couldn't decipher a word; she had to grab hold of the corner of the fruit and vegetable display to steady herself. He was a devil, that Jimbo. An absolute devil. He'd known all the time. Prosecute! He wouldn't dare! But she had a sneaking suspicion he would. He was a typical businessman who had no thought for his employees. As the moment passed, she saw Maggie Dobbs and went across to have a word.

'You didn't mean it about no more,' she nudged Maggie with her elbow, 'you know, evenings? I was really frightened. Anyway, Don isn't dead, is he? Someone was saying he's coming round fine, at last.'

Maggie turned to look at her. Her face had lost all its colour. 'I said no more and I mean it.'

'No need to be like that. We pay yer, don't we?'

'If you see any of the others tell them it's over. Maggie Dobbs has had enough.'

'Oh, come on, don't be daft. We all like it. Can't say enjoy, but we do like it.' She shuddered. 'Gives us such a thrill. Bet *you* had a thrill prancing into the Rectory in your nightgown. You knew exactly where to go; straight to the most handsome man in the village. I'm shocked! Anyway, you'll miss the money. Wish I could earn thirty pounds in an hour. Great. See yer Friday.'

'How many times do I have to say it before it sinks in? Eh? I'm not doing it no more. Full stop.'

Linda folded her arms and, blocking Maggie's way to the chill counter, said, 'Well, we shall all turn up, believe me. With our five pounds at the ready. So you'll have to.' She rubbed the fingers and thumb of her right hand directly under Maggie's nose and pursed her lips mockingly.

'I'm not! I'm not!' Maggie dropped her wire basket and fled for the exit. Emitting hoarse shrieks, she flung the door open wide and rushed out down Stocks Row. Linda was livid. The silly cow! Well, she'd show her come Friday night.

By Friday night Linda had contacted everyone to let them know that Maggie was holding a seance, despite what she'd said at the last one. She was there early, and at ten minutes to nine she rattled at Maggie's door. When there was no reply, she tried opening it. Everyone in the village was somewhat lax about locking their doors and she fully expected that Maggie's door would open when she lifted the latch. But it didn't. The curtains were drawn, but then they always were when they had a seance. She waited a few moments and then spotted the Senior sisters coming along Church Lane. They came slowly, huddled together as though afraid. Honestly, with their black headscarves, they looked like two refugees from one of those old Second World War films on telly that her Alan liked to watch 'cos of his grandad.

Linda waved enthusiastically and the two of them peered quickly over their shoulders to check if anyone had seen her waving. They each gave a discreet acknowledgement of her greeting and then scurried towards her.

In stage whispers they asked, 'Is there really one tonight?'

'Is it on then?'

Linda nodded. 'I can't get a reply though. Knock on the window, Miss Senior, and see if she's there.'

The two of them knocked timidly and waited.

'She won't hear that! Here, give it a good knock like this.' Linda rapped loudly on the glass three times. But there was no reply.

Venetia came, then Greta Jones. 'Good evening. Isn't she in?'

The Senior sisters shook their heads.

'Well,' said Venetia, 'she did say she wouldn't. I was surprised when you said she was, Linda.'

Mrs Jones asked Venetia about Jeremy.

'Thanks for asking, he's much better at the moment. Gave us another scare a couple of days ago, but he's hoping to be out by next weekend. Fingers crossed.' She crossed all her fingers and held them up, smiling, Mrs Jones thought, a little too bravely.

They stood huddled in a group at the door, whispering together a while longer. They felt conspicuous and Venetia and Mrs Jones wanted to go home. 'No, don't do that,' said Linda. 'Let's go round the back. She has a gate on to the Green. We'll get in that way.'

She led the way round the back, opened the bolt on the little gate and marched up the back garden path. Before she knocked, Linda peered in the kitchen window, shading her eyes to see better. 'There's no one there. No one at all.'

'Saw her Thursday and thought she didn't look too good.' Mrs Jones looked in the window but could only see the tidy kitchen, still looking as fresh and beautiful as the day Don Wright had modernized it. 'It's funny, hope she's all right.'

Linda tried the door but it was also locked. 'She hasn't gone into Culworth because there's no bus after seven for her to come back. I wonder where she is?'

Venetia declared she was going home, and Mrs Jones agreed. 'So am I. She said she didn't want one so obviously she doesn't. Goodnight.'

Venetia hooked her arm in Mrs Jones's. 'I'll walk with you. I left the car by the school. Would you like a lift?'

They went, leaving the Senior sisters and Linda standing in the garden. Linda rattled on the door again, tried the handle. 'She's in there, I'm sure. I'm going to force the door.'

'You mustn't.'

'No, no, no.'

'I am.' To justify her actions she added, 'She might be

233

ill, needing help.' She looked round the garden for some instrument with which to force the lock and found what had been Dave's trowel for his window boxes in the old flat. Linda rammed the pointed end at the door frame by the lock and with several almighty heaves sprang the door open. There was an horrendous cracking of wood as the frame gave way, which made the Senior sisters tremble with fear.

'You shouldn't have, Linda.'

'Right, come on.' Linda led the way in, stepping quietly and listening for some sound of Maggie. Tabitha fled between their legs and out through the back door and under the shed. It startled Linda and for a split second she almost changed her mind, but somehow the thought of Jimbo allowing her to work for him knowing she'd stolen had empowered her that day and she marched to the foot of the stairs.

'Maggie? You there?'

Maggie had heard everything. Every single word. At first she'd been sitting on the bottom stair where she knew they couldn't see her, but when they'd come round the back, she'd quietly crept upstairs and got into the wardrobe. She'd managed to get the door almost closed and was crouched down among the shoes, desperately trying to stop herself from wailing. She was so afraid. It was stifling in there and she didn't know how long she could hide before she suffocated. She could clearly hear footsteps coming up the stairs but didn't know how many of them there were. It sounded like the whole of her seance group, if not the entire Culworth Constabulary.

When they got in the bedroom, she heard Linda's voice. Whoever else was there remained silent.

'Well, she doesn't appear to be here, does she? I can't say I like her bedspread. Candlewick! I mean. Nasty pink, too. They went out with the ark. Ooh! Just look at them crocheted mats, they match the bedspread. Aren't they awful? She's got no taste.'

Maggie could hear her heading for the bathroom. 'Look at this! My God, it's far too good for a pokey old house like this. A shower as well.' She could hear them having a practice pull on the shower curtain, heard someone turn on a tap. Her home. Her sacred home. Her beautiful bathroom. No one had a right. Moving very, very slowly, Maggie stood up among her clothes, pushed them aside and reached out in the pitch black for Dave's golfing clubs, which she hadn't been able to part with, propped in the far corner of the wardrobe. She slipped a club out, gripped it tightly and softly pushed open the wardrobe door. Her heart was beating so fast she thought she'd die, but before she did she'd give them the fright of their lives. Touching her things, mucking up her home.

She sprang on them just as they were leaving the bathroom. In the tight confines of Maggie's landing there wasn't much room for escape. She beat about the air with the golf club, screaming like a banshee.

'You interfering old besoms, I'll show you. Here, take that. And that. You nosy-parking old bitches, get out, get out!' The Senior sisters, nervous to begin with, shakingly mustered their strength and raced each other to be first down the stairs, but jammed together at the top, shouting for help.

'I'll give you help. How dare you force your way into my house? Get out. Go on, get out.' Maggie swiped at them with the golf club until they unknotted themselves

235

and hurried down the stairs one after the other. But where was Linda? She was found in the bedroom, hiding behind the door, half laughing, half crying with fright.

Maggie shouted, 'It's all your fault. I told you I wasn't doing another seance, but oh no, Linda Crimble wouldn't listen. Now, get yourself down those blasted stairs before I stove your head in.'

She slapped Linda twice on the back of her head before Linda managed to get out of the bedroom, then she clattered down the stairs, catching her high heels in the carpet more than once, with Maggie behind, lunging at her and screaming abuse. Linda shot out of the back door faster than light. Maggie shouted after her, 'And put the bolt on the gate, you nasty bitch, you.'

She sat down beside her fireplace and rocked herself furiously until her temper had cooled. Then she began to laugh. She laughed as she hadn't since Dave died. How she giggled, peel upon peel, and when she stopped to hold her side from the pain, she started again almost immediately. It would be a while before that Linda Crimble tried anything like that again. She'd send her the bill for repairing the door frame. Nasty pink candlewick! How dare she? But the surprise on Linda's face when she appeared waving the golf club was worth it! What a laugh. My, it was a while since she'd enjoyed herself so much.

When, finally, she'd laughed herself to a standstill, she went to the cupboard beside the fireplace and took out the squares of paper she'd used for the Ouija board, found some matches and, methodically placing the logs on the hearth, she threw the pieces of paper in the grate, lit a match and set fire to them. Just before the flames died down, she remembered the red square of cloth she'd used

236

to cover the lamp shade and burned that too. Then she got the tulips out of the cupboard, cut the plastic stalks in half with her old dressmaking shears and bunged them in the bin. The wine glass she'd already got rid of so now there was nothing left of the seance sessions except her memories.

She went upstairs and took a shower, using some shower gel her sister had given her for Christmas. When she was sweet-smelling all over she went into the bedroom for her nightgown, blushed at the thought of the Rector seeing her in it, and decided that too had to go. As her hand touched the bedspread to pull it back she recalled Linda's scathing comment, so she pulled that off, screwed it into a ball and flung it down the stairs. It narrowly missed Tabitha, who was padding upstairs now the excitement was over, to climb into bed for some TLC after her shock.

The two of them settled down under the blankets and Maggie's last thought was she'd go to Culworth on the bus on Saturday and indulge herself with a duvet at that sale in Bishopgate. From now on she was keeping her word about going to church and there'd be no more communicating with the spirits, definitely not.

Now she'd put things right she felt so much better. Like Peter had said, if she truly was sorry for what she'd done, then Him up there would give her a new beginning. She was and He would. So now she could sleep proper like. She tucked a gentle arm around Tabitha and they both fell asleep.

Chapter 15

Kate stayed late that night at the school, putting the finishing touches to her plans for the anniversary. She was admiring the programme proof just come from the printers and thinking about any loose ends she hadn't tied up when the telephone rang.

'Kate?'

'Craddock, is something the matter?'

'Just wondered if you were coming home.'

'Right now.'

'Good. Drink?'

'Gin and orange.'

'Right.'

Kate picked up the programme proof, checked she'd locked the filing cabinet, and left the school by the main door. She paused for a moment after she'd locked it and looked up at the sky. It was a fine, clear night with the full moon shining brightly in a magical, midnight-blue sky. It was far later than she'd realized. When the celebrations were over, she'd spend far more time with Craddock. He deserved it, he'd been so thoughtful about her late nights at work, but obviously he was feeling lonely tonight. Kate drove home, parked her car and walked towards the front door to find it opening and Craddock standing there waiting for her.

He kissed her cheek, took her hand and drew her inside. The door to the students' bar was wide open and their shouts and laughter could be heard all over Turnham House. Venetia came hurrying across the hall. 'Sorry about this, Mr Fitch. I'll turf them out.'

'That's all right, but they are over-running their time.'

'I realize that. Sorry.'

Kate and Craddock went upstairs, closing the flat door firmly behind them and shutting out the noise.

'Here's your gin. Show me the proof.'

While Kate sank into a chair and took her first sip, Craddock put on his reading glasses and read. He looked at her and smiled.

'This is excellent. Absolutely excellent. You've got it just right. Everyone will want one for a souvenir. They'll sell like hot cakes. Just the right number of photographs, and the text is absolutely bang on the nail.'

Kate blushed with pleasure. 'Thanks. That's praise indeed.'

'Don't make it sound as though I'm not ready to give praise. I always do where praise is due.'

'You do. I'm beginning to get quite nervous about this anniversary. I am doing the right thing, aren't I?'

'Of course you are. You've got all my support and if there's anything you need doing on the day, just say the word.' He tapped some ash from his cigar. 'I'm a good man in a crisis.'

'You are. Like a rock. Best day's work I did asking you to marry me.'

He spotted the smile on her face and grinned back,

remembering how many times he'd asked her before she'd agreed. 'Same for me. First time in my life I've really been loved.'

'Oh come on, Craddock, surely your parents loved you?'

He looked down at his glass. She waited, realizing that, without thinking, she'd asked him a very crucial question. The silence lasted for almost a minute before he answered.

'My mother would have if she hadn't had love beaten out of her. As for my father, he spent most of his time with his brains addled by drink. He was a drunken, brutal bully, self-obsessed, coarse, domineering, the son of another drunken, brutal bully. He hadn't a single redeeming feature. The six of us lived in terror of him.'

'My darling! I'd no idea.'

'And my mother made seven. She never had a happy moment for as long as I can remember. In the end she gave up the struggle and consequently we lived in a hovel. Who could blame her? I certainly couldn't. All I did, smart Alick, Henry Craddock Fitch, was walk out on her at sixteen and never go back. As a grown man I could have made her life so much better, at least in the material way.' He looked up at Kate, those ice-blue eyes of his filled with tears.

He held out a hand to her and she got to her feet and went to kneel in front of him. Putting her arms around him, she laid her head on his chest and remained quiet for a while until she'd found the right words. 'You're loved now. Right this very minute. You always will be while I have breath in my body. Don't ask me why. The age difference is huge; you're rich, I'm not. I'm bloody-minded when it comes to it, independent and tough and

240

like my own way, and I'm having to learn about living with someone, but I wouldn't change things, not for the world.'

Again he was silent, stroking her hair, holding her tightly, communicating without words. Eventually he said, 'I remember my mother's birthday, I must have been about seven at the time. The six of us had scraped some money together and managed to buy her some cheap perfume, something perfectly appalling, I've no doubt. We couldn't wait for the morning to come to give it to her. We must have had the bottle out of its box a dozen times, desperate for her birthday to dawn, desperate to witness her delight. My father, who'd slept downstairs because he couldn't get up them to go to bed properly, woke up when we sang "Happy Birthday" and when he saw what we'd bought her, he snatched the bottle from her just as she was smelling it and telling us how delighted she was. I remember,' his voice broke and he had to pause, swallowing hard to control his emotion, 'she had this beautiful smile on her face, it was lit up, even her eyes were glowing with her pleasure and we felt so delighted for her . . . then he staggered to the sink and poured it away. "She's not bloody having that," he said. "It'll make 'er smell like a tart." How I hated him for that. How hard we'd tried to save the money for it. How precious it was to us and to her. Had I been bigger I would have killed him. I remember it was a lovely bottle with a kind of frosted glass top. It seemed to me to be the very height of elegance, a thing of real beauty. We were so proud of it.'

'I'm sure it was. I'm so sorry, Craddock. And still it hurts after all these years. How dreadfully painful. Why

241

have you kept this all hidden away? You could have told me.'

'It is the only way I can deal with the shame. The absolute shame that I never went back to see to her, to make her life easier. Me with my millions! I'm not worth much, am I? Not in any real way.'

'Darling!'

'That was why I did Mrs Bliss's house up. I saw my mother all over again, the smell of desperation, of having given up because the odds were unsurmountable. My God! It was like going back in time. The moment I saw her, I knew.' He explained to her what he'd found out about Mr Bliss. 'A wonderful, spirited husband, selfish perhaps when he'd fathered so many children, but brave and courageous, filled to the brim with enthusiasm, but not very practical. If only he'd attended to the money he'd have come back from the South Pole and been applauded for it. But he went without enough of the right supplies and some unexpectedly severe weather defeated him. Thought he was invincible, I expect. Money is the very devil.'

She picked up his cigar from the ashtray where he'd put it when she'd knelt down to hug him, handed it to him and watched that sexy ring of smoke float away up to the ceiling. 'Only if you let it be your master. You may not have helped your mother but you have helped Mrs Bliss.'

'I have. She's taking that job, you know. She can attend to the school computers, too, if you have a problem.'

'Thanks. That'll be wonderful. They've been a tremendous asset for the school. For a village school to be capable of giving the children such a tremendous start is fantastic. When I meet other teachers and tell them what computers

242

we have, they almost faint. One or two I swear have turned several shades of green. "In a *village* school?" they say very scathingly, so as to let me know my humble place in the scheme of things. I don't let on my husband gave them to us as bait to get me to marry him.'

Craddock grinned a schoolboy grin. 'I wasn't even *thinking* of marrying you at the time. I do know when I realized what you meant to me, though.'

'When was that?'

'Remember I was given those tickets to a VIP do at the Globe? You know, Shakespeare's doodah? You were dressed in the most flattering dark blue dress, almost black but not quite, and you were talking to someone, animated and thoroughly enjoying yourself, and I caught your eye and you raised your glass to me and a gorgeous smile came over your face. That was when I realized you were the woman for me and come hell or high water I'd marry you before the year was out.'

'I remember that. I was thinking you weren't a bad old cove and that I quite liked you. I thought you could be fun if you'd just lighten up a bit. But I never expected you to propose. Really, in truth, we are an outrageously mismatched couple, but it works, doesn't it? The first time you asked me, I went to bed that night absolutely floored. How could he possibly imagine I should want to marry him? I thought. I can't, can I? It would be ridiculous. Then I decided to cold-shoulder you and refuse your invitations, just to see if I could manage without seeing you.'

He laid a gentle hand on her cheek and kissed her lips. 'I remember that. You were cruel. I believed I'd lost you and kicked out at everyone and everything in sight. I must have been a total pain. You know old Ted, who's been with me since the beginning? He's never deferential, ever, and he said, "What's bloody getting at you? Anybody'd think you were in love." And I thought, he's damned right, is Ted. I am. I must be.'

'I liked old Ted when I met him, you know that time you took me round your offices and on site at the new arts complex you were building? I thought, there's a man who knows the world as it really is, no frills, no sentiment, just plain honest to goodness truth.'

'Oh! Ted knows about truth all right. He never spares my feelings. He said after he'd met you that I should get married to you sooner rather than later because he could see you'd keep my feet on the ground, like he'd always tried to do.'

Kate sat back on her heels, smiling.

'Bless you.' Craddock bent forward and kissed her again. She got to her feet and returned to her chair.

Kate finished her gin and orange, then said out of the blue, 'I have an idea. Let's pay for ballet lessons for Una Bliss. She's exceptionally talented and well worth encouraging.'

'If you could devise a way I can pay without anyone knowing. My Sadie Beauchamp Education Fund is looking for some good causes now Dean Jones has finished at Cambridge, and Michelle Jones at horticultural college. Rhett Wright finished too, of course, some while ago.'

'I shall elect myself as searcher of good causes in the education field. Can't have good money going to waste. Talent must be positively encouraged.'

'Bless you. When this anniversary is finished we shall go

on holiday, the honeymoon we never had. Will you leave the destination to me?'

Kate nodded. 'You'll sit on the platform at the anniversary won't you? You know, Craddock, each time I think about the old headmasters and their wives coming, I wonder how on earth Peter and Caroline will cope. Worse still, how will the children cope?'

'You didn't make him bed Suzy Meadows, did you? Eh? So let them sort it out as best they can. It won't be easy but they'll have to do it as best as they can. They're both intelligent people . . . and . . .'

'Being intelligent doesn't mean you know how to handle emotions that deep.'

'I know. Don't worry.'

Kate nodded slowly. 'OK. So you will sit on the platform? As the benefactor who has promised to buy some new playground equipment you must.'

Surprised, Craddock said, 'I don't remember promising that. It's the first I've heard of it.'

'I know, it's just occurred to me.'

Craddock sighed. 'Hen-pecked, that's what I am.' He stood up, holding out his arms to her, and she rose to her feet, put down her glass and walked towards him, her face alight with pleasure. He kissed her again and then said with an amused grin on his face, 'My wife can twist me round her little finger.'

'And aren't you loving it?' They both laughed until the tears ran down their cheeks. When Kate could finally draw breath she said, 'I told you it would be fun.'

Craddock wiped his eyes and stuttered, 'I haven't laughed like that in years. You must be good for me.'

★

The next morning Kate went to school to find Maggie Dobbs full of life. There was a new spring in her step and a strength in her voice.

'Good morning, Mrs Fitch! How're things?'

'Very well, thank you and better for hearing you sound so happy.' She raised a questioning eyebrow at Maggie.

'Well, I've got a temporary job shelf-filling on Saturday nights at the Store. Only temporary until I get my finances sorted out, but it's relieved my mind.'

'And the seance business?'

Maggie leaned on her polishing mop and said, 'Well, that's all sorted too.' She told Kate about the incident with the golf club and they both had a laugh. 'And having turned over a new leaf, there's going to be no more arguing with the dinner ladies. I've made up my mind. I shall be as nice as pie to 'em.' She looked into the distance. 'Though that might be a bit difficult, them being how they are.'

'Goodwill, that's what's needed. You set the standard, and they'll be eating out of your hand.'

Maggie nodded, gave a final flick to the hall floor, glanced at the big clock on the wall, which had been measuring time since the day the school opened, to make sure she wasn't running behind with her jobs, and said, 'You'll give me instructions about the anniversary, won't you? I want things to be smart and that. It's wonderful thinking about all that learning going on all these years. Just wish I'd had the sense to pay more attention in school. Still, you can't put an old head on young shoulders, can you?'

'No, you can't, but it's never too late.'

'Suppose not. Time that clock was overhauled. Bel Tutt

said it had to be done every two years, on account of its age, and I'd hate it to be stopped when the anniversary came along. They'll all look at it, if only for old time's sake, and expect it to be keeping time. Only three weeks, you know.'

'Three weeks! Good heavens, you're right. Three weeks, and none of the displays done. Help.' Kate dashed off into her office as though there wasn't a minute to spare.

That day Hetty Hardaker rehearsed the school choir for the umpteenth time, Muriel played again for the Maypole dancing practice, Kate's class revised, *again*, the play they were doing and the little ones rehearsed as the butterflies. Miss Booth exhibited a butterfly costume she'd done over the weekend, which the children thought was so magnificent that some of the older girls even wished they were small enough to be butterflies.

'Them's huge wings. Just like that Notting Hill Carnival, isn't it, Miss Booth? All glittery and kind of papery,' Karen from Year Seven said.

Kate finally got round to planning the display material for the hall wall. She needed photographs. A comment Caroline had once made reminded her that Peter had the parish photos in albums and she wondered if there were any suitable for a school display.

She went out of school and walked along Church Lane, hoping that either Peter or Caroline would be home.

Peter answered the door. 'Come in, Kate. How can I help?'

'I'm looking for photos of the school, past and present. I don't suppose you have any in your parish albums I could possibly borrow? I'd be so careful with them.'

247

'I'm sure we have. Come in the kitchen. I'm making tea for the children. They apparently die from starvation at school and require immediate sustenance on their return.'

'I remember the feeling. I was just the same. I thought I might use a few photos from the early days, but the rest will need to cover the last fifty years. Do you think I'm right?'

'I think so. I don't know how far back they go, though I suppose we only need to look at the dress to hazard a good guess.'

She watched while he cut two slices of bread and filled the kettle. Should she say anything? Why not be frank and open about it. Craddock would be. 'I had never been told about the twins and I do hope that my inviting Michael Palmer and his wife won't be too upsetting. They have e-mailed me and they are both coming, as well as their daughters. I do hope I haven't upset things. When I heard about . . . the . . . situation, I was surprised they'd agreed to come.'

Peter stood with his back to her, getting cups out of the dishwasher. 'So am I. But it has to be faced. Perhaps it's better this way. There'll be lots of people . . .'

'Yes, maybe they won't meet.'

'Beth is so much like her mother, there's no mistaking.'

'I see.'

Peter heard Alex's key in the door. 'Here they come.'

They bounded into the kitchen.

Beth flung her arms around her father and kissed him.

Alex said, 'Hi Dad. Have you got my toast ready? I'm starving.'

Kate said, 'Just the people I need to see.'

'Good afternoon, Mrs Fitch,' the two of them said together.

'I'm needing someone with a smattering of intelligence to give me a hand at the school this Saturday. Could you possibly help?'

Beth, who was already seated at the table munching her toast and peanut butter, said, 'What do you want us to do?'

'Help me put up the displays in the school hall. I'm hoping to find pictures of school events in your dad's albums. I need someone with an artistic eye.'

Alex said almost before she'd finished speaking, 'Can't help. Sorry. I've got a rugby match on Saturday.'

Peter gave him a long look. 'I didn't know you'd been chosen for the team?'

Alex concentrated on his toast, not wishing to look him in the eye and acknowledge he'd just told a big fib. 'Well, I have.'

'Well, that's excellent news. I am pleased. Will you help Mrs Fitch, Beth?'

'Of course. I'd love to.' She didn't comment on Alex's refusal to help. They'd talked about the albums in the weeks after they'd been shown their mother in a couple of the photographs. Alex had said he didn't want to meet her. Never ever. His mother was Caroline and someone who could give their children away was nothing to do with him.

But she, Beth, had been more sympathetic and was secretly looking forward to seeing her real mother. She knew she would recognize her because she was so much like her. She hadn't let on to anyone that she knew they

249

were coming to the school anniversary and said nothing at all about the small burst of excitement inside her.

Peter offered to get the albums and asked Alex for help. But he shook his head. 'Haven't finished my toast. They're not that heavy, Dad.'

So it was Peter who sought out the albums and carried them into the kitchen. 'There we are, Kate. This one on the top is the latest. Shall I carry them across to the school for you?'

'No, thanks, I'll be all right. I'm fairly tough. I will take great care of them and replace the photos afterwards. It's most kind of you. I do appreciate it. See you Saturday, Beth, nine-thirty?'

'Yes. See you, Mrs Fitch.' When Peter came back from letting Kate out, Beth swallowed the last of her tea and disappeared upstairs, knowing full well that Alex would be in trouble for fibbing, and she was best out of the way as she would only jump to his defence and complicate matters.

Peter sat down and watched Alex eating his toast. 'Well?'

Alex looked up and Peter saw not the child he knew and loved, but the man he would be.

'Well? I'm waiting.'

'I know I fibbed. I've not been chosen. There isn't even a match. But I'm not helping. I don't ever want to see those albums again. And if she comes to the school anniversary, I don't want to meet her, or have anything to do with her, ever, and I won't, whatever you say. Not even to be polite.'

'If you didn't want to help, there was no need to lie in order to cover up your reluctance. Just say it.'

250

Alex pushed his empty plate away and said, 'Please, Dad, don't talk to me about lies. Doing it with Suzy Meadows was the biggest, most enormous, terrible lie to my mum. So don't talk to me about lies ever again.'

'Alex!'

'It's the truth, Dad. The absolute truth, don't kid yourself.' He got up, lifted his satchel from the floor and said, 'I've got work to do.' He walked out.

Peter was stunned. He hadn't realized until that moment that his son had grown up, not enough to see shades of grey, as yet he still only saw in black and white, but he was right, there were no shades of grey in this matter. He'd been profoundly unfaithful, and though he might know he'd been forgiven by his God and his wife, it was certain that Alex never would forgive him. Peter went to look out of the kitchen window at Caroline's country cottage garden, and he wondered if it might be better if they moved to another parish and left behind the whole tangled mess.

Chapter 16

When Saturday morning came round, Beth was off to the school by twenty minutes past nine and had to sit on the doorstep of the main entrance waiting for Mrs Fitch. She'd left Alex still in bed. Mum had called him several times but he'd ignored her, something she could never remember him doing before.

Mrs Fitch arrived at twenty-five minutes past the hour, bright and welcoming and armed with huge, brightly coloured sheets of card for the displays. As she put the key in the lock she said, 'Thank you for helping. What do you think of the colours I've chosen?'

'They're lovely. I like the yellow best.'

'So do I.' They walked into the hall and Kate laid the sheets of card on a table she'd borrowed from the dinner ladies. 'I've made sure it's absolutely clean. The albums are on my desk. Can you get them for me?'

Beth carried them into the hall for her and laid them at one end of the table. 'Dad says there might be some photos of the playgroup in here.'

'Oh good. I have some pictures belonging to the school in my bag, which I've already sorted out. It's such fun looking at the really old pictures; for some reason the

252

children all look dreadfully unhappy. I don't think there's a smiler among them.'

'Children smile nowadays though, don't they?'

'They do. Now . . . here we go. Alex gone to his match?'

'Yes . . . No. He doesn't have one. He just didn't want to help'

'I see. Well, never mind, we'll manage, won't we?'

Back at the Rectory Alex had got up, showered and was downstairs in the kitchen eating his breakfast. Caroline was sorting out the freezer while he ate. She'd made up her mind she wouldn't ask his reasons for not helping at the school.

'Mum?'

'Mmm?'

'Is she coming? This . . . Suzy person?'

There was only a slight hesitation before Caroline answered, 'Yes. So I'm told.'

'I shan't speak to her.'

'That's all right, but you must be polite if she speaks to you.'

'Why?'

'Because you must.'

'Why?'

'Well, for one thing, she gave you life and carried you for nearly nine months.'

'She didn't want me though, did she? She gave me away.'

'She gave you to your father and to *me*, and I needed you so desperately.'

'Did you?'

'Yes. I wanted Dad's children because I love him so, but I couldn't have them with him.'

Alex lingered over his cup of tea, thinking about what his mother had said. He poured himself another cup, rested his elbows on the table and drank. After a few sips he said quietly, 'How did you find out what had happened?'

'Your father told me as soon as he knew you were expected.'

'What did you think?'

Caroline shut down the lid of the freezer and propped herself against it. 'If you want the truth, my world fell apart. I went home to Grandma's and had a big think and I decided I couldn't live without your dad and I'd have to forgive him.'

'And you did?'

'Yes.'

'I don't think I could forgive my wife having a secret like that.'

'Well, there we are, that's you but not me. Best of all, I got the two of you and I loved you from day one. It wasn't difficult, believe me. I saw you being born and held you immediately, and instantly felt right here in my heart you were mine. You see, your mother couldn't tolerate even seeing you, not because she hated you, or wanted rid of you, but because she knew if she did see you she'd never give you to us. Which she knew was the best because being widowed, this was before she married Mr Palmer, and having her three girls to feed and clothe, tiny twins would have been impossible financially. Praise be, Alex! You're ours, Dad's and mine, and I can't begin to describe how full of gratitude I am for her generosity. So remember that when you think of her.'

He sat silently gazing out of the window absorbing what she'd said. 'But he—'

'Yes?'

'Never mind.' Alex cleared the table, put his dishes in the dishwasher and went to leave the kitchen. He hesitated in the doorway and turned back. 'Thanks for talking, Mum.' He disappeared up the stairs to sit at his desk in his bedroom, staring out of the window and thinking about grown ups and how wrongly they could behave and yet be forgiven for it. Then he recollected how when he was nine, or was it ten, he'd been so defiant and rude to his mother every day for a week that in exasperation his dad had banned him from eating with them for a whole weekend and he'd had to stand at the kitchen worktop to eat his meal after they'd all finished. But his mum had forgiven him that. He couldn't even remember now what it was that had made him swear and be so cruel. Now he couldn't believe he'd done it and when he recollected some of the words he'd used to her, he wondered how on earth she could have forgiven him. But she'd forgiven his dad for . . . with that Suzy Meadows so . . .

Alex leapt to his feet, cleaned his teeth, looked in the mirror as he combed his hair and realized how like his dad he was. He very much liked the idea of that.

He ran down the stairs, jumping the last four in one leap as he loved to do, landed at the bottom with a thud and shouted, 'I'm off to the school.' He shot out of the door at the speed of light. He pondered what he would say to Mrs Fitch, thinking it might be good to have a kind of rehearsal of how very polite he could be, in preparation for speaking to that Suzy.

Mrs Fitch beamed a great big smile at him. 'Why hello, Alex! So pleased you could come. You've arrived at just the right moment. We really want someone to climb up on the piano and fasten this card to the wall below the clock. Could you do it for us, please? This one, look.'

So before he knew it he was doing a balancing act on top of the piano with Mrs Fitch and Beth gazing up at him, admiring his athleticism. There was no need for an apology and altogether he spent a very satisfying morning being male and useful.

The three of them had coffee and biscuits halfway through the morning in Mrs Fitch's office, talking nineteen to the dozen about school, their new schools and what would happen on the 'big' day.

'Beth, I have an idea. Would you present flowers to the headmasters' wives on the Saturday?' The moment the words were out of her mouth Kate could have bitten her tongue out. What a stupid, stupid thing to have suggested.

Alex caught Beth's look of panic and answered for her. 'I think it would be better if someone from the top class did that. People might think it favouritism if Beth did it, mightn't they?'

'Of course, I think perhaps you're quite right.' Kate almost sweated with relief at the wonderful reason he'd given. 'Yes, you're quite right. I did say I wanted someone with a smattering of intelligence to help. Thank you, Alex. Shall we get on?'

By noon the hall was looking festive. They'd had such fun choosing which photographs to put up and where to place Mrs Fitch's graphs of school numbers over the years, of scholarships won to Lady Wortley's and Prince Henry's, of careers chosen by old pupils and any number of facts about the school. There were even copies of some of the school log book pages scanned by Mrs Fitch and printed out on her state-of-the art computer. In fact, Beth was of the opinion that they'd all be so interested in the hall displays, especially looking for themselves in the photos, they'd never move outside to watch the play and the dancing and to listen to the choir and to take advantage of the buffet in the church hall

'Thank you so much for helping. I'd never have got it all done by myself.' Mrs Fitch gave them a box of toffees from the toffee specialist in Culworth as a thank you and Beth and Alex went to sit on the seat by the pond.

With her speech impaired by the rather large piece of toffee she'd chosen, Beth said, 'You came then.'

'Yes.'

'Why? You said you wouldn't.'

Alex shrugged. 'Don't know really. Just thought I'd help. But I'm not speaking to her on Saturday, even if she speaks to me.' He glared at Beth, daring her to persuade him otherwise.

Beth chewed her toffee and gazed at the geese.

Alex offered a piece of information on the subject foremost in their minds. 'Mum just said the Suzy person daren't look at us when we were born in case she wanted to keep us.'

'Mummy said so? You've talked to her about it then?'

'Yes, just now before I came to school.'

'She must have wanted us then. Really.'

It was Alex's turn to stare at the geese.

'But she couldn't work to feed her family and look after

two babies. Mummy says we were very small when we were born so we needed a lot of care.' Alex muttered something she didn't catch and then he added, 'Will you speak to her?'

'I don't know. I shan't be rude, if that's what you mean.'

'Mum said we mustn't ever forget that she made us and carried us for nine months.'

Beth asked for another piece of toffee and this time chose a smaller piece. 'Let's go home and give Mummy and Daddy some.'

Alex closed the lid of the box. 'We'd better not eat any more anyway or we shan't want lunch.' He stood up to go but Beth didn't make a move. 'Come on then.'

Beth said almost to herself, 'They'll all be watching us. Everyone in the village knows.'

'They never say.'

Beth stood up. 'That's because they don't want to hurt Mummy and Daddy. They love them so much.'

'I *might* speak to her, but I shan't make a fuss because I don't want to upset Mum.'

Beth looked at him for a moment and then she said in a whisper, 'Do you think Mummy and Daddy will speak to her?'

'I haven't thought about that.'

'Neither have I till just now.'

They stood close together, the two of them, puzzling over their problem, both of them envisaging watching their real parents speaking to each other, aware that everyone there knew what was between them. It was more than they could cope with so they brushed the idea

258

aside and set off for home, Beth saying hopefully, 'They might not bump into each other.'

As they were about to cross the road to the Rectory they saw Maggie Dobbs heading there too.

'Hello, Mrs Dobbs. Are you wanting Daddy?'

'Hello, you two. How're things? I'm wanting anyone who can lend me a couple of light bulbs and no one seems to be in today. They haven't got the bayonet kind I want in the Store, just fancy ones. And I can't spend the whole weekend with no light, now can I?'

'I'm sure Dad's got some.' Alex put his key in the door and opened it up. 'I know just where they are.'

He disappeared into the kitchen. Beth offered Mrs Dobbs a piece of toffee.

'Thanks very much but no, I'm trying to lose weight. A moment on the lips, a lifetime on the hips, they say.'

Peter appeared carrying two light bulbs. 'Here we are, Maggie.'

'Thank you, Rector. I have such trouble with light bulbs; they're always going. Spent a fortune, I have.'

'Is it the wiring, do you think? Don Wright modernized the cottage but perhaps he didn't think to rewire.'

'Do you know, I bet that's it. You could be right. I'll let Vera know. He's home this weekend, you know, Don. Isn't it great? Fully recovered, they say, all because he's a fighter and didn't give in. He'll never be quite the same again, climbing ladders and that, but his brain's working OK and with a bit more physio he'll be in the Royal Oak same as usual and driving his car. Same for Jeremy Mayer. He's fighting fit and home this week too. Isn't it good news?'

'It most certainly is.'

'See you Sunday, Rector. Thanks for this. I'll go into Culworth next week and get you replacements.'

'Don't worry, I shan't go bankrupt over a couple of light bulbs.' Peter laughed.

Maggie said, 'Well, I shall get you some, I don't like to be in debt to anyone, least of all the Rector.' She turned to leave and then changed her mind. 'I want to thank you, Rector, for what you've done for me. You've made things so clear. It's good to have someone who makes me feel reassured. We're all well blessed with you. Perhaps people don't say it often enough, but we are.' She held up the light bulbs. 'And thanks for these.'

Peter went into his study after she'd left and didn't see Alex hovering indecisively by the study door. Finally Alex made up his mind, knocked and went in.

'Dad?'

Peter looked up from his desk, 'Yes?'

'Dad . . . '

'What is it, Alex?'

'Dad, you know this weekend with the school anniversary, I don't know what to do.'

'What about?'

'Speaking to Suzy Meadows.'

Peter put down his pen and leaned back in the chair. 'Neither do I.'

'Oh!'

'Whatever takes place, we must be very careful not to upset Mummy, Caroline I mean. I think the best approach is to be utterly polite. If you bump into her then . . . speak politely. I don't want to have a scene. It is the school's anniversary and that should be paramount, not our private business.'

'"Our private business." But everyone knows.'

'I'm aware of that. But the matter is never mentioned and that's how I want it to stay. I don't want anything to happen that will cause tongues to wag.'

'So I've to shake hands politely and say good afternoon. Or how nice to meet you or something.'

Peter nodded.

'Right. Will you speak to her?'

'If the occasion arises. I shan't seek her out.'

'And Mum?'

'That's for her to decide. OK? It's going to be difficult for us all. She'll understand though.'

'She will? She won't cry and go all mushy?'

Peter had to smile. 'I hope not. But she will be upset, I expect. Old pain, you know.'

'Yes, of course.' Alex burst out of the study as quickly as he'd come, leaving Peter to his work, but somehow Peter couldn't concentrate. In his mind's eye he could see Suzy with her platinum hair and those rounded cheeks of hers and her eyes looking so pleadingly at him when he refused her request to see the children the weekend she'd come back to visit Michael Palmer before they married, believing he and Caroline were on holiday with the children. A lump came in his throat at the memory of her. She'd left herself with him in Beth's face and hair. The telephone rang. 'Turnham Malpas Rectory, Peter speaking.'

'Hi, Peter. It's Kate from the school. I've got a problem I need to tell you about. You know the Tranter family from Penny Fawcett? Well, they've sent a complaint about the school to the education office.'

'What about?'

'In a nutshell, we're not doing enough for their children.'

'In the circumstances you couldn't have done more than you have.'

'Exactly. They're really special needs children but of course there isn't a school for them within fifty miles. I'm very upset about it. We've all tried so hard to help. Frankly, the Education Committee has let them down all through their school lives. Just thought I ought to let you know in case someone mentions it to you. However, they are right in that they haven't had the special teaching they need, but it can't be laid at our door. We've done all we can. Anyway, change of subject. I can't wait for the anniversary weekend.'

'Neither can I. Sorry you're having this difficulty. Keep me in the picture, won't you? If there's anything you need or anyone I can have a word with on your behalf, and indeed anything at all about the anniversary weekend, just let me know. Sorry about the Tranters.'

'Thanks. That's great. If I come up with someone who might be more amenable to a word from you rather than me I'll let you know. Be seeing you.'

Peter put down the receiver sick at heart. Thank God it was Saturday. He leapt to his feet, intent on finding Caroline and suggesting they all went out somewhere. Anywhere to escape his anguish.

'Who's for an outing? Lunch in Culworth then a visit to the open-air pool? It's hot enough.'

'How about lunch at home as it's almost ready, then a visit to the pool, followed by the new museum in Culworth and then an evening meal out?'

'Excellent! Beth, Alex? Come down, we're going out!'

262

But a day out of the village only served to push their problems to the back of their minds for a while. When they returned, all four of them realized they'd only had a temporary respite from the critical situation they faced on the anniversary weekend.

Chapter 17

If you lived in Penny Fawcett or Little Derehams and were planning an important family picnic or some outdoor activity then you knew to choose the day Turnham Malpas was having a special event because they always had good weather. The weekend of the school anniversary was no exception. It had rained on and off every day that week but come Saturday morning they opened their curtains to a brilliant, cloudless sky and the hint of mist arising from the fields, which augured a beautiful day.

At first light, the cricket pitch was inspected, the pavilion's shutters were opened and the windows flung wide to air it after all the damp, and the ladies of the cricket team were busy preparing the tables. Colin Turner's idea of a cricket match, the Village against the Old Boys, was going to give a rousing start to the day. The scratch team of Old Boys he'd managed to cobble together had some cracking bowlers in it, to say nothing of Colin who was well known for his prowess at the crease. When he opened his shoulders and sent the ball flying to the boundary at the threat of fading light and thirty runs needed to win, he was a sight to behold.

In the village hall, Pat Jones was in charge. She never tired of facing the challenge of providing food and good service for her customers. This time she was doing it on a voluntary basis, but the enthusiasm was present just the same. She'd gathered a good volunteer team to serve food from four o'clock onwards and soon had them folding paper napkins, stacking plates, polishing any lacklustre cutlery and checking that Jimbo had provided everything she needed in the way of rolls, meats, cakes and desserts. Her team might not be earning money today, but she was determined to make money for the school and provide a memorable feast.

'Another table in that corner, Willie. Jimmy, bring in more chairs, we'll have four chairs at each small table and six chairs at the bigger ones.'

'We've got to leave room for people to get between.'

'I know that. Willie, put a few tables in the small hall for the VIPs.'

'How many?'

'Three, I reckon. See what it looks like. That sounds like the food arriving.'

At the end of a busy morning arranging plates, cups, glasses, cutlery, napkins, tea urns and soft drinks, in came Jimbo with some of his staff, all laden with trays and shiny catering plates holding a wide variety of pastries, both savoury and sweet. Flick and Fran followed, each carrying a huge gateau carefully screened from the air by a clear plastic dome.

'Where would you like these, Mrs Jones?' asked Flick.

'End table. Leave the domes on, please. Sweet stuff on the end table, savoury here at the start by the piles of plates.' Everyone then disappeared outside to bring in the rest of the supplies. Pat cast a critical eye over the first consignment and decided Jimbo had lived up to his reputation. The individual quiches looked so tempting she could have eaten one there and then. As for the desserts! They were breathtaking. There was still more to come and she had to get Willie to put tables up behind the main buffet table to hold replacement supplies.

For a moment Pat wondered if he'd over-provided, but she was to find out by six o'clock that some swift thawing in the microwaves of more pastries would only just save the day.

Mr Fitch had opened up Rector's Meadow for car parking only to find that Home Park had to be opened up too as the cars were overflowing on to Church Lane and Stocks Row. He was beside himself with nerves. Kate had spent a very restless night worrying over just about everything to do with the smooth running of the day. She even had notepaper and pen by her bedside to jot down her last-minute thoughts. So come seven o' clock in the morning, they were both feeling not only exhausted, but frantic with anxiety.

The selling of the souvenir programmes was in the hands of Ralph and Muriel. They'd recruited Sir Ronald and Lady Bissett, and Tom and Evie Nicholls to assist as Ralph was determined to sell every single one. To his consternation, Ralph found some of the photographs brought back memories he would rather have forgotten. There was one of his father presenting the end-of-year prizes at the school, and, judging by the date, it must have been his very last official engagement before he was killed in Malaysia. Ralph had already opened the church safe several times to store the money they'd taken and was altogether feeling very pleased with their efforts.

But Muriel couldn't concentrate easily on her brochure-selling. She had the Maypole dancing to play for later on. She just knew her fingers would be all thumbs and her nerves would get the better of her. Chaos, she knew for certain, would reign and the ribbons would get all tangled up and her days of playing for the school would come to an abrupt end. Her head ached at the prospect and she knew she'd have to pull herself together.

Trundling the piano out from the school hall and round on to the Green was a marathon task and several members of the victorious Turnham Malpas cricket team, which despite Colin Turner's gargantuan efforts had beaten the Old Boys by nineteen runs, were called in to help. A useful wooden trolley on four large rubber wheels had been constructed to help with this very problem and the piano arrived in Stocks Row to cheers from the crowd. Muriel placed her unsold brochures and her money bag in Ralph's guardianship and marched over to it.

Half past four Mrs Fitch had said and it was. But the piano stool, with her music safely placed by her inside the lid the previous day, had not arrived. She signalled frantically to Jimmy Glover, who waved nonchalantly back to her and gave her a thumbs-up. She waved her arms even more frantically and sensing there was some-thing afoot he walked over to her. Muriel hissed, 'The piano stool. They've forgotten it!' She grew even more desperate when out of the corner of her eye she saw the children marching out in pairs ready to begin dancing. Then she realized the Maypole wasn't in place either. She called out, 'The *Maypole*!' But no one appeared to understand what she was saying. The children got closer and closer and it was Miss Booth shepherding them out who saw the problem. She halted the children, grabbed Rhett Wright and Dean Jones by their arms and said firmly, 'The *Maypole*. Now!'

The crowed began to laugh and mutter and Muriel could tell it was all going to be a fiasco. Poor Kate. She'd be devastated.

But Rhett and Dean had no need to run to the school because around the corner into Stocks Row came Mr Fitch, staggering along at one end of the pole with Sir Ronald at the other, both of them panting fit to burst. A cheer went up when they placed it at the right spot on the Green. The piano stool arrived and Muriel whipped her sheet music out from under the lid. She sat down hastily only to find that the stool was far too low for her to reach the keyboard comfortably. She said 'giddy godfathers' to herself, twiddled the appropriate knobs at each side of the stool, sat down again, played a wonderful, given the circumstances, peal of chords and notes from one end of the keyboard to the other, gave a nod to Miss Booth, and the dancing began.

Unfortunately, in her panic, she'd played the introduction of the second dance, 'Barber's Pole', not the first. Some of the children realized what she'd done and began the movements of the second dance but others didn't and they started to dance the first one. Mayhem reigned. Ribbons were knotted, children were tumbling about, and not a few hefty pushes were exchanged.

Miss Booth clapped her hands to bring everyone to a standstill while she unknotted the ribbons. She glanced across at Muriel who by now was redder than the geraniums below the dais. Muriel found the right music, gave another nod to Miss Booth, and the children began again. But they hadn't bargained on a sudden gust of wind, which made an errant sheet of music blow away. Hetty Hardaker had to burst into a run to retrieve it. Finally, with Hetty anchoring the music with one hand and turning the pages with the other, they began again, for all the world as though there hadn't been a single hiccup.

Muriel played merrily throughout the performance, loving the dances, 'Gypsy's Tent', 'Barber's Pole' and 'Three in Hand'. At the end, when she'd played 'Chrysanthemum' as the finale to the performance, they were clapped and clapped, and the children bowed and curtsied as instructed. Miss Booth waved a hand in Muriel's direction and she got an extra clap. All told, the dancing went off well, but Muriel was left feeling shattered. She vowed that was it. Never again, not even for a practice. This was truly her swan song.

Beth and Alex had been in the crowd clapping the dancing. 'They did it much better than we ever did,' Beth said.

Alex agreed. 'Just glad I'm too old to do it. Imagine dancing like that. Kids' stuff.'

'I liked it when I was there.'

'Well, I didn't.'

'You did. You were quite upset one year when you didn't get chosen.'

'I wasn't.'

'You were.'

Alex saw his dad but couldn't see who he was talking to so earnestly because his father was shielding the person and the sun was in his eyes. There was something very tense about the way his dad stood and a dreadful suspicion came over Alex. He watched him move to let someone pass by

269

and Alex's heart sank to his socks. He nudged Beth but she was tucking her T-shirt into her trousers and didn't bother to look up.

'What? What's the matter?'

Alex turned his back to his father and said, 'Look who's speaking to Dad.'

The Scout band struck up to announce the beginning of their performance. Beth's heart bounded in her chest. So it was to the sound of 'March of the British Grenadiers' that Beth saw her mother for the first time. The stirring music added drama to the event. After all, thought Beth, it's not every day you meet your mother. She studied her body language, saw how tense she was, trying to laugh naturally but at the same time . . . she was wearing a dress Beth could admire, so that was a plus, but she was shorter than she'd imagined. She'd always thought that only tall women would be attracted to her very tall father. He looked uncomfortable . . . then someone stood in front of her and she couldn't see any longer.

Alex surreptitiously put a hand on Beth's shoulder, gripping her as though trying to ease the moment. 'She's like you, Beth.'

'Same colour hair.'

'Chubby cheeks.'

'Mine are not chubby, just rounded.'

'It is her though, isn't it?'

'Yes. Look the other way. I don't want her to see us.'

'Neither do I.' Alex turned away from the band performance and hastened Beth away towards the church hall and food. 'They'll have begun serving, let's go in there.'

They carefully skirted the Green to avoid contact with

their father and Suzy. While they were choosing what they would like to eat from the laden buffet table, Beth spotted Caroline, sitting by herself at a table in the far corner, sipping a cup of tea, looking for all the world as though she were hiding herself away.

'Let's sit with Mummy. You pay this time.'

'OK.' Alex carried the tray across to Caroline's table. 'Hello, Mum.'

He saw Caroline visibly make the effort to speak naturally. 'Hello, darlings. I really did begin to think the Maypole dancing had flopped, but they did very well in the circumstances, didn't they?'

Hearing the tension in her voice, Beth encouraged her by saying, 'Well, I just wished I were still at the school and then I might have been chosen to dance. I loved it.'

Her mummy placed a warm hand on hers. 'I know you did.'

'Would you like some of my pastry, Mum?' Alex cut his Danish pastry in half.

'Just a corner, darling, please. That'll be enough, I have to think of my figure.'

Alex reassured her. 'Daddy thinks your figure is lovely.'

'He does? He might not if I got fat.'

'He would because he loves you like I do.' Beth entwined her fingers with Caroline's and smiled at her, but there were memories of her real mother in her eyes.

With dread deep in her heart, Caroline asked, 'You've met her?'

There was a short silence before either of them answered her.

Alex spoke first. 'In the distance. We haven't spoken.'

'Was she with her husband? Mr Palmer?'

271

Beth and Alex exchanged a swift glance.

'Yes.'

'No.'

'Well, was she? Yes or no.'

'No. We didn't know to whom she was speaking.' Alex glared at Beth to shut her up.

Caroline finished her tea, put down the cup and said, 'Things to do. Things to do.' Then she hurried off like the Red Queen in *Alice in Wonderland* or was it the White Queen in *Through the Looking Glass*? Alex couldn't remember. Whichever it was, his mother was distinctly harassed.

The tables were rapidly filling up now as the band had paused for an interval, and to his absolute horror, Alex spotted the Suzy Meadows person in the queue with a man he recognized from the school photos as Mr Palmer. He gave Beth's foot a slight tap with his and nodded towards the queue.

Beth saw the two of them and her heart gave that great bound it had done earlier. It was no good, she couldn't face them. But it was too late to escape; Suzy was coming directly towards them, a tentative smile on her face. As she got nearer, the two of them realized Beth was not entirely like her, similar but not the same.

Alex got to his feet. 'Good afternoon,' he said, sounding more like a frog croaking.

'Good afternoon. Would you mind if I sit with you for a moment?'

'Not at all. There's really nowhere else to sit.' Alex pulled out a chair for her, and then sat down again.

Beth was staring into her teacup. Now the moment had come she couldn't find any words to say. She just wanted her to go away and stay away and not upset her mother or any of them any more.

'My husband, Michael Palmer, is paying for our tea. I see Jimbo Charter-Plackett's catering is still coming up to scratch. His cakes look lovely.'

'They are,' Alex agreed.

'I've chosen a cream puff. Have you tried one?'

'No.'

Almost pleadingly she asked, 'Am I right? You're Alex and Beth Harris?'

Neither of them answered her.

'You won't know me.'

'No,' Alex replied. He wasn't going to make it easy for her. How he wished his dad was there to help. He'd have known what to say.

'You're like your father, Alex.'

'I am?'

'Oh yes. The absolute image. Which school do you go to now?'

'Prince Henry's.'

'Then you must be clever.'

'Mediocre.'

'No. Much better than mediocre I think.' The Suzy person turned to Beth and asked, 'And which school are you at, Beth?'

Beth didn't reply. The excitement that had been in her ever since she'd realized she might meet the Suzy person had quite melted away. Now all she felt was a terrific let-down, and stubbornness too. So Alex answered for her. 'She's at Lady Wortley's.'

'Another clever person then. Your mum and dad must be very proud.'

273

'They are.' And then the words tripped off his tongue before he could stop them. 'Are you?'

He shouldn't have said that, it was too grown-up for someone his age. But who did she think she was kidding, behaving as though they had no connection? Beth wasn't helping with her stubborn silence. A mist came down over his eyes and all he could see was the Suzy person's face. Then he heard the thump of a tray and a rattle of teacups. Someone was pushing his cup aside, and mentioning how tempting the cakes were. 'Jimbo hasn't lost his touch, has he? Should I know you two young people?'

'Michael! This is Beth and Alex Harris. From the Rectory.' The emphasis she put on their names and where they came from was very obvious, she might as well have said 'you know who I mean, be careful what you say'.

'I see. Lovely day for such a lovely event. When I've drunk my tea I'm going to see the exhibition in the school hall. I used to teach here, before your time, of course.'

Alex answered, 'You will be interested then.'

'Of course. This lady used to teach in the playgroup, didn't you, Suzy?'

'Yes, I did.'

A silence began, which grew longer and longer. Mr Palmer was taking huge bites of his cream puff, the cream oozing out on to his lips. The Suzy person was nibbling hers and Alex could see she was at a loss to know what to say next and not really knowing if the children realized just exactly who she was.

But Alex knew all right. 'We've got to go. We told our mum we wouldn't be long. Nice to have met you.' He did what his dad would have done and offered to shake hands with the two of them. The Suzy person gripped his

274

tightly as though she would never let go. As for Mr Palmer, well, using a phrase he'd heard his mother use once, it was like shaking hands with a piece of wet fish. Beth got up and followed him. The moment they got outside she burst into tears. Alex took her down the side wall of the church hall and stood in front of her so no one could see. He normally hadn't much patience with her when she cried but he felt like crying himself so he protected her while she did his crying for him.

'I want to find Mummy.'

'Not while you're crying.'

Beth gave several huge sniffs, rubbed vigorously at her cheeks to rid herself of tears, stored her hankie away in her trouser pocket and stood tall. 'There, I'm not crying now. Let's go find her.'

'We'll go home and you can wash your face, otherwise she'll see you've been crying.'

'I didn't like him, did you? I'm glad he's not my daddy.'

Alex put his key in the door and opened it, pushing Beth in the direction of the kitchen. He followed her in to find Beth hugging her mother.

'There, there, darling. What's the matter?'

'Nothing. I couldn't find you.'

'I'm only getting some more tea towels for the church kitchen, they're beginning to run out.'

But Alex knew differently. She might be getting the tea towels but she was also using it as an excuse to hide. And no wonder. The hurt she must feel. 'Mum, do we have to go back?'

Caroline hesitated for a moment and then said, 'I think we must. Better face everything and get it over and done with.'

275

Beth tightened her grip. 'I don't want to see her again.'

'You've met, then?'

They both nodded.

'In that case, let's be off. Alex, will you take the tea towels for me? It could be urgent by now. I promised Lady Bissett I would take a look at her flowers in the church, I'm told they're spectacular.'

'OK. Come on, Beth. Let's go to the fair. I've still got some money left.'

Beth released her mother reluctantly. 'Have *you* seen this Suzy person?'

'In the distance.'

'We spoke.'

Caroline didn't ask what she said.

'She didn't say much really. I'm like her but not quite.'

'Right.'

'She knew us when she saw us.'

Alex urged Beth to leave.

'OK. Where are you going when you've seen the flowers, Mummy?'

'Don't know. I'll be around.'

Beth vigorously threw water on her face and then dried it on the kitchen hand towel. 'There. I'm ready.'

The three of them went as far as the lychgate together and Caroline went up the path to the church. She stopped to greet several old pupils who remembered her and then was free to make her way in. Sheila Bissett had said something about school pupils being all over the world by now, thinking of our Kenny and Terry Jones, so she'd introduced an international flavour to her flowers.

Caroline gasped when she went in. The air was heady with the perfume of the blooms and her eyes were dazzled by their magnificence. Sheila must have spent at least a whole day arranging them. The church was filled with vivid displays. She paused to inspect the one by the font. It was made entirely of white flowers, Sheila's favourite colour, and began in the font, trailing right down to the floor and down two steps in an unbroken stream of white flowers and green and silver foliage. Caroline crouched down to find out how she'd achieved it and didn't hear someone's footstep on the stone flags of the church aisle.

The person who'd come in didn't notice her and wandered down to stand in front of the altar. Then she turned to face the body of the church, looking up into the rafters and remembering, oh yes, remembering, studying the old banners hanging wispily threadbare. She turned to look at the old memorial chapel and recollected the last time she'd stood here, in this very spot. She'd been at a loss for words when Peter had surprised her by coming from behind the screen that shielded it; she remembered the touch of his hand, his glorious presence, his endearing vulnerability, but most of all his spiritual strength. Such was her love for him that day, if he'd even only half suggested it, she'd have gone to the ends of the earth with him.

Startled by Caroline's movement as she stood up, Suzy froze with surprise. She half raised her hand in greeting and then let it fall to her side. What did you say to the woman who'd taken the children you couldn't cope with? Maybe she could have managed somehow. Perhaps she ought never to have let them go. Having met them, she knew so positively that she should have kept them. Especially Alex. He was so bewilderingly like Peter; his gestures, his protectiveness to his sister, that same kind of caring.

It was Caroline who opened their conversation. 'Hello.'

'Hello.' Suzy saw that Caroline's arms were held rigidly by her sides so she didn't hold out her hand to shake. 'Lovely day, as usual when there's an event at Turnham Malpas.'

'I'm amazed by all the people who've come. We didn't expect such a huge response.'

'No. It's surprising.'

'I understand lots of people are staying over for the service tomorrow.'

'We're going home tonight.'

'Right. Your girls, Rosie and Pansy and Daisy, are they well?'

Suzy gave her a huge smile. 'Yes, thank you.'

'And Michael?'

Suzy's face lost its smile. 'He's well.'

Caroline, seeing the discomfort, had to know. 'Has it worked out with him? Are you happy?'

'Tolerably. I've known worse.'

'I'm sorry.'

An uncomfortable silence followed in which Suzy contemplated asking about the twins and Caroline decided they couldn't stand here much longer avoiding the subject.

'The children say you've spoken to them.'

A great ball of emotion lodged itself in Suzy's chest. 'Yes, I have. They are lovely. Beth doesn't have much to say, does she?'

'She never stops talking usually.'

'Alex is obviously in charge.'

'I don't know about that.'

'That's how they came across to me.'

'I expect they felt embarrassed. Awkward, you know.'

'You've told them everything?'

Caroline nodded. 'Yes.'

Suzy sighed. 'I'm glad, it's only fair.'

Caroline asked sharply, 'To whom?'

'To them, of course.'

'It didn't seem fair to *me*.'

'I'm sorry.'

'Is that all you have to say? On a whim you all but trashed my marriage, decided you could give your children away very conveniently to their father and then you went off into the blue for a new start with your next husband. And you say *sorry*? It is hardly adequate.'

Suzy jerked back with the shock of Caroline's onslaught. 'But I thought you wanted them.'

'I did. I do. But in here,' she patted her chest, 'in here I'm desperately sad because Alex can't get over you giving him away. I explained your circumstances to him, but he still came to the conclusion that you couldn't have wanted him. That's a terrible thing for a child to feel.'

'Haven't you compensated for that? Do you not love him then?'

'Of course I do. I love both of them like they were my own. And don't you dare entice them while you're here with promises of this and that. You understand? I can't even begin to get my mind round why you've come today. Michael, yes. You, no. Do you have any idea how hurtful it is? To me, to the children and especially to Peter.'

Suzy hesitated. 'I've spoken to Peter; he seemed all right.'

'That's Peter, having consideration for everyone as usual and not wishing to wound.'

Suzy opened her mouth to apologize yet again, realizing for the first time that the anxiety she'd felt about coming was justified and she should never have allowed Michael to persuade her. But in truth she'd been easily persuaded. She'd desperately wanted to see her twins, just this once. 'I . . . I . . .'

'Why *did* you come? Just to hurt us?'

Someone came in, their heels busily tip-tapping on the stone floor. 'Oh! Ah, yes. Just coming to check my flowers but I'll come back later. Sorry.' Sheila Bissett turned to go.

'That's all right, Sheila. We've finished,' Caroline called out.

But Suzy hadn't. As she walked down the aisle with Caroline she said loudly, with almost hysterical passion, 'You've got *everything*. The loving husband a *million* women would die for and the two beautiful children I gave you.'

It was the note of hysteria in her voice that alerted Caroline to the truth. She loved him. After all these years, Suzy *loved* Peter. That was a complication she hadn't anticipated. She had persuaded herself, in order to ease her own terrible pain, that it was a transitory thing, a moment of lust between them. Caroline wished she hadn't been so outspoken about her marriage being trashed and Alex's anguish, because Suzy had suffered, three times over: giving the twins away, the misfortune of an unsuccessful marriage and loving Peter . . . She trembled inside. Uncertain. Afraid. She'd have to find Peter.

She found him in the school hall, deep in conversation

with the two old headmasters, the ancient Mr Browning and Michael Palmer. As she listened to them talking, it seemed as though Mr Browning was the younger man of the two. With age his voice was frail, but the words were as forceful as ever they had been.

'Wonderful improvements to the school. Central heating! My word! That old stove was the bane of my life. Just here it stood. I see the same clock still ticks away the hours. Are you the new head?' His bright brown eyes sparkled his appreciation of Caroline.

'No, I'm Peter's wife.'

'What a delight you are, my dear. You have children?'

Very positively Caroline answered, 'Two.'

'You should have more. Young intelligent folk like yourselves should have armies of children. It's what the nation needs, bright, healthy children brought up by godly parents. Yes, indeed.'

This statement, coming as it did after her altercation with Suzy, was almost too much for Caroline. She simply nodded and smiled.

Peter drew closer to her, sensing her unease, and diverted Mr Browning from his population theories by saying, 'Now, Mr Browning, what do you think of our computers? Bit of a change from using slates, eh?'

'My word! Wonderful. State of the art. They even outshine mine and I thought that was good when I bought it. But then it's two years old now so it's old hat, I suppose. Mr Palmer, are you computer literate? You must be, of course.'

Mr Palmer, now greying and somehow faded, shook his head. 'No, no. Can't be bothered with all this new technology. I leave that to my younger staff.'

Mr Browning playfully punched his arm. 'Come on, man, get to it. Younger staff indeed! If I can learn, so can you! At your age you should be at the forefront of it all. I haven't met the present head yet. Where is she?'

Peter saw Kate coming across the hall as though on cue. 'She's here. Kate, a wonderful day! You've done a great job.'

Kate wasn't feeling as though she was doing a great job. The notes she'd jotted down during her ghastly night of tossing and turning had all been gobbledegook when she'd read them this morning and it had unnerved her. She braced herself for further social chit-chat.

Holding out her hand, she grasped Mr Browning's and was surprised to find how strong it was. She said, 'I think you must be Mr Browning. Welcome back to Turnham Malpas School. So good of you to find time to come. And Mrs Browning?'

'My grandson has found a nice quiet corner for her and she's sitting on a chair remembering. How nice to meet you. What a wonderful idea to have a celebration! I loved working here. Do you?'

Kate nodded. 'I do. So rewarding and everyone in the village is so supportive. I love it. I shan't go until they force me out.'

'I'm glad, my dear. You'll never be happier. Now, take me round this display and point out people I might know.' Old Mr Browning crooked his arm and invited Kate to escort him. They trotted off followed by Mr Palmer, leaving Caroline and Peter alone for a moment.

Peter watched Mr Browning as he stopped Kate beside a display of photographs. 'He's a feisty old chap, isn't he? I really admire old gentlemen like him.'

'So do I. He's years younger than Mr Palmer in his mind. They're not all that happy, you know.'

'Who?'

'Suzy and him.'

'What makes you say that?'

'She said as much.'

Peter tried hard to be casual. 'You've spoken then?'

'We met by chance in the church.' Caroline, to others, might have appeared to be studying the display of triumphs of old pupils at the school but she was saying, 'I think she regrets giving us the children. They've spoken to her but she couldn't make out if they knew who she was. But they did, of course. From what I can gather, Beth refused to speak.'

Peter joined her pretence of looking at the display. 'I'm so sorry about today. Be brave, see it through, and then we can get back to normal.'

'I understand you've spoken to her.'

'How do you know?'

'She said so.'

'We passed the time of day.'

'Peter, tell me honestly. You don't feel . . . attracted to her, do you?'

He gripped her hand and looked at her. Today he was wearing a casual jacket and trousers with his clerical collar and she couldn't remember him looking more handsome than he did just then. His smile scrambled her insides as it always did. He said, 'Absolutely not. There is no point in speaking of anything other than trivialities, because there's nothing between us. That's the absolute truth.'

Kate returned just as they were pulling themselves back

from their ragged emotions. 'Platform time! Come along. Make haste or we shall be running late.'

They went with her out into the bright sunshine to be faced by the large crowd all waiting on the Green, with more coming out of the village hall and even more streaming from the school to swell the gathering. The last few scurried across Stocks Row in time to watch old Mr Browning and his wife and Mr and Mrs Palmer climbing the steps and taking their places. Kate tested the microphone, looked around the platform and realized Craddock wasn't there, spotted him in the crowd and signalled to him to come up the steps and take his place. She crooked an imperious finger at him and then pointed to his chair on the platform. The crowd roared their approval. They had never seen Mr Fitch bossed about like a naughty child before and it amused them. He got several pats on the back as he made his way through to the platform, all in good humour, and Craddock began to wonder if he might, just might be getting accepted. When he was seated, a small cheer went up and the speeches began.

Kate drew on her rapidly diminishing resources and began her speech. 'Ladies and gentlemen, welcome to Turnham Malpas School's one hundred and fiftieth anniversary. I am amazed by the wonderful response you have given to our invitation. There are dozens more of you here than I had ever hoped for. Thank you so much for your support. We celebrate a century and a half as a centre of learning. The school is so well equipped I am the envy of all my colleagues. Our computers are the best of the best, obviously a tremendous tool for broadening our children's education. By the beginning of the next school year we shall have new playground equipment, generously

284

donated by a benefactor, which will be the envy of every school in the county. All these things contribute to the rich experience a school needs to provide to ensure we send well-rounded, engaging pupils with enquiring minds and sound morals out into the world. In the school hall you will see that we have two boys and three girls who have won places this year to Prince Henry's and to Lady Wortley's. A record number.'

There was a burst of congratulatory applause.

'Hands up all those who remember attending the school when Mr Browning was Head? Here he is, as sprightly and forward-thinking as ever.' A round of applause for Mr Browning followed. 'He'll be speaking shortly. Hands up all those who remember being taught by Mr Palmer? He's as kind and authoritative as ever, and still playing cricket, which we all know was a great passion of his.' An even more substantial number of hands went up. 'He'll speak after Mr Browning. Remember to look round our memorabilia in the school hall and when in need of sustenance visit the church hall, where the food is as glorious as ever.

'At six-thirty there will be the quiz, organized by Hetty Hardaker and her husband Theo. Old pupils versus the newcomers, that is, people not educated in our school. That will be held in the school hall. But before then, Years Six and Seven are to entertain us with a play and the infants with choral singing, trained by Mrs Hardaker. They've worked tremendously hard to fine-tune their performances and I know you can all look forward to some excellent entertainment. Thank you.'

Kate sat down to enthusiastic applause. She beamed with delight. All in all, everything had gone off without a

285

hitch, so far, that was, if you discounted the problem with Muriel's music, Maggie Dobbs loudly scolding two children who had dropped chewing gum on the hall floor just as they were going out to start the Maypole dancing, Pat Jones catching the Misses Senior stealing meringues from her buffet, and Hetty and Margaret Booth having a flare-up over the choir. Minor matters in the grand scheme of things. She smiled at Craddock and saw he was grinning from ear to ear, obviously thoroughly enjoying himself. He caught her eye and winked and, for a moment, there was no one else there but him. She resisted the urge to kiss him as a thank you for making her so happy when she'd had such doubts about marrying him, for indulging her with her school, and for trying so hard to be accepted. Quite a few of the sceptics saw him grip her hand and give it a squeeze. It looked as though they might be married for far longer than anyone had supposed.

Epilogue

Kate wriggled her bare toes and felt the fine, warm sand filter between them. The book she'd bought at the airport lay unopened in her bag. Even a lifetime habit of reading a newspaper every day had been abandoned. She checked her watch. It was just about time for afternoon tea. Craddock would keep to these traditional English habits and she humoured him. To tell him he was being ridiculous would only hurt him and causing him pain was not on her agenda. She shielded her eyes and searched along the beach where the sea was softly creeping up the sand, small ripples giving way to waves the further out she looked.

Ah, there he was, walking quietly up the beach and stepping tidily between the sunloungers. She waved and he quickened his step. No one seeing him relaxed and happy would even pause to comment on their age difference. He looked so fit and lean. Kate held out his beach towel to him and he thanked her with a kiss.

'Do you know, I'm lying here with a completely blank mind.'

'Is that possible?'

'No, not really. All too frequently, thoughts pop up like a jack-in-a-box.'

'Such as?'

'That Peter and Caroline may very possibly be leaving us this time next year. It's just too terrible to contemplate. However shall we manage without them?'

'I must say it came as a shock to me, well, to all of us.'

'I know they'll be coming back, but a whole year away seems a long time.'

'Too long.' Craddock saw the waiter with a laden tray about fifty yards away searching for them. He waved.

When the waiter had seated them to his satisfaction, Craddock gave him a tip and shoo'd him away. 'Never got used to servants standing over me.'

'Me neither. Peter always feels like a rock to me, like in the Bible. How shall we cope with his replacement? But no one could replace him. He's unique.'

'Sandwich, before they curl up in the heat?'

'Yes, please. I must say, I have never in the whole of my life stayed in such a spectacular hotel.'

'It won't be the last. You'll see.' Craddock washed his sandwich down with a drink of tea, returned his cup to its saucer and added, 'I just wish he hadn't been tempted. Africa! All that heat and those flies. Still, after all these years in the village, maybe it's time for him to be shaken up a little.'

'It's what he wanted. Something to get his teeth into. Lots of initiatives to start up, new faces, a greater need for his particular talents. I admire him for contemplating the whole idea when he has such a cushy number in Turnham Malpas.'

'Mmm.'

'I think he's searching for new fields to conquer because

he wants to get away from . . . well, I don't know how he sees it, but to get away from his . . . sin?'

Craddock refilled her cup and handed it to her. 'Careful, it's hot. You'll scald yourself if you spill it on your skin. They appeared to manage very well at the anniversary considering what an explosive situation it was.'

'Yes, but apparently Sheila Bissett interrupted Caroline and Suzy talking in the church. She said they were arguing and it was very embarrassing.'

'She'd say black was white if it made a good story.'

'Sheila was genuinely upset.'

'Maybe.' Craddock sat gazing out to sea, occasionally selecting another sandwich. They were so damned small, more like postage stamps. 'Kate?'

'Mmm?'

'I have the feeling I'm accepted a little more since you and I—'

'I thought so too. When they cheered?'

'Yes . . . When we've finished our tea we'll both need more lotion. The sun is very intense.'

'You might, having swum, but I've stayed under the umbrella all afternoon.'

'I've a mind to rub some on you just for the pleasure.'

He eyed her up and down, thinking how beautiful she was. She saw his look and smothered a smile.

Kate searched in her bag for the lotion. 'Here we are. Sit on the end of my lounger and I'll re-do you now you're dry.'

'I understand the children will be going with them and attending an English school. We shall miss them very much.'

'We all will.'

289

When they'd both massaged each other with the lotion they lay back, gazing idly at the beach and watching people pick up their belongings and head for their hotels.

Craddock played a game of guessing who was staying in the same place. 'He wouldn't dare, not in those shorts. Nor her with that dreadful hair. How does she get it to look like a crow's nest? This one walking up now is a definite. He shouts money. So does she.'

'Craddock, you really are a snob. It's unworthy of you. Does it matter where they're staying? Not one jot.'

He had the grace to look embarrassed. 'Sorry.' He reached across and took hold of her hand. 'I hope no one thinks of me as not staying at the best hotel. It's partly that I don't like to remember my beginnings.'

'I don't care two hoots about your beginnings. I love you as you are. Even if you are predictable.'

'Are you saying I'm boring?'

Kate smiled. 'No, not at all. Not since you married me. I've even got you laughing sometimes.'

'Yes, you have. What plans do you have for the school for its next fifty years?'

Kate looked up at the sun burning down and almost, but not quite, wished the school was a million miles away. 'I could get used to this lazing in the sun, it feels very beneficial.'

'It is, but the mind turns to porridge. These people in their fifties who leave England to buy homes in the sun and live with nothing to do must be mad.'

'You're not thinking of retiring then?'

Craddock sat upright, his blue eyes ablaze. 'Retire? Me? Not ever. I shall drop in harness.' He laid back down again. 'Having married you, the best years are yet to come.'

'I'm going in. I've laid here long enough. I'm having a shower and then I'm lying on the bed for an hour before dinner. Join me?'

'Did you hear what I said about the school?'

'Yes.'

'Well?'

'I need time to consider. Do you know we have people registering their children for the school when they're only two years old? I'm thinking of moving the playgroup out to the church hall and using the classroom to accommodate the extra children. Get another teacher. What do you think?'

'Why not? Good idea.'

'I didn't tell you before we left because I didn't want to spoil things after such a spectacularly successful weekend, but there's been a consultative paper sent round and the "education", as Maggie Dobbs calls it, are considering the closure of village schools and concentrating the children in schools in the towns. More equipment, greater concentration of teaching talent and so on.'

'Did they specifically mention Turnham Malpas?'

'No, but we are a village school. Here and now, I am saying, and don't let me go back on my word, I am prepared to stand stark naked outside the education office with a placard in protest.'

Craddock had been drifting off to sleep during this conversation but when he heard that, he remembered thinking that being married to Kate would mean a life full of surprises, but this was one surprise too far. 'You will not.'

'Who's to stop me?'

'Me! I won't have it.'

'You won't be there.'

'Doesn't matter. I shan't allow it.'

'Not even when it means so much to me?'

'No. That's my promise. I shan't allow it.'

'How else can one show how serious one is? A few petitions, a couple of marches, a TV interview achieves nothing now; everybody does it. But sacrifice and determination do. Showing them you mean it.'

Horrified, Craddock stood up. 'Kate! You will not.'

She squinted up at him, shielding her eyes. 'I'm not having my school closed, not when it's a centre of excellence.'

'Think of the scandal.' He hesitated and then added, 'It wouldn't be tasteful.'

'Are you saying . . .' Then she laughed until her sides ached. 'Oh, Craddock! Your face.'

'Oh! I see you were teasing me.'

Wickedly, knowing she'd caught him on the hop, she replied, 'To save you embarrassment I'd hold the placard in a strategic place.'

Appalled, he asked, 'You weren't teasing me?'

'Yes, I was, but I am determined no one shall lay a finger on my school.'

'Quite right,' he said, busily thinking how he might out-manoeuvre her and keep the school open. He had influence and would use it, no matter what it cost in brown envelopes or anything else. Maybe Kev, his mole in the council offices who he had used in the past without even a momentary feeling of guilt, could find out the lie of the land, if needs must. Then he recollected how beautifully Ralph Templeton could get his own way, with his breeding and his aristocratic manners, without once breaching the gentleman's code of honour. Yes, he might be the best ally if closure ever became a serious threat.

He glanced across at Kate intending to reassure her, but she'd fallen asleep. The sun had crept lower in the sky and now the shade she'd had all afternoon had almost gone. He stood up, gently laid her sarong over her and altered the tilt of her sun umbrella. He never thought he would say this, not even to himself, but she was worth all his money, all his projects, all his property investments; he'd sacrifice the whole bally lot for her. Craddock bent to place a kiss on her forehead.

22 (2) — £20
6 bread rolls £1   No change?
Liqu're   56p. —